Long Time Coming

Long Time Coming

ROCHELLE ALERS

ARABESQUE®

LONG TIME COMING

ISBN-13: 978-0-373-83052-7
ISBN-10: 0-373-83052-1

www.kimanipress.com

Printed in U.S.A.

The Whitfield Brides series

You've met Ryan, Jeremy and Sheldon—the Blackstones of Virginia—and now it's time to meet the Whitfields of New York. In this Arabesque trilogy, you will meet Signature Bridals' wedding divas: Tessa, Faith and Simone Whitfield. These three women are so focused on their demanding careers that they've sacrificed their personal happiness. Within a year, though, each will encounter a very special man who will not only change them but change their lives forever.

In *Long Time Coming,* wedding planner Tessa Whitfield never imagined that opening the doors of Signature Bridals to Micah Sanborn would lead to their spending the next twelve hours together after a power outage hits her Brooklyn, New York, neighborhood. Her vow never to mix business with pleasure is shattered when the Brooklyn assistant district attorney offers Tessa an extraordinary friendship with a few special surprises that make her reevaluate everything she's come to believe about love.

Wedding cake designer Faith Whitfield, who owns the fashionable Greenwich Village patisserie Let Them Eat Cake, has all but given up on finding her prince, and refuses to kiss another frog. But when she least expects it she discovers love in the passionate embrace of pilot to the rich and famous, and modern-day knight-in-shining-armor Ethan McMillan in *The Sweetest Temptation.*

After a disappointing marriage and an ill-fated reconciliation with her high school sweetheart, floral designer Simone Whitfield wants nothing to do with men. She's content to run her business, Wildflowers and Other Treasures, in the greenhouses on her White Plains, New York, property. In *Taken by Storm,* Simone witnesses an attack on a federal judge and suddenly finds her cloistered suburban life turned upside down when U.S. Marshal Raphael Madison from the witness protection unit is assigned to protect her 24/7. Although they are complete opposites, Simone and Raphael come to share a heated desire and a love that promises forever.

Yours in romance,
Rochelle Alers

Dedicated to Lieutenant Robert Gonzalez—
a special thanks to one of the NYPD's
best and brightest.

For this cause shall a man leave his father and mother, and shall be joined unto his wife, and they two shall be one flesh.

—*Ephesians* 5:31

Chapter 1

Tessa Whitfield unlocked the front door to the Brooklyn Heights brownstone where she lived, had set up Signature Event Planners Inc. and Signature Bridals—where she'd established a reputation as the consummate wedding consultant.

It was mid-October and, to her relief, the wedding season was winding down. Four months ago she'd coordinated the wedding of the season for sports hero Ashton Cooper and bestselling African-American novelist Jadya Fyles. The elegant ceremony was held in the Grand Hall of the New York Public Library, where the high-profile couple had met three years earlier.

Tessa had arranged for a reception for a thousand in Bryant Park under gauzy multicolored tents that turned the half-acre park in the middle of Manhattan into a wonderland. Media coverage included *People* magazine, which reported the wedding was "Exquisite! Lavish! Joyous!" The *New York Times* society section gave it a full page, and it was reported that Oprah had called for an interview for her magazine *O*.

The spectacular wedding had catapulted Signature Bridals to Manhattan's elite A-list of wedding planners, and Tessa's phone rang constantly for her services with requests from hip-hop stars, high society and the Euro elite.

Closing the self-locking door, she walked through the foyer, down a hallway and into a gourmet kitchen. She set her canvas bag filled with fresh fruit and vegetables on a stool at the cooking island, then made her way into her office to check her telephone. A blinking light indicated a message. Tessa pressed a button on the console.

"This is Bridget Sanborn. I was scheduled to meet with you tonight at six-thirty, but I can't make it. I told you that I was on jury duty, and now I've been sequestered. I know this is the third time you've rearranged your schedule to accommodate me, but I've come up with an idea where you won't have to cancel tonight's meeting. I've asked my brother Micah to keep the appointment for me. I hope to meet you soon, and thank you again for your infinite patience."

"You're welcome, Bridget," she whispered, then blew out a breath at the same time she shook her head.

Tessa had only agreed to accept Bridget Sanborn as a client because the frenetic spring and summer wedding season was over. She hadn't met the children's book editor but knew instinctively she had her work cut out for her. Bridget had gotten engaged over the Labor Day weekend and planned to have a formal New Year's Eve wedding at her parents' Franklin Lakes, New Jersey, home. Most brides planned their wedding a year in advance, but Tessa had less than three months to coordinate the Sanborn-Cohen nuptials.

An antique clock on the fireplace mantel chimed the half hour. It was five-thirty. She had an hour before Micah Sanborn's arrival. Unlike his sister, she hoped he'd keep the appointment.

Tessa thought about preparing and eating a hastily prepared dinner but changed her mind. She would wait until after she met with the prospective bride's brother, then sit down at the table in her dining room instead of the one in the kitchen's breakfast nook and eat without having to watch the clock for her next client.

Returning to the kitchen, she removed a New York steak from the freezer. It was too large for one portion, so she decided to save half for another meal. Forty-five minutes later, the marinated steak and bowls of mixed baby greens and wedges of yellow pear tomatoes and sliced potatoes in cold water sat on a shelf in the refrigerator.

Micah Sanborn mounted the steps to the brownstone in the tony Brooklyn neighborhood. He glanced at the shiny brass plate affixed to the wall of the three-story structure, engraved with Signature Bridals. Admiring the solid oak door with stained-glass insets, he rang the bell and waited as the seconds ticked off.

"Who is it?" a woman's voice came through the small speaker over the mail slot.

"It's Micah Sanborn."

Seconds later, a soft buzzing disengaged the lock. Micah pushed opened the door and stepped into a foyer. Pale oak floors reflected the warm glow from wall sconces and an Art Deco-inspired ceiling fixture. A winding staircase with a mahogany banister led to the upper floors. Turning to his left, his gaze lingered on an exquisite bouquet of fresh flowers in an orange-glazed clay vase on a side table. The vibrant hues of pink, coral, red and yellow lilies, roses, peonies and orchids with folded palm leaves tucked in between the blooms added warmth to the crisp autumn weather.

"Mr. Sanborn?"

Micah's gaze shifted from the flowers to the woman standing several feet away. He inhaled a deep breath, holding it until the pressure in his lungs forced him to exhale.

He extended his hand. "Micah."

Tessa stared at the large, well-groomed hand with clean square-cut nails for several seconds before placing her smaller one on the broad palm. She affected the practiced professional smile she did not feel at that moment. She'd met a lot of men since starting up her business—prospective bridegrooms, groomsmen, fathers and brothers of the bride and groom—but this was the first time in a very long time that she experienced a feeling of unease.

There was something in the way Micah Sanborn stared at her that had slipped under her barrier of professional poise. Everything about the tall, dark-skinned man in a navy-blue pin-striped suit with equally dark eyes was intriguing, compelling and magnetic. He wasn't what she considered handsome but attractive nevertheless. His features were neither broad nor sharp and would've been considered nondescript if not for his eyes—eyes that were large, deep-set and penetrating.

"I'm Tessa Whitfield, coordinator of Signature Bridals," she said after what seemed an interminable pause when in reality it'd been only seconds.

Micah tightened his grip on Tessa's slender fingers before he released them. He smiled, and the gesture flattened his top lip against a set of incredibly straight, startlingly white teeth.

He inclined his head. "Miss Whitfield."

Tessa smiled. "Please call me Tessa."

Micah lifted a thick, black curving eyebrow. "If it's Tessa, then I insist you call me Micah."

Nodding, her practiced smile in place, Tessa said, "Okay, Micah. Please come with me."

He followed her down a hallway to the rear of the house. He missed the carefully chosen furnishings in the rooms he passed because he couldn't take his gaze off Tessa's freestyle hairdo. It looked as if she'd washed the gold-tipped brown strands, then let them air-dry where the soft curls framed her round face like a regal lioness.

In fact, she reminded him of a feline with her exposed gold-brown skin still bearing the results of the summer sun. He thought her more bronze than golden. Her slanting catlike brown eyes under a pair of arching eyebrows, her lithe body swathed in a black-yellow-and-orange-print wrap dress ending midcalf made her look exotic.

He followed Tessa into a large room with French doors and a wall of floor-to-ceiling windows. Pale silks drapes were drawn back and afforded a glimpse of the brightly illuminated backyard with a patio and flower garden.

Tessa gestured to an off-white armchair. "Please sit down, Micah."

Micah waited for Tessa to sit on a matching love seat, but before he sat down, the room went completely dark. The lights had gone out in the room, the backyard and also in the buildings facing the rear of the brownstone. He heard Tessa's soft gasp.

Her heart fluttering wildly in her chest, Tessa stood up and tried making out Micah's face. "I have to flip the circuit breakers."

"Forget about circuit breakers, Tessa," he countered softly. "We're in the middle of a blackout. Do you have a backup generator?"

She realized for the first time the total darkness surrounding her. The last blackout to hit New York had been August 14, 2003, and the memory of her having to walk from Greenwich Village and across the Brooklyn Bridge in an oppressive humidity had not faded.

"No, I don't," she said, moving closer to the heat emanating from Micah's body. "What are you doing?" she asked when she felt him search inside his jacket.

"I have to call a friend."

With an arm circling Tessa's waist, Micah retrieved his cell phone. He flipped the top and a bright blue light shimmered eerily in the blackness. They were in luck, unlike the last blackout when the multistate power outage knocked out cellular telephone satellite communication.

He pressed the speed dial, and seconds later he heard a familiar feminine voice. Tightening his hold on Tessa's slender body, he said, "Sylvia, Micah Sanborn. What's happening with the electricity?"

"OEM just informed us that a fire in a substation knocked out power to lower Manhattan, all of Brooklyn and portions of Staten Island. Where are you?"

"I'm still in Brooklyn."

"Are you at the D.A.'s office?"

"No."

"The mayor just issued a citywide emergency, and it'll be easier for you to get back to the courthouse if you're needed if you stay in Brooklyn."

Micah ended the call and returned the cell phone to his jacket pocket. He had recently turned over his Bronx condominium to his sister, moved to Staten Island and had signed a one-year lease on a furnished studio apartment because he hadn't decided whether he wanted to purchase or build a home in that borough.

Lowering his chin, he inhaled the floral fragrance of the hair grazing his chin. The pleasure he derived from Tessa's curvy body molded to his overshadowed the seriousness of the situation. Smiling, he told her what his contact at One Police Plaza had informed him.

"Do they have any idea how long it's going to last?" Tessa asked.

Micah shook his head before he realized she couldn't see him. "No. By the way, do you have a flashlight?"

"I have one, but it's upstairs."

"What about candles?"

"I have tons of them. Getting to them will prove somewhat difficult."

"Where are they?"

"They're in the pantry off the kitchen."

"Lead the way and I'll follow you."

Turning in the direction she hoped led out of her office, Tessa took small, halting steps, one hand held out in front of her, Micah following closely behind. She found the hallway, her fingertips trailing along the wall. At the end of the hallway she turned to her left and walked through a small antechamber and into the kitchen.

"Don't move," she said in the blackness that seemed to swallow her whole. "I have to get my bearings."

Micah stood completely still, all of his senses operating on full alert. He heard Tessa moving about the space, then a soft moan of pain followed by a whispered expletive. "What happened?"

"I bumped my shin."

"Are you okay?" His voice sounded abnormally loud in the eerie silence.

"I will be as soon as I locate the stove."

His brow furrowed. "What's up with the stove?"

"I have a gas range."

Micah's frown vanished. Not only was Tessa Whitfield beautiful but he found her levelheaded. She hadn't panicked or dissolved into hysterics once the power went out. One by one the jets to the stove-top range in a cooking island came on. There was enough light for him to see Tessa's shadowy figure move to a corner of the kitchen. He was galvanized into action as she gathered up candleholders from a drawer under the countertop.

Working quickly, Tessa set out more than two dozen holders and tea lights on the cooking island, the countertops and a table in a breakfast nook, while he lit them with an automatic lighter.

Micah shrugged out of his jacket, draping it on the back of a tall stool at the cooking island as Tessa stared at the man staring back at her.

Smiling, she said, "It's not the first time I'm thankful that I don't have an all-electric kitchen."

"Do you always keep so many candles on hand?"

She nodded, crossed her arms under her breasts and rested a hip against the countertop. "I have hundreds of them. I usually eat outdoors during the warmer weather and use them for illumination rather than spotlights." What she didn't tell Micah was that she found candlelight calming, relaxing.

Affecting a similar pose, Micah crossed his arms over his chest. "Are you the outdoorsy type?"

Tessa's pouty lips formed an attractive moue, and Micah's midnight gaze lingered on her mouth. He'd found her face incredibly beautiful in the light, but with the glow of flickering candlelight she'd become mesmerizing.

A mysterious smile crinkled the corners of Tessa's eyes as she stared at the tall man standing only a few feet away. "My favorite outdoor activities include sitting under an umbrella sipping a tropical concoction or grabbing a few winks with the sound of water lapping up on a beach as background music."

Throwing back his head, Micah laughed, the warm sound bubbling up from his broad chest. "I suppose I'd never find you on a ski slope."

She wrinkled her pert nose. "Never," she confirmed. "Do you ski?"

He nodded. "Yes. My parents are avid skiers."

It was obvious the Sanborns liked cold weather. Why else would Bridget schedule a New Year's Eve wedding in the northeast? Thinking of Micah's sister reminded Tessa why he was in her kitchen.

She straightened. "Speaking of cold weather, I think we'd better talk about your sister's wedding." She'd planned to give Micah an informational packet for his sister, but that along with the other literature she usually gave to prospective brides was in her office.

Reaching for his jacket on the stool, Micah withdrew a folded sheet of paper and handed it to Tessa. "I took a few notes when I last spoke to Bridget."

She unfolded the single sheet of paper, holding it close to the flickering flames. She could hardly read the scribble. Her arching eyebrows lifted. "What language is this?"

Micah's jaw tightened. "It's English," he ground out between clenched teeth.

Tessa handed him the paper. "You're going to have to translate this for me."

He scowled. He knew he didn't have the most legible handwriting, but no one had ever mistaken it for a foreign language. "You've got jokes, *Ms-s-s.* Whitfield?" He had drawn out the *Ms.* to several syllables.

"No, I don't. And it's *Miss* Whitfield."

"I thought running your own company would make you a liberated woman."

Tessa pulled back her shoulders. "I am liberated—but not so much so that I don't expect a man to hold a door open for me, push and pull back my chair and stand up whenever I enter a room."

A slow smile parted his mobile mouth at the same time he angled his head. "That's what I like—an old-fashioned woman."

"I'm not old-fashioned," she countered. "It's just that I like my men to have home training."

"Does your man have home training, Tessa?"

There was a pulse beat of silence before she said, "No." The single word was barely a whisper.

"And why doesn't he have home training, Tessa?" Micah asked, his deep baritone voice dropping an octave.

Because right now I don't have a man, she mused.

She wanted to tell Micah he should mind his business but couldn't. He was the brother of her client, and the courtesy she afforded her clients extended to family members. Ninety-five percent of her business came from referrals.

Tilting her chin in what she hoped was an arrogant gesture, she affected a supercilious smile. "Correct me if I'm wrong, but I was led to believe your purpose for coming to Signature Bridals was to discuss your sister's upcoming nuptials."

Micah went completely still. Nothing moved. Not even his eyes. "Your assumption is correct."

Moving closer, close enough for several strands of her wayward hairstyle to graze his chin, Tessa gave him a direct stare. "Then it should be your sister's wedding that we should be talking about, not what I like in a man."

Micah inhaled the sweet scent clinging to her hair and a different woodsy fragrance on her body. Not only did she look good but she also smelled delicious.

"You can say that I'm just curious."

"I hope you're familiar with the saying about curiosity and the cat."

"I am," he shot back smugly, "but I'm also quite familiar with what brought her back."

"Wasn't the cat a *he?*"

Micah's mysterious smile was back. "Not in this case."

"Why would you say that?"

"Your hair, eyes and coloring remind of a lioness."

Tessa wanted to tell Micah that he also reminded her of a predatory jungle cat but wanted to steer the conversation away from that of a personal nature.

"Have you eaten dinner?" she asked him.

He blinked once, seemingly startled by her question. "No, I haven't. Why?"

She turned and walked over to the refrigerator and opened the door. "I don't know how long the electricity is going to be out, and rather than have my dinner spoil, I'm going to share it with you. Meanwhile you can tell me about your sister." She glanced at Micah over her shoulder. She knew she'd surprised him with her offer. "Do you eat red meat?"

"Yes, I do."

"How do you like your steak?"

"Medium-well."

He peered at Tessa's slender body outlined in a flickering golden glow. There was something about Tessa Whitfield's exquisite face, beautifully modulated voice and aloof manner that he liked—a lot.

"Would you like some help?"

Tessa removed a platter with the marinated steak from a shelf. "No, thank you. I have everything under control," she said, placing the platter on the counter next to the stove-top grill.

"What if I set the table?" Micah asked. He wanted and needed to do more than just stand around and stare at her.

She gave him a warm, open smile for the first time. "Okay."

"Where can I wash my hands?"

She pointed to the cooking island. "Use that sink. I'm going to put a few candles in the downstairs bathroom before I go upstairs for the flashlight."

Turning back his shirt cuffs, Micah washed his hands in a stainless-steel sink. He knew Rosalind Sanborn would have a hissy fit if she saw him washing his hands in the kitchen, but he was certain she would forgive this one infraction. What would have shocked his mother more was that he'd finally met a woman who had caught his interest even before she'd opened her mouth. And when she did speak, she'd enthralled him with the low, throaty timbre.

He smiled. Tessa Whitfield's voice was the perfect match for her sultry look.

Tessa handed Micah a towel to dry his hands. "The dishes are in the cabinet above the dishwasher. And you'll find flatware in a drawer under the butcher-block counter."

She turned on the oven, then concentrated on draining the water from the potatoes and patting them dry before she placed the wedges in a plastic bag filled with an herb-and-olive-oil mixture. What she didn't want to do was think about the tall man moving about her kitchen as if he had done it before. She placed the potatoes on a cookie sheet and put it into the preheated oven.

"What would you like to drink?" she asked.

"What are my choices?"

"You can have either water or wine."

"Wine is good."

"Red or blush?"

Micah halted putting steak knives on the table. "Red."

"Come and select one."

He crossed the kitchen and stood in front of a built-in subzero wine cellar. Dozens of bottles lay on their sides in precise rows. He opened the door, selected a Merlot and closed it quickly. If the power stayed off for any extended period of time, then there was no doubt Tessa's perishable foodstuffs would have to be discarded.

Chapter 2

The distinctive ringing of the wall phone shattered the silence, and Tessa answered it. "Hello."

"Thank goodness you're home. I just turned on the television and heard about the blackout. Are you all right, Theresa?"

She smiled. Only her mother called her Theresa. "Yes, I am, Mama."

"Don't forget to tell her to check the windows and doors," her father's voice boomed in the background.

"Tell Dad they're locked."

There came a pause on the other end of the wire. "Your father said if the power is still out in the morning, he'll drive down and bring you home."

Tessa rolled her eyes upward. "My home is in Brooklyn, not Mount Vernon." Why couldn't Lucinda Whitfield accept that she was no longer a child but a thirty-one-year-old woman running a very successful business? "I don't want to cut you short, but I have a client I have to talk to."

"You're conducting business during a blackout?"

"Yes. I'll call you tomorrow."

"You promise, sweetheart?"

"Yes, I promise."

"Love you, Theresa."

"I love you, too, Mama."

She hung up before her mother could lapse into a diatribe as to why she shouldn't have set up Signature Bridals in Brooklyn. After all, her sister Simone ran a successful floral business out of her home in White Plains. All of her life she'd fought for her independence. Her parents—her father in particular—believed a woman couldn't survive without the protection of a husband.

Although Tessa refused to conform to their outdated views, her older sister had. Simone had married her high school sweetheart, yet the union didn't survive their fifth wedding anniversary. Tessa smiled. What she found incredible was that Simone and her mother had perfected the role of vapid female to an art form.

Micah thought because she owned and operated her own business she *had* to be a liberated woman. She *was* liberated—not in the literal sense of the word; however, what she'd done was fight a long and at times arduous battle to determine her own destiny. And during her personal struggles she'd had to make sacrifices in order to make Signature Bridals a success.

She had sacrificed love and marriage.

Tessa turned to find Micah staring at her as if he had never seen her before. "Do you need something?"

Micah blinked as if coming out of a trance.

I love you.

Whenever he heard a woman say the three words, he usually turned and headed in the opposite direction. He was able to accept a woman's passion and companionship until she opened her mouth to profess her love for him. It was thirty-six years and he still hadn't accepted his biological mother's abandonment.

Evelyn Howard had hugged and kissed him as they'd sat waiting to be seen in a large, noisy hospital clinic; she'd told him that she loved him and that he was not to move while she went to the restroom. He'd sat in the same spot for more than four hours waiting for her return. It wasn't until a nurse noticed he'd been alone that he'd realized his mother wasn't coming back.

He became a ward of the state of New Jersey for three years, until at age seven he was adopted by Edgar and Rosalind Sanborn. His new mother learned quickly that although he would permit her to hug and kiss him, she couldn't tell her adopted son that she loved him.

Micah successfully camouflaged his inner turmoil with a smile. "I need a corkscrew."

Tessa searched a drawer and gave him the corkscrew, checked the potatoes and then turned on the stove-top grill to heat up. At that moment she wished she had a battery-powered radio on hand to break the stilted silence. She did have a small portable TV/radio, but it was in the space on the top floor that was her sewing room. She wanted something—anything—to distract her from Micah's presence.

Micah Sanborn was the first man in a long time whose presence reminded her that she was a woman, one who'd denied her femininity for far too long. She would share her dinner with him, address some of his sister's concerns about her wedding and then escort him out the door.

Picking up a candleholder, she cupped her hand around the flicking flame. "I'm going upstairs to get the flashlight."

"Do you want me to come with you?"

Tessa forced a smile. "No, thank you. I'll be back in a few minutes."

"Are you sure you don't need an escort?"

Her smile widened. "Yes, I'm sure," she said as she took small, measured steps and she left the kitchen.

Micah sat opposite Tessa, thoroughly enjoying his meal and his dining partner. The grilled steaks were the perfect complement to the oven-baked seasoned potato wedges and accompanying salad. As soon as he drained his second glass of Merlot he felt more relaxed than he had in a very long time.

"Thank you for dinner. You're a very good cook."

She inclined her head in acknowledgment. "Thank you."

Her cooking skills were adequate; but it was her first cousin Faith Whitfield who, as a professional chef, had become a renowned cake designer. Tessa, Faith and her floral-designer sister Simone completed the threesome that made up Signature Bridals.

The sheet of paper with his scribbled notes lay next to Micah's plate. He moved a candle closer, glancing at the first notation. "Bridget and Seth want an interfaith service. My sister is Catholic and her fiancé is Jewish." He ran a hand over his close-cropped hair. "Will that pose a problem for you?"

Tessa shook her head. "No." And it wouldn't because she'd coordinated countless interfaith marriages. "Have they selected a priest and a rabbi?"

"Seth's cousin is a rabbi, and Bridget has requested her

local parish priest be present, along with a coworker who is also an ordained minister."

Tessa laughed. "It looks as if they've covered all of the bases."

He glanced at the paper again. "She'd like you to take care of everything with the exception of food. Mom has a friend who's a caterer."

"What about a cake?"

Micah studied his notes, attempting to decipher what he'd written. Tessa was right. His handwriting did look like hieroglyphs. "She didn't say anything about a cake."

"We'll take care of the cake," Tessa told him. "How many attendants do they plan to have?"

"They've planned on a maid of honor and a best man."

She mentally filed away this information. "How about a ring bearer or flower girl?"

Micah shook his head. "No."

"Do they plan on having music?"

He smiled. "What would New Year's Eve be without music?"

Lowering her gaze, Tessa smiled. "You're right about that. How many guests do they expect to invite?"

"The last count was eighty."

"I'll plan for one hundred just in case they want to add a few more names," she said in a quiet voice. "Signature Bridals will assume responsibility for mailing the invitations and securing the services of a photographer, a florist and a reputable band. Does she have a dress?"

Micah shook his head again. "I don't believe she has because I recall her telling Mom that she had to go look for a dress."

"I have dresses."

"You have dresses *here?*" he asked.

Tessa smiled. "Yes. I have at least twenty dresses on hand at any given time. However, it is imperative that I meet with Bridget as soon as she's off jury duty to set up a realistic wedding budget and timeline."

Tracing the rim of his wineglass with his finger, Micah fixed his gaze on the delicate glass. "Money's not an issue. My parents are prepared to pay for whatever Bridget wants."

Tessa wondered if Bridget Sanborn's impulsiveness came from her being spoiled and/or pampered. "Time is more important than the money. Your sister has less than twelve weeks in which to plan a formal wedding. Do you have any idea when she'll be available?"

Lifting a broad shoulder under his white shirt, Micah said, "The judge has just sequestered the jury, so hopefully they'll reach a quick decision."

Propping her elbow on the table, Tessa rested her chin on the heel of her hand and stared directly at Micah. She had to admit that the diffuse light flattered the sharp angles in the face of the man sitting opposite her. He was well-spoken and urbane—two traits she'd found missing in some of the men she'd come in contact with. Either they were one or the other.

"There's not much I can do until I meet with her. There are too many questions and details to go over that only she'll know. But there is something I could check out now."

"What's that?"

"I need to see the wedding site."

"How soon do you need to see it?"

"Like yesterday." There was a hint of laughter in Tessa's voice.

A small smile played at the corners of Micah's firm mouth. "That can be arranged." He stood up and reached for the jacket he'd left on the stool. Retrieving his cell phone, he scrolled through the directory. Within seconds he heard Rosalind Sanborn's dulcet greeting.

"Mom, I'm here with the wedding consultant." It took less than three minutes for Micah to give his mother an update on what Tessa needed for Bridget's wedding, Rosalind promising to help when and wherever she could. There was no mistaking the excitement in her voice.

Covering the mouthpiece with his thumb, he met Tessa's questioning look across the table. "Are you available to come to New Jersey with me on Sunday?" She nodded. He removed his thumb. "Yes. We'll see you Sunday." Ending the call, he placed the tiny phone in his shirt pocket.

Tessa expelled an inaudible sigh. She'd just scaled one hurdle in the Sanborn-Cohen nuptials. She didn't have to scramble to look for a place in which to hold the reception for eighty.

"What time is your mother expecting us?"

"My mother is always up early, so maybe we'll get there in time to share brunch with her and my father. And if Bridget is finished with jury duty, she'll also be there."

Tessa spent the next hour outlining minute details of a formal wedding, from invitations, prewedding parties, hair and makeup to ceremony, reception flowers, photographs of the ceremony, reception and music. Some of the candles on the table were sputtering when she finished.

She pushed to her feet and Micah stood up with her. "I need to clean up the kitchen."

Micah caught her wrist as she picked up a plate. "Sit. I'll clean up."

"No."

He tightened his hold, registering the fragile bones under his loose grip. "You cooked, so I'll clean."

She shook her head. "No, Micah."

Not releasing her hand, he rounded the table. "Yes." He hadn't raised his voice, but the single word was pregnant with authority.

"Must I remind you that you're in my home?"

Attractive lines fanned out around his eyes when he smiled. He let go of her hand. "There's no way I'd ever mistake your place for mine. I live in a studio apartment above a garage that's about the size of your kitchen and pantry. The bathroom is no larger than a closet. It's a good thing I'm not claustrophobic, because there's only enough room for a convertible sofa, a table and *a* chair."

Tessa's naturally arching eyebrows lifted as she smiled. "A single chair?"

Micah returned her smile, nodding.

"Have you always lived in Staten Island?"

"No." Taking the plates from her, Micah walked over to the sink. "I moved there four months ago."

Tessa gathered up the glasses and silver. "Where did you live before?" She wasn't chatty by nature, but talking was preferable to complete silence.

"*Da* Bronx. "

She laughed softly. She'd grown up hearing Bronxites refer to their borough as *da* rather than *the*. "I assume you're a Yankees fan?"

Shifting, Micah stared at Tessa in the muted light. The flickering flames turned her into a statue of gold. "I didn't grow up a Yankees fan, but after living in the Bronx for almost half my life it was safer to root for them than the Mets."

Tessa joined Micah at the sink, filling it with water and adding a dollop of dishwashing liquid. She rinsed the dishes and glasses, passing them to him as he stacked them in the dishwasher.

"Did you grow up in the city?" Tessa asked, continuing with her questioning.

His eyebrows lifted when he realized she'd called New York City *the city.* "No. I grew up in New Jersey."

She gave him a sidelong glance. "How did a Jersey boy find his way across the river to the Bronx?"

His hands halted placing serving pieces in the dishwasher. "My, aren't you inquisitive."

"You can say that I'm just a little curious about a man willing to do dishes." She was very curious about Micah Sanborn because he was the first man who'd offered to help her in the kitchen.

"Good home training."

She smiled. "Good for you, and kudos to your mother."

"You can tell her when you meet her Sunday. To answer your question as to how I came to live in the big city, I lived with an aunt in Manhattan while I went to college. After graduating, I rented an apartment in the Bronx. Eventually I bought a two-bedroom condo not far from the Throgs Neck Bridge. Earlier this year I moved from the Bronx to Staten Island. Where did you grow up?" he asked, deftly shifting the focus from himself to Tessa.

"Mount Vernon."

"What brought you to the city?"

"It's the same as you. I came to go to college."

"What college did you go to?"

Before Tessa could answer the question, the power returned; the lights flickered off and on for several seconds, then went out again. She let out an audible sigh. "It looks as if this is going to be a long night."

Several of the tea lights sputtered, fizzled and went out. Micah replaced the burned-out candles from a supply in a large plastic bag. "I'd better light a few more candles or we're going to be in the dark again."

The doorbell rang, startling Tessa and Micah. They stared at each other as a slight frown appeared between her eyes. She wasn't expecting anyone. Reaching for the flashlight, she flicked it on.

"I better see who that is." She turned to make her way out of the kitchen, Micah following. Without warning, she stopped. He plowed into her and she dropped the flashlight. "What are you doing?" The query came out in a hissing sound.

Micah picked up the flashlight. "I'm coming with you."

"There's no need for you to follow me."

Ignoring her reprimand, he held her hand in a firm grip. "There's no way I'm going to let you answer the door when you don't know who's standing on the other side."

"You're a bossy somebody, aren't you?" she said accusingly.

"Hell, yeah." There was laughter in his confirmation.

She struggled to free herself, but she was no match for his superior strength. What little she'd been able to glimpse of Micah Sanborn before the power went out was a tall, slender man whose tailored clothes artfully concealed a lean, muscular physique. When he'd held her during his call to One Police Plaza, she hadn't been that traumatized that she hadn't taken note of the comforting crush of his solid body.

"I'd answer the door by myself if you weren't here with me," she countered angrily.

Training the beam of light from the flashlight on the floor, Micah steered her down the hallway to the front door. "Thank goodness that I *am* here. There are some folks who'll use a blackout as an excuse to act the fool."

Tessa rolled her eyes at him even though he couldn't see her. "This happens to be a safe neighborhood."

"No neighborhood is *that* safe. There *is* crime in Brooklyn Heights."

"I suppose you would know the statistics." A tapping on the door and a man's voice calling Tessa's name cut off Micah's reply. "It sounds like one of my neighbors. May I open the door?" she asked facetiously.

He stepped back and handed her the flashlight. She unlocked and opened the door. Intermittent flashes of light sliced through the pitch-black streets. He could make out the shapes of people out with flashlights or candles, standing around in small groups. A slow-moving car with high beams came down the street, the slip-slap of tires on the roadway breaking the eerie silence.

Tessa smiled at the man standing on the top step, his luminous blue eyes illuminated in the glow of a lantern. "What's up, Jacks?"

Micah peered through the opening in the door. He wanted to tell Tessa that he knew her neighbor.

"Some of the folks have gotten together to throw a block party."

Tessa gave him an incredulous look. "How are we going to party in a blackout?"

"I bought a generator after the last blackout. Come on over and get your eat and drink on."

It wasn't often that Tessa socialized with the residents

of her close-knit neighborhood because of her hectic schedule, but she decided getting together with the people who lived on her block was preferable to sitting in the dark waiting for the power to come back on.

"I'll be over as soon as I lock up here."

"Do you want me to wait to walk you over?"

Micah stepped from the shadows for the first time. "That's all right, Jacks, I'll see that she gets there safely."

Jackson's smile faded as his gaze narrowed. "Sandy?" Those familiar with Micah Sanborn had shortened his name to Sandy.

"Long time no see, Jacks," Micah said to the man who'd entered the police academy with him and later graduated with him. Time appeared to have stood still for Jackson Cleary.

Jackson reached for Micah and grabbed him up in a bear hug. "Where the hell have you been? Since you left the department it's like you dropped off the face of the earth."

Tessa watched in astonishment as the two men greeted each other like long-lost buddies. She knew Jackson Cleary was a New York City police officer, and when she registered his comment about Micah leaving the department she assumed Micah also had been a police officer.

Micah thumped Jackson's back. "I'm working with the Brooklyn D.A. Where are you now?"

"Internal Affairs."

"So you decided to join the rat squad," Micah said softly.

Frown lines appeared between Jackson's eyes. "Look, why don't we talk about this when we're alone?" His frown vanished quickly. "I didn't know you knew Tessa, but you're welcome to come."

Micah turned and stared at Tessa, who nodded in agreement. "We'll be over in a few minutes."

"Later," Jackson called over his shoulder as he made his way down the stairs.

Tessa stared up at Micah, trying vainly to see his expression. "I need to put out the candles before we head over to Jacks's place."

"I'll help you." He held out his hand. "Please give me the flashlight."

She handed him the flashlight at the same time his free hand went to the small of her back. She stiffened before relaxing against his splayed fingers, the heat warming her skin through her cotton dress.

Chapter 3

Tessa and Micah, his suit jacket draped over her shoulders to ward off the cool night air, joined the modest crowd that'd gathered in the backyard of the brownstone in the cul-de-sac. Floodlights lit up the area like daylight.

The smell of broiling meat was redolent in the crisp autumn night as Jackson manned a gas grill, flipping franks, hamburgers, sausage links and steaks. The waning full moon in a clear sky competed with the flickering flames from lighted candles in the many windows of the buildings lining both sides of the street. After the 2003 blackout most New Yorkers had learned to stockpile candles and battery-operated devices in the event it would happen again. And it had, but not to the proportions that had affected the entire city.

Tessa found it ironic that the brother of a client she had yet to meet was on a first-name basis with one of her neighbors. The adage about it being a small world was certainly true. What were the odds of her running into someone she hadn't seen in years in a city that boasted a population of nearly eight million?

Grasping the proprietary arm Micah had draped around her waist, Tessa smiled up at him. "I'm going inside to see if Irena needs some help."

More people had begun to crowd into the Clearys' backyard; they hadn't come empty-handed, many carrying trays of meat, fruits and vegetables.

Lowering his chin, Micah smiled at the alluring woman pressed to his side. "Are you sure you're going to be okay?" he teased.

She affected an attractive moue. "Why wouldn't I? Especially with several members New York's finest in attendance. Yours truly included in the mix."

"Former NYPD," he corrected softly.

"Are you still in law enforcement?"

Dipping his head, he pressed his mouth close to her ear. "Instead of arresting the bad guys, I now prosecute them."

There was something in his voice and the way he stared at her that permitted Tessa to shed her professional persona and enjoy the moment and the man under whose sensual spell she'd fallen.

Her family always complained that she was too serious and that was why men tended to stay clear of her. What most had refused to understand was that her priority was growing her business, and that love and marriage—if it was in the cards for her—was always a possibility no matter her age.

"I have a parking ticket I need you to fix for me."

Micah went completely still. "You're kidding, aren't you?"

"No, I'm not," she replied, her voice even and her expression deadpan.

"I can't help you. And even if I could, I wouldn't."

A hint of a smile touched Tessa's lips. Micah Sanborn had just gone up several more notches in her approval category. He was no doubt quite ethical.

"And I wouldn't want you to."

He lifted black expressive eyebrows. "Then why did you ask me to help you?" His gaze narrowed. "You were testing me," Micah said intuitively as she placed a hand over her mouth to muffle the giggles. Tessa nodded. "And did I pass?"

Lowering her hand, she placed it on his shoulder, feeling the heat from his skin through his shirt. "Yes, you did."

"What do I get as a prize?"

She angled her head. "I don't know. I suppose I'll come up with something appropriate."

"If you can't come up with anything, then may I make a suggestion?"

Sobering, Tessa kept her features deceptively composed. Seeing Micah in the light, albeit artificial, had changed her opinion of his looks. He *was* handsome *and* very sexy, the combination having a lethal effect on her senses. Before the loss of electricity she hadn't been able to glimpse the attractive slashes in his lean cheeks, the stubborn set of a strong chin and the smooth texture of his close-cropped hair.

"What?" The single word came out in a breathless whisper.

"Let me return the favor of you cooking for me by taking you out to dinner."

"I…I can't," she stuttered.

"Why can't you? It's only dinner."

She flushed like a nervous schoolgirl and remained silent for several seconds, pondering how she was going to reject Micah's offer when she knew she would continue to come into contact with him until his sister's wedding.

"I don't date." The three words rushed out of their own volition.

"You don't date?"

The heat in her face increased. "What I mean is that I don't date or get involved with a client or anyone associated with that client. It's not good for business." Her gaze was drawn to his teeth when he smiled. "What's so funny?"

Micah dipped his head. "You are," he said in a quiet voice. "I'm not asking you out on a date or to get involved. I just want to repay you for your very gracious offer. You didn't have to share your food with me."

"What did you expect me to do? Show you the door?"

"You could've, but you didn't."

There was a spark of some indefinable emotion in the dark eyes staring at Tessa, and in a moment of madness everything she professed about maintaining a professional perspective toward her clients was forgotten.

"Okay. I'll go out to dinner with you."

Micah wondered why it sounded as if Tessa were doing him a favor when he'd felt as if it were the reverse. He *did* want to repay her for sharing her dinner, but what he couldn't admit to her and didn't want to admit to himself was that Tessa Whitfield fascinated him.

She was beautiful, intelligent, reserved and confident. At forty-one, he'd known his share of women, but there was something about the wedding planner that was different from any other woman he'd ever known.

He inclined his head. "Now, that wasn't so hard, was it? It will be at your convenience—of course."

Tessa visually traced the outline of his mobile mouth and said, "Of course."

She felt the heat of Micah's midnight gaze on her back as she went in search of Irena Cleary, silently berating herself for breaking her own rule. She'd lost count of the number of men who'd tried coming on to her since she'd established Signature Bridals with her sister and cousin—men she normally wouldn't have met if not for her business.

Once burned, twice shy.

She'd gotten in over her head with Bryce Hill, but swore it would never happen again with another man.

Tessa found Jackson's wife Irena in the kitchen. Pregnant with her third and what she claimed was her last baby, the elementary school teacher was engaged in a heated conversation with her preteen daughter, who wanted to know why she couldn't invite her friends over to the impromptu cookout.

Turning on her heel, Tessa retraced her steps. She didn't want to witness what was certain to become a volatile confrontation between mother and daughter. She remembered her own disagreements with her mother, but it always ended with Lucinda declaring, *I had you, not the other way around, so that makes me the boss of you.* And it wasn't until she'd matured that Tessa realized every decision her mother had made on her behalf was for her daughters' benefit and protection.

Returning to the backyard, she saw Micah with Jackson Cleary, the two men standing apart from the others and deep in conversation. She was stuck in the dark with a former New York City police officer who'd taken an oath to protect and serve.

She smiled.

How lucky could she get?

Hours later, Tessa unlocked the door to her home and found the dark silence eerie. It was after eleven; the block party had wound down and her neighbors had retreated to their darkened residences.

She handed Micah his suit jacket, the lingering scent of his cologne still wafting in her nostrils. "You're welcome to hang out here until the power comes back or sunrise. Whatever comes first," she added.

Raising the flashlight, Micah stared at Tessa, photographing her with his eyes. Slowly, seductively, his gaze slid downward to the hollow of her throat, where a runaway pulse revealed she wasn't as composed as she appeared.

"Thank you."

"Come upstairs with me."

He didn't move. "That's all right. I'll hang out down here."

"You can't hang out down here because there's no place for you to lie down, and I don't think you'd want to spend the night sitting up in a chair." Tessa extended her hand. "I'm going to need the flashlight."

They climbed the staircase together. There was only the sound of their footsteps muffled in the carpeting on the stairs and the rhythmic ticking of the massive grandfather clock in a corner at the top of the staircase. The narrow beam of light illuminated the Oriental runner on the second-story parquet floor hallway. Tessa led the way into her bedroom, stopped and turned to face Micah.

"You can sleep in here."

He frowned. "Where are you going to sleep?"

"I'll be in one of the guest bedrooms."

"Why can't I sleep in the guest room?"

Her frown matched his. "Are you always so contrary, Micah?"

His frown deepened. "You think I'm contrary?"

"Yes," she countered. "Everything I suggest, you refute. I'm offering you my bedroom because it has the largest bed and I believe you would be more comfortable sleeping in a king rather than a full- or twin-size bed."

Micah's expression softened. "It's not that I don't appreciate your hospitality, but I don't want to inconvenience you."

"Everyone affected by this blackout is inconvenienced. We're lucky because we could've been trapped in a subway tunnel or in an elevator. And like in so many other unfortunate situations, I've learned to go with the flow."

When Tessa directed the beam of light to a corner of the room, Micah could make out the outline of a chaise, a table and a lamp. "I can't sleep in your bed. I'll take the chaise."

Tessa clamped her teeth together. She couldn't remember the last time she'd met someone as exasperating at Micah Sanborn. And that included a few over-the-top brides-to-be. She'd gone above and beyond social protocol to make him comfortable, and still he challenged her every proposal. What she should've done when the lights went out was show him the door, but she'd accommodated him because of his sister. There was no doubt the Sanborns were going to test her patience and work her last nerve.

"How tall are you, Micah?"

"Why?"

"How tall?" she repeated.

"Six-one."

"You just struck out. The chaise is configured for someone less than six feet in height. Therefore the bed is yours."

"If that's the case, then why don't we share the bed? I give my word that nothing will happen," he teased.

"And I give *you* my word that I'll jack you up if you tried something."

"*You* jack *me* up?" he asked incredulously. "I'm at least half a foot taller and I'm willing to bet that I outweigh you by eighty pounds—and you claim you can jack me up."

Tessa wrinkled her nose. "There may be some truth in your statistics, but I know a way of changing you from a baritone to a soprano in one-point-two seconds with a well-aimed knee to your—"

"Please don't say it," Micah said, interrupting her. "I get the point."

She walked over to the sitting/dressing area. The seconds ticked off as she lit candles on two low tables in the inviting space. There was enough light coming from the candles in the alcove for her to gather a pair of pajamas from a drawer in an eighteenth-century Louis XV armoire made of walnut that included the original hardware. She'd refused to reveal to anyone how much she'd paid for the magnificent piece she'd found in the historic city of Arles, where van Gogh painted *Starry Night* and two hundred other canvases. The armoire matched the sleigh bed and the bedside tables she'd purchased at an estate sale two years before.

Tessa made her way into an adjoining bathroom, lighting the many candles lining the marble ledge surrounding the garden tub, and gathered towels from a marble slab mounted under the counter of a porcelain basin and took out a cellophane-wrapped toothbrush from a shelf concealed behind a wall mirror, placing them on a table next to a freestanding shower stall.

She left the bathroom to find Micah sitting in an upholstered club chair, one leg draped over the opposite knee. He stood up. Tilting her head, she smiled up at him. "I left towels and a toothbrush on a table next to the shower." There was a beat of silence, then she said, "Good night, Micah."

He returned her smile. "Sleep tight and don't let the bedbugs bite."

Tessa's sultry laugh swept over him like a light breeze as she left the bedroom, closing the door behind her. He liked hearing her laugh. It was unrepressed and free. Something she hadn't allowed herself to be—at least not with him. From the moment he'd stepped into the building housing Signature Bridals Tessa Whitfield was the consummate professional. She hadn't permitted the professional persona to slip over dinner. Even when she'd questioned him about where he'd grown up her tone was neutral, almost impersonal, as if she were conducting an interview.

He'd watched her interact formally with her neighbors as if she feared letting them see another side of her personality. If she'd accused him of being contrary, it was because he wanted her to relax, not to take herself or life so seriously. The events following 9/11 had changed him and his outlook on life forever.

Micah stood, staring at the door, thinking about the woman under whose roof he would spend the night—a woman whom he didn't know but wanted to get to know. Tessa's rule that she didn't date or get involved with anyone associated with her clients had become a challenge, one he readily welcomed.

All of his life he'd faced challenges: abandonment by his biological mother, becoming a ward of the state of New Jersey, serving and protecting the citizens of New York City for twenty years as a police officer and now as an assistant district attorney for Kings County.

He liked challenges and he was patient—patient enough to wait until after his sister's wedding, when she would no longer be a Signature bride.

Micah walked into the bathroom and took in a quick breath. Aside from indoor plumbing and electricity—or lack of the latter at the present time—he felt as if he'd stepped back in time. The French-inspired bathroom was a retreat—a place to relax and while away the hours in the oversize marble tub or in a corner with an overstuffed chaise covered in a pale-blue-and-cream-striped fabric.

A nearby table held a crystal vase filled with a profusion of colorful fresh-cut flowers. A terra-cotta floor and walls covered with pale-blue-and-cream wallpaper reflected the French influence Tessa seemed to favor. He picked up a book off a stack on the table and smiled. He and Tessa had similar reading tastes.

As he unbuttoned his shirt, pulling it from the waistband of his trousers, he didn't want to think of what else he had in common with the seemingly elusive woman who'd aroused his curiosity. Perhaps it was because Tessa was so unapproachable that she'd piqued his interest. He'd never viewed women as sexual objects or regarded them as receptacles for his lust, but that also didn't mean that he hadn't had his share of affairs or one-night stands. There were women he'd liked—a lot. And there were women who'd liked him—a lot.

He brushed his teeth and undressed, leaving his clothes folded neatly on the chaise. Opening the door to the shower stall, he stepped in and closed it behind him. Turning on the cold water, Micah gritted his teeth as the icy spray pebbled his flesh. Then he turned on the other faucet, adjusting the water temperature until it was lukewarm. He picked up a bar of soap and lathered his body.

The scent of flowers and fruit filled the space. He recalled the Aerosmith classic hit, "Dude Looks Like A Lady." He may not have looked like a lady, but he sure smelled like one. The first thing he had to do when he returned to his apartment was take a shower using his own bath gel.

Micah completed his shower, toweled off, extinguished all of the candles and carefully made his way out of the bathroom. He repeated the action, blowing out the candles in the alcove. He managed to get into bed without bumping into chairs or tables.

The moment he pulled back the duvet and the sheet everything about Tessa came rushing back. Her scent clung to the linen. He recalled her flyaway hairstyle and bohemian style of dress, things that were incongruous to her very controlled personality.

He lay in the darkened room, listening to the sound of his own breathing, when he heard a noise. Sitting up, all of his senses on full alert, Micah saw the outline of Tessa's body in the beam of light coming from the flashlight where she'd opened the door.

A grin split his face. "Are you coming to join me?"

"I just came to check on you."

"I'm glad you did, because I forgot to tell you that I'm afraid of the dark." Tessa laughed softly, the sound sending a myriad of emotions racing through Micah.

"I can't help you there, buddy. But if it would make you feel better, I'll leave the flashlight with you."

He patted the mattress beside him. "Come sit with me a while."

"Aren't you sleepy?"

"No. I'm too wound up to sleep."

Tessa walked into the bedroom. "So am I." She approached the bed. "Move over." He shifted and she crawled atop the sheet beside him. She didn't know if he was naked under the sheet and she wasn't anxious to find out. Placing the flashlight in the space separating her from Micah, she leaned over and sniffed him. "You smell like a woman."

Folding his arms under his head, Micah chuckled softly. "I'll put up with smelling like a woman only if I don't turn into one."

"What's wrong with being a woman?" There was no mistaking the censure in her tone.

"There's nothing wrong with being one, but I like being a man, thank you very much."

Shifting slightly, Tessa stared at Micah. "Why?"

"Because we can belch, scratch and adjust ourselves with impunity—because that's what men do."

She scrunched up her nose. "That's disgusting, Micah."

"Well, it's true."

"It's true because that's what society has permitted men to do. Meanwhile if a woman chooses to breast-feed her baby in public—and even if no one can see her breast or nipple—she's rebuked and castigated for something that is the most natural thing in the world. And some of those same narrow-minded people will go to the zoo and see animal mothers nursing their babies and claim it's so cute."

"You're preaching to the choir, Tessa. I'm not a sexist. How did you get into the wedding business?" he asked, deftly steering away from the controversial topic of differences between male and female.

"I'm second-generation wedding business. My mother is a wedding dress designer, and my father and uncles own and operate a catering hall in Mount Vernon. My sister, cousin and I set up Signature Bridals four years ago. I'm the coordinator, my cousin Faith's specialty is wedding cakes and my older sister Simone is a floral designer."

"You come highly recommended, because when Bridget attended the Jadya Fyles-Ashton Cooper wedding in Bryant Park she couldn't stop talking about how spectacular everything was."

Tessa had addressed the invitations for the Fyles-Cooper wedding, and because there had been so many invited guests she'd hadn't remembered Bridget Sanborn's name until Bridget called to tell her that she wanted Signature Bridals to coordinate her upcoming wedding.

"It took more than a year of planning to pull their wedding together. What helped was that Jadya knew exactly what she wanted from the onset."

"What about Ashton?"

"The prospective grooms usually adopt a hands-off attitude. It's the brides who become the Bridezillas."

"How do you handle them when they go ballistic?"

"It varies from bride to bride. You'll get an up-close-and-personal view when I deal with your sister."

"Bridget is a pussycat."

Tessa snorted delicately. "Don't forget that a cat also has claws. I usually can tell within fifteen minutes of meeting a prospective bride what I'm up against."

"Have you ever turned anyone down?"

There came a pause. "Yes. There was one woman who punched out one of her bridesmaids because she refused to agree on a color that was totally wrong for her complexion."

"What did you do?"

"I gave her back her deposit, tore up her contract and told her to find another wedding coordinator. I wasn't willing to run the risk of her hitting me if something I said or did offended her."

"What did she say?"

"She cried and pleaded, but I wouldn't change my mind."

"You're tough, aren't you?"

There was another pause before Tessa said, "I'm all business when it comes to business."

"What happens when it's not business?" Micah asked.

Tessa smiled. "I'm a pussycat."

"A pussycat with claws?" he teased.

She wrinkled her nose. "But of course."

Tessa entertained Micah with stories about some of the more bizarre weddings she'd coordinated that made him laugh and/or speechless. It was after one when her voice faded and she closed her eyes. She never knew when Micah turned off the flashlight, pulled the duvet up over her shoulders and draped an arm over her waist.

Tessa woke hours later to see light coming through the silk-lined drapes and the space next to her empty. She stared at the impression on the pillow beside her own.

It was the first time she'd shared her bed with a man who hadn't made love to her. A knowing smile tilted the corners of her mouth.

Unknowingly Micah Sanborn had earned a seal of approval from Theresa Anais Whitfield.

He was a man she knew she could trust.

Chapter 4

Micah drove from downtown Brooklyn to Staten Island in record time. The trip that would've normally taken anywhere between twenty and thirty minutes, depending upon the flow of traffic, was accomplished in ten.

It was Saturday. The power hadn't been restored, and at six-thirty in the morning he was one of a dozen motorists on the Verrazano Bridge.

He'd woken up in bed with Tessa Whitfield, her huddled to his chest like a trusting child, him experiencing a gamut of emotions he hadn't wanted to feel at that time. It was when he felt a rush of desire for the woman whose bed he'd shared that he knew it was time to leave Brooklyn.

Maneuvering into the driveway, Micah activated the remote device under the visor, raising the garage door. Less than a minute later he opened the door to his studio apartment and walked in. Streaks of gold had pierced the veil of night as the rising sun filtered through the skylight over a utility kitchen with a sink, a two-burner stove and a portable refrigerator.

Whenever he returned home he made it a practice to look in on his landlady. However, the eighty-two-year-old former schoolteacher was currently in Florida with relatives.

Diane Cunningham had complained of a pain in her side for several days, but when he'd offered to take her to the doctor she'd balked, saying she'd probably pulled a muscle from lifting a laundry basket.

She'd proudly announced that she'd waited more than a year to travel to Sarasota to see her newest great-grand-daughter and a little old pain was not going to stop her from making her scheduled flight. Two days ago he'd gotten a call from Mrs. Cunningham's daughter telling him that her mother was in the hospital recuperating from an emergency appendectomy.

Micah made a mental note to check on his landlady's place as he emptied his pockets of loose change, keys to his office, credit card case and money clip, leaving them on the bistro table. He also had to call Tessa and give her an approximate time when he would pick her up on Sunday to take her to New Jersey.

He undressed and walked into the closet-size bathroom to shower. A slow smile parted his lips as he soaped his body with a bath gel in a scent that matched his aftershave and cologne, washing away the scent of fruit and flowers. His smile faded when he remembered waking up to find Tessa's face pressed to his shoulder. The velvety smoothness of her body, the moist whisper of her breathing on his exposed throat and the soft crush of her breasts against his bare chest had elicited lascivious thoughts that were truly shocking.

What he did like about Tessa was her spontaneity. She was candid, without a hint of guile—attributes he hadn't experienced with most women he'd dated. Her beauty and intelligence aside, it still didn't explain why he'd reacted to her like a randy adolescent boy. Well, he thought, he didn't have too much longer to wait to uncover why, because in a little more than twenty-four hours he would see her again—this time in the light and away from her cloistered sanctuary.

Minutes after eight on Saturday morning electrical power was restored to lower Manhattan; Brooklyn a little before ten; and portions of Staten Island an hour later. Tessa trained her gaze on the television, channel surfing and listening to the same rendition of the possible and probable causes of the blackout from network correspondents.

Experts reported that a Con Ed work crew had cut through a feeder cable, while other reports attributed the blackout to a fire in a substation. The result was that New Yorkers in three of the five boroughs had lost power for more than twelve hours, and the owners of restaurants and smaller eateries were particularly vocal because they were forced to dispose of food worth estimates exceeding twenty million dollars.

Sitting on a stool in the kitchen and sipping her second cup of coffee, Tessa's attention was diverted when the telephone rang. Leaning over, she picked up the cordless instrument and peered at the display. Smiling, she pressed a button.

"Hello, Simone."

"How was the blackout?" drawled a low, sultry voice.

"I managed to survive," Tessa told her sister. "At least this time I was home when the lights went out."

"Mama told me you were with a client. How on earth did you manage to conduct business in the dark?"

"I used candles."

"Damn, Tessa. It's not that critical. Couldn't you've postponed the meeting?"

"Not when *we* have ten weeks to put together a formal interfaith wedding for more than eighty guests."

"That's really cutting it real close."

"Tell me about it. I haven't met the bride, so right now I have no idea what she wants."

"Who were you meeting with last night?"

"Her brother."

"Where's the bride?"

"She's on jury duty." Tessa told Simone that Bridget had canceled two meetings and went over what she'd discussed with Micah. However, she didn't reveal that Micah had spent the night or that they'd shared the same bed without making love.

"The girl sounds ditzy. The fact that she's canceled twice could be a cry for help that she really doesn't want to get married."

Tessa rolled her eyes upward. Simone had enrolled in college with the intent of becoming a psychologist but changed her major from psychology to a liberal arts degree program. She never became a psychologist, and when her marriage ended she channeled her pain and frustration into flower arranging. The result was wannabe psychologist Simone Whitfield had become a much-sought-after floral designer and the official florist for Signature Bridals.

"Don't go Dr. Phil on me, Simone. She just got engaged six weeks ago."

"Now that proves she's certifiably ditzy. Formal

weddings usually take more planning than a few months. When's her big day?"

"New Year's Eve."

"And I suppose she wants you to book a room at the Waldorf-Astoria or Tavern on the Green?"

"Thankfully, no," Tessa drawled cynically. "She's getting married at her parents' house in Franklin Lakes, New Jersey."

A soft whistle came through the earpiece. "Nice neighborhood. A lot of homes in that community start at a million and go as high as eight to ten."

Tessa thought about Micah saying money's not an issue, which meant the Sanborns were willing to pay for whatever Bridget wanted. "Well, I'll find out how much her folks are willing to spend when I meet them tomorrow."

"How old is baby girl?"

Tessa laughed. Simone always referred to spoiled, pampered brides as *baby girl*. "I don't know. I didn't ask her brother."

"Then how old is baby boy?"

"I don't know," Tessa said. She didn't want to tell Simone that if Micah had put in twenty years with the NYPD, then he had to be at least in his early forties. "I'll let you know what I come up with when I see you and Faith Monday night."

"Faith called me early this morning from Vegas—"

"Don't tell me she's not coming," Tessa moaned, interrupting Simone. Of the three, it was Faith Whitfield who'd become the most elusive. Faith had missed their last two bimonthly Monday-night dinner meetings. At any given time she could be asked to create a cake for a surprise birthday celebration or for a high-profile celebrity's impromptu gala.

"She's coming, but she's flying into Westchester instead of LaGuardia. I'll pick her up, and she can ride back to Manhattan with you."

"If she calls you again, please tell her that we're going to need a wedding cake for New Year's Eve."

Tessa talked to Simone for another quarter of an hour before ending the call. As soon as she hung up, her phone rang again. Micah's name came up in the display.

She smiled and said, "Good morning, Micah."

"Is it really a good morning?" came his velvet baritone query.

"Yes. I have electricity. How was your drive home?"

"Quick. It took about ten minutes door to door."

"You were speeding," she said accusatorily.

He chuckled softly. "Guilty as charged. I called to let you know I'll pick you up around ten. If that's too early, then I'll let my mother know we'll come for an early dinner."

"Ten is fine."

"Dress casually and wear comfortable shoes."

"Why?"

"You'll see when you get there," Micah said cryptically.

"I don't like surprises, Micah."

"This one I'm certain you'll like…." His voice trailed off. "I'm going to have to take this call, Tessa. I'll see you tomorrow."

Tessa held the receiver to her ear until she heard a programmed voice telling her to either hang up or try her call again. She hung up, wondering what it was Micah wanted her to see.

She couldn't begin to think of the possibilities, so she decided to concentrate on the laundry list of things she had to do: glue crystal beads and faux pearls to the bodice of a sample gown she'd designed in her spare time, put up several loads of laundry and go through her closets to take out winter clothes and put away her summer wardrobe. The leaves on the trees lining the streets had begun changing color, a blatant indicator that the summer was over.

Tessa walked down the steps at ten on Sunday morning, cradling a large envelope in one hand, at the same time Micah drove up in a low-slung, two-seater BMW convertible Roadster in a subtle charcoal gray. A hint of a smile softened her mouth. He'd just gotten another gold star: he was on time.

He waved to her as he got out of the car. A pair of jeans, an off-white cable-knit pullover sweater and running shoes had replaced his tailored suit and imported footwear. Her smile widened when she noticed the well-worn New York Yankees cap on his head. Her smile faded as quickly as it'd come. Micah hadn't shaved, and the stubble on his jaw enhanced his overt maleness.

Recovering quickly and holding her arms out at the sides, she spun around. "Is this causal enough for you?"

What Micah hadn't been able to see in the dark was now blatantly on display for his viewing pleasure. His midnight gaze moved slowly over the curly hair Tessa had brushed off her face and secured in a twist on the nape of her neck, down to her face with a subtle application of makeup that highlighted her gold-flecked eyes, high cheekbones with a light sprinkle of freckles and a lush mouth outlined in a soft rose-pink shade. A single strand of pearls matched the studs in her pierced ears.

He stared at her lush, compact body in an apricot-pink cashmere tank top with a matching cardigan, brown body-hugging stretch slacks and matching suede slip-ons. Even her brown pony-and-calfskin leather shoulder bag complemented her elegant sense of style. The epitome of casual-chic, she looked as if she'd stepped off the pages of *Town and Country.*

What she wore wasn't casual enough for what he'd planned for them, but he couldn't tell her that. "You look beautiful."

Caught off guard by the vibrancy of Micah's voice, the tenderness in his eyes, Tessa was helpless to stop a rush of heat darkening her face. She lowered her gaze in a demure gesture. "Thank you."

Micah winked at her. "Don't thank me, Tessa. I had nothing to do with the way you look." Cupping her elbow, he helped her into the car, closed the door and got in beside her. Pressing a button, he raised the convertible top, shifted into gear and maneuvered through the quiet Brooklyn neighborhood as the soothing sounds of jazz filled the racy sports car.

He took a quick glance at Tessa as she pressed her head to the leather headrest and closed her eyes. "Do you want me to put on a different CD?"

Tessa recognized the melodious horn of Wynton Marsalis playing a bluesy piece perfect for a nightclub setting. "No, please don't. It's nice." The music was nice, Micah's car was nice and he looked and smelled very nice.

Stopping at a red light, Micah reached for a pair of sunglasses off the console and slipped them on against the brilliant autumn sun. "Do you like jazz?"

She smiled. "I love it."

"Cool or hot jazz?"

Tessa opened her eyes and stared through the windshield. "Both. I grew up listening to my father and uncles playing

Coltrane, Miles Davis, Charlie Parker, Dizzy Gillespie, Art Tatum, Thelonious Monk and, of course, the incomparable Ella Fitzgerald, Billie Holiday and Abbey Lincoln."

"What about hip-hop?"

"It depends on the artist. I prefer R & B to hip-hop." Shifting on her seat, she stared at Micah's distinctive profile. She preferred him dressed down because he appeared less intimidating. "Why did you ask?"

"I've been thinking about places where we could go for dinner and I'm leaning toward one that features live music. If you have a favorite place or are partial to a particular cuisine, then let me know."

"I'll let you pick the place."

She didn't want to give him the names of places where she'd eaten with the men in her past—Bryce Hill in particular. Once she'd ended her relationship with Bryce she'd promised herself that she would never look back.

Micah gave Tessa a quick glance behind his dark lenses. "I'll pick the place and you can let me know when you're going to be available."

"I'm free this coming Saturday and Sunday."

He took his hand off the gearshift, leaned over, opened the glove compartment and handed Tessa a PDA. "Please check and see what I have for next weekend."

She scrolled through his calendar filled with entries of meetings and reminders. "You've blocked out Saturday."

"What does it say?"

"'Check heating system.'"

He smothered a groan. He'd forgotten about his upstate vacation home. He hadn't gone up this past summer because he hadn't had the time with moving to Staten Island and settling into his new position with the Brooklyn D.A.'s office.

He didn't want to put off having dinner with Tessa any longer than necessary because, as a new prosecutor, his hours were slated to change from days to nights, and with most weddings taking place on weekends he wasn't certain about her timetable. Perhaps, he mused, he could check on the house *and* have dinner with her.

"How would you like to go apple picking next Saturday?"

Tessa shot him a confused look. "Which one is it, Micah? Are we going apple picking or out to dinner?"

"We can do both. I have a place upstate, and across the road is an apple orchard where you can pick whatever variety you want. We can pick apples, I'll winterize the house and then we'll go out to dinner. But if we eat up there, then it's not going to be fancy."

"Is the food good?"

Giving her a quick glance, Micah smiled. "It's very good."

Her smile matched his. "That sounds like a plan to me."

Micah covered her left hand with his right, bringing both to rest on the gearshift. He continued to hold her hand as he shifted gears. They lost track of time when they talked about the evolution of music from the early days of blues and jazz to the advent of pop, rock and roll, R & B and soul and the sampling and crossover of artists to different genres.

He was so engrossed in their conversation and the sensual pull of the woman sitting inches away that he hadn't noticed he was in Bergen County until he saw the signs indicating the number of miles to Franklin Lakes. The landscape had changed, along with the size of the homes.

Tessa eased her hand from the protective warmth of

Micah's when they entered the city limits for Franklin Lakes. Judging from the number of gated properties, there was no doubt he'd grown up in a privileged environment.

He maneuvered off a local road and onto a private path with four mailboxes bearing the names of homeowners at the bottom of a steep hill. She peered through the copse of towering trees lining both sides of the unpaved path like sentinels on guard duty and filtering out the sun's rays.

"You grew up in the woods."

A soft chuckle rumbled in Micah's chest. "It's not the woods."

Resting a hand on her hip, Tessa gave him a look that dared him to refute her. "Anytime trees grow high enough to block out sunlight, then it's the woods."

"Okay, you win. It's the woods."

Her delicate jaw dropped. "I don't believe it!"

"What don't you believe?" he asked.

"I can't believe you conceded," she teased.

"I only conceded because you hurt my feelings when you said I was contrary."

Tessa leaned close enough for her shoulder to touch Micah's. "I'm sorry. Will you accept my apology?"

Slowing, he pressed one of two remotes attached to the visor, and the iron gates protecting the property at the top of the hill opened smoothly. He drove through, continuing along a paved path and coming to a stop behind one of several SUVs parked in the rear of a three-story manor-style house.

Micah shut off the engine, got out and came around to assist Tessa. He didn't give her time to react when he wrapped an arm around her waist and pulled her close to his side.

Lowering his head, he stared at her parted lips. "I'll think about it."

Tessa shivered noticeably despite the warmth from Micah's body. She had no intention of permitting herself to fall under the spell he wove just by their sharing the same space. She imposed an iron control on her emotions she hadn't known she possessed.

"Don't think too long, Micah."

A hint of a smile tilted the corners of his mouth. "I won't." Reaching for Tessa's hand, he said, "Let's go inside. Once you meet my family, then you'll know what you have to deal with."

Chapter 5

Tessa followed Micah as he led her around to the front entrance, and within seconds of walking into the great room with a ceiling rising upward of three stories she understood Micah's claim that his parents were prepared to pay for whatever Bridget wanted. The size of the house and surrounding acreage confirmed that Bridget Sanborn didn't need a room at the Waldorf or a catering hall for her reception because the Franklin Lakes house with a massive chandelier and elaborate winding staircase was the perfect setting for a formal wedding and reception.

Micah studied Tessa's reaction to seeing the house where he'd grown up, but nothing in her expression revealed what she was thinking or feeling. "What do you think?"

Tilting her head, she flashed a warm smile. "It's wonderful." Opening her handbag, she took out a slim digital camera and snapped pictures of the entryway, the great room and the staircase. "Is your sister here?"

Micah shook his head. "I didn't see her car." He took her hand again. "Whatever happens, don't let my mother talk your ear off."

"I heard that, Micah Edgar Sanborn. And you know it's not nice to gossip about your mother behind her back."

Tessa and Micah turned around at the same time. Standing in the entryway was a petite woman with stylishly cut silver hair and laughing blue eyes. She'd come up behind them without making a sound, looking every inch the suburban housewife in a pair of khakis she'd paired with a pale blue button-down shirt, navy-blue cardigan tied over her shoulders and leather slip-ons. Attractive lines fanned out around her eyes.

Micah released Tessa's hand and scooped up Rosalind Sanborn, kissing her cheek. "Good morning, beautiful."

A rush of pink suffused Rosalind's porcelain complexion as she patted her son's shoulder. "Don't try to get over on me, you silver-tongued devil. I owe you a dressing-down for standing me up for dinner last week."

Setting his mother on her feet, Micah winked at her. "We'll talk about *that* later." He turned and smiled at Tessa. "Tessa, this is my mother, Rosalind Sanborn. Mom, Miss Tessa Whitfield of Signature Bridals."

Tessa slipped her camera into her purse and offered her hand. "It's a pleasure meeting you, Mrs. Sanborn."

Rosalind shook Tessa's hand while rolling her eyes upward. "Please call me Rosalind. The title of Mrs. Sanborn has been reserved for my mother-in-law."

Tessa felt an instant liking for Rosalind Sanborn. She was friendly and unpretentious, and although there was nothing in her physical appearance to substantiate that she was Micah's biological mother, the intangible bond between mother and son was strong enough to be palpable.

"Why are we standing here talking when Tessa's probably starving? Are you ready to eat, my dear?"

Tessa's gaze met Rosalind's. "Yes, ma'am."

Taking her arm, Rosalind led Tessa across the marble floor. "You'll get to meet everyone except Bridget. It's not often that Edgar and I get to have all of our children together at the same time, but we take whatever we can get." She glanced over her shoulder, giving Micah a knowing look.

Tessa entered the kitchen with Micah and Rosalind and found herself bombarded by a cacophony of noise, voices and a variety of tantalizing aromas. Adults and children ranging in age from a toddler sitting on the floor banging on a pot to an adolescent sat around an oval counter in the middle of the expansive kitchen, waiting to eat. An older man with salt-and-pepper hair stood at the cooking island. He alternated flipping pancakes with checking omelets for doneness.

"Hurry up, Grandpa," urged a young boy with a shock of unruly red curls. His identical twin brother drummed his elbows on the table as he brandished a fork like a rapier.

"Put down that fork before you put someone's eye out," warned a slender freckled-face woman with hair a darker shade of red.

"Hold on, champs. Grandpa is cooking as fast as he can."

A teenage girl with a sun-browned gold complexion, waist-length curly black hair and large, slanting eyes glanced up and stared at Tessa. She'd been lip-synching to the song coming through the earbuds of her iPod Nano.

"Are you my uncle Micah's new honey?" Snickers and giggles followed her query.

"Marisol Sanborn!" Rosalind chided, her eyebrows crinkling in a frown.

Finding herself the object of curious stares, Tessa's gaze flitted from one face to another with a myriad of expressions ranging from shock to embarrassment to amusement. She managed a half smile as she stared at the incredibly beautiful teenager.

"No, I'm not. I'm your aunt Bridget's wedding planner."

Micah glared at Marisol. "Tessa, please forgive my niece's lack of manners." The girl hung her head, seemingly embarrassed by her outburst. He moved closer to Tessa, meeting the curious gazes of his relatives. "This is Tessa Whitfield of Signature Bridals. Her company has earned the reputation as an A-list wedding planner, which means Bridget is very lucky to have her coordinate her wedding. Now that everyone knows you're *not* my girlfriend, let me introduce you to my family."

"What's a honey?" asked one of the ten-year-old twins.

"Duh, baby brother. Someone you kiss on the mouth," Marisol drawled.

Micah shot his niece a warning look. "Maybe you should make the introductions, Marisol, because, after all, you're the factotum."

Marisol smiled, exhibiting the colorful bands on her braces. "That's okay, Uncle Micah. You do it."

"Thank you, Marisol."

She waved a hand. "What*ever.*"

Taking a deep breath, Micah slowly counted to three. He loved his niece, but there were times when she truly tested his patience. "Tessa, I would like to introduce you to my father, Edgar Sanborn, aka chef and Grandpa."

Edgar deftly slipped three pancakes off a stove-top griddle and slipped them onto a platter. He winked at Tessa, his dark eyes sparkling like polished onyx. "Welcome, Tessa. I'd shake your hand, but that would be a little risky with this wild bunch."

She smiled at the man who bore an uncanny resemblance to one of Hollywood's late great leading men, Clark Gable. "I understand," she said. "It's nice meeting you."

Micah pointed to his redheaded sister-in-law. "This is Melinda, but everyone calls her Lindy. Standing behind her is my brother, William. Will and Lindy are the parents of my bottomless-pit nephews, Isaac and Jacob, and my niece, *la princesa,* Marisol."

Marisol affected a curtsy with Micah's compliment. Tessa acknowledged William and Lindy with a warm smile. "You have a beautiful family." The twins looked like their mother, and Marisol had inherited her father's rich olive-brown coloring and raven-black hair.

Bending down, Micah scooped up the toddler whose intent was to make as much noise as she could when she pounded a pot with a wooden spoon. Her sandy-brown hair, braided in cornrows, resembled orange sections, and the braids, held together with a length of red ribbon, looked like a stem.

"This future percussionist and indisputable boss of her family is Kimika." The chubby little girl squirmed, holding her arms out to her mother, who'd affected a similar hairstyle. "Kimmie belongs to my brother Abram and my sister-in-law Ruby."

Abram, who claimed the height and girth of a football linebacker, looped an arm around his petite wife's waist and pressed a kiss on her braided hair. His clean-shaven dark brown head gleamed like polished teak.

Abram winked at Tessa. "I think I can speak for everyone else in the family, but I hope you have the patience of Job. Dealing with our little sister is certainly going to try your soul."

Edgar, using a pair of tongs to remove strips of crisp bacon from the heated griddle, shot his youngest son a warning look. "Watch it, son. You're talking about my princess."

"Dad, you know your princess is spoiled rotten."

"And you're not, *mama's boy?*" Edgar teased.

"Edgar, please," Rosalind said softly, blushing. "We have company." Her husband had accused her of spoiling Abram, while she'd blamed him for indulging their only daughter's every whim.

Micah's hand cradled the small of Tessa's back. "Let me show you where you can wash up before we sit down to eat."

Tessa stood in an all-white bathroom with pale blue accents, next to Micah at twin blue-veined pedestal sinks, washing her hands. She met his amused gaze in the mirror. He'd taken off his cap and placed it on a table with a half dozen others bearing the logos of baseball and football teams.

"What's so funny, Micah?"

He lifted his eyebrows. "Go ahead and say it."

She smiled. "Say what?"

"That my family is a little off the chain."

"They appear quite normal to me."

"Didn't you notice something that was just a bit unconventional?"

"By *unconventional* do you mean that the Sanborns are a multiracial family?"

Reaching for a towel on a stack on a low table, Micah handed it to Tessa. "Yes."

"Your family is anything but unconventional, Micah. I've interacted with families with two mommies or two daddies, transgender, families where the bride and groom are visually- or hearing-impaired and I'm forced to bring in someone fluent in Braille or American Sign Language. That's what I'd consider unconventional. My focus will be on the bride, the groom and the mother of the bride. And if Bridget and Seth want a traditional interfaith ceremony wedding, then there are certain customs and traditions they have to follow."

Micah dried his hands as he watched Tessa's reflection in the mirror. The more sedate hairstyle displayed her features to their best advantage, but he much preferred seeing her hair loose and framing her face in sensual disarray.

"When my brothers got married, all I had to do was put on a tuxedo and show up."

"You've never been a best man?"

He shook his head. "I've been a witness a few times but never a best man. What about you, Tessa? Have you ever been a bride?"

She met his steady gaze in the glass. "No."

"Have you come close?"

"No. What about you, Micah?" she asked, shifting the focus from herself to him. "Were you ever married?

"No, and I've never come close."

"Do you like women?"

Her query must have startled him, because he went completely still. The frown lines that appeared between his eyes were replaced with a knowing smile. Resting a thigh against the pedestal sink, he crossed his arms over his chest. "You think because we slept together and I didn't touch you that I'm not into women?"

Tessa blushed, the color temporarily concealing the spray of freckles across her velvety cheeks. "This is not about me."

His smile widened. "Isn't it, Tessa?"

"No. It's about you, Micah."

"What about me?"

"I've come into contact with together sisters every time I coordinate a wedding. Bridesmaids and maids of honor looking for a together brother like you. But when they do marry, it is to *settle* because they don't want to be alone and they don't want to become just a baby mama."

Micah angled his head. "By *settle* you mean they marry brothers who don't come correct?"

"Yes. The men they marry don't measure up, will never measure and have no intention of ever measuring up. Instead of becoming a partner, she's thrust into the role of working overtime emotionally to make her marriage a success."

Micah had lost track of the number of times he'd overheard black women complain about not being able to find a "good black man." He'd worked and gone to school with good black men. His brothers were good black men, loving husbands and protective fathers.

"Thank you for the backhanded compliment, Tessa. But, unlike Will and Bram, I'm not the marrying kind."

"You don't believe in marriage?"

"It's not that I don't believe in marriage. In fact, I believe it's a very important societal institution necessary for creating and preserving families. However, marriage is just not for me."

Tessa's mouth curved into an unconscious smile. "I admire your honesty. Most men would be reluctant to admit that. But I'm glad you're not in the majority or I'd be out of business."

"Sorry about interrupting, Uncle Micah, but Grandma is waiting for you before we say grace."

Micah turned to find Marisol lounging in the doorway. "Tell her we're coming."

Tessa walked out of the bathroom with Micah. His statement, *Marriage is just not for me,* lingered with her during the brunch she shared with the Sanborns, and nagged at her when she sat down with Rosalind to discuss what they needed for Bridget's upcoming wedding.

Tessa sat at a lace-covered table in Rosalind Sanborn's sun parlor. The room was an exquisite retreat. The near-white furnishings and accessories and bright autumn sunlight filtering through white-on-white awning-striped voile drapes at the many-mullioned windows brought the outdoors inside.

She handed Rosalind a bridal information guide. "It looks more daunting than it actually is. You can read it at your leisure. However, I'm going to give you a brief overview so you'll know what I'll need to start the process of planning Bridget's wedding. Please stop me anytime you need to ask me something."

Rosalind gave Tessa a direct stare. "Even before you begin, I'd like to know whether it's humanly possible to plan a formal wedding in ten weeks."

Tessa saw doubt and fear in the blue eyes peering at her over a pair of half-glasses. She smiled. "Signature Bridals has been known to perform minor miracles given less time than what Bridget is giving us."

Rosalind, pressing her palms together, exhaled audibly and whispered a silent prayer. "Edgar doesn't like to hear it, but Bram's right when he says that Bridget's spoiled. Unfortunately, I've spoiled all of my children," she said in a voice that seemed to come a long way off.

"Isn't that what parents are suppose to do?"

Rosalind observed Tessa through lowered lids. "Are you speaking from experience, Tessa?"

"No, I'm not. I don't have any children."

There was a pregnant silence as the two women regarded each other. Tessa cleared her throat. She knew she had to steer the focus back to Bridget's wedding.

"I'd like to cover the different elements that make up a wedding. I'll begin with the breakdown of roles and responsibilities of the members of the wedding party, the ceremony, the reception and, last but certainly not least, is money and who pays for what. I believe it's better when the bride and groom stick to tradition, given the time frame, but if they want to break the rules, then it can't be something catastrophic."

Rosalind's expression brightened. "We don't have to discuss money because Edgar and I will pay for the invitations, Bridget's dress and accessories, flowers, music, the reception, including food and drink, the cake, photographer, accommodations for out-of-town guests and, of course, your fee."

"Have you compiled a mailing list for your guests?"

"Yes. I'll get it for you."

"Please don't get up," Tessa said when Rosalind pushed back her chair. "You can give it to me before I leave."

The two women spent over an hour going over the wording for the wedding stationery—the invitations, the place and reply cards. "Keep in mind," Tessa suggested, "that with formal invitations guests' names are handwritten in the top left corner or in the space provided within the wording of the invitation, and full titles are used. It's going to be time-consuming, so Bridget will have to decide whether she wants to use them."

Rosalind jotted notes on a legal pad. "What's the latest we can send out invitations?"

"They should be sent out two or three months before the day, and certainly no later than six weeks before. I recommend including the preprinted reply cards and addressed envelopes with the invitations because they encourage guests to reply promptly. And the fact that Bridget and Seth are marrying New Year's Eve may be to their advantage, because those who haven't made plans for the holiday will have the perfect excuse to celebrate it at a black-tie affair."

"So the invitations have to go out before the end of the month," Rosalind mumbled under her breath.

"Realistically they should," Tessa confirmed. "You'll be given the choice between engraving, letterpress, offset lithography and thermography. Paper can be made of many different materials and come in all sorts of textures, finishes and weight. It's the same with shapes. If Bridget and Seth want an unusual-shaped invitation, then they must keep in mind that it will call for custom-made envelopes. I always tell my clients that wedding stationery should be printed at the same time. Would you like a printed menu?"

"Yes. That's something you can take with you along with the guest list. I—" A soft tapping on the door preempted her words. Turning, she glanced over her shoulder at Edgar. "Yes, dear?"

He walked into the room. He'd changed into a pair of sweatpants, a shirt and running shoes. The faded logo of Princeton University was barely legible. "Are you almost finished?"

Rosalind looked at Tessa, who nodded. "Give us a few more minutes."

Edgar nodded, smiling. "Tessa, I hope you're going to join us."

"Join you for what?"

"Micah didn't tell you?"

Tessa shifted her gaze from Edgar to Rosalind, her expression mirroring confusion. "I'm sorry, but I don't know what you're talking about."

Rosalind rested a hand on Tessa's shoulder. "On Sundays the family gets together after brunch to play touch football."

Tessa's jaw dropped as she opened her mouth but no words came out. She couldn't believe Micah had asked her to dress casually just so that someone could tackle her. If he'd mentioned football, then she would've told him that she didn't do grass and dirt.

"I—I'm afraid I'm not dressed to play football," she stammered.

Rosalind waved her hand. "Don't worry about ruining your lovely twinset. You're about the same size as Bridget. I'll find something in her closet that's certain to fit you."

Seething and cursing Micah inwardly, Tessa forced a smile when she felt like grimacing. She'd come to New Jersey to coordinate a wedding, not play football.

Chapter 6

Tessa, wearing sweatpants and a Smith College sweatshirt and running shoes belonging to Bridget, studied the framed photograph of the woman whose clothes she wore. Rosalind had given her a new bra-and-bikini-panty ensemble to change into after the football game. The older woman appeared embarrassed when she disclosed her daughter's obsession with frilly, delicate undergarments. The six-drawer lingerie chest was filled with bras, panties and camisoles in every fabric and color, many with the sales tags still attached.

Tessa discovered she and Bridget were *almost* the same size. She had an inch or two on her client in the hips, but Bridget was a cup larger in bra size.

She smiled. Now Tessa had a face to go along with the name. Smiling and staring directly at the photographer, dark-haired, green-eyed Bridget Sanborn radiated a youthful exuberance that enhanced her delicate beauty.

There was something else she'd discovered when Rosalind had directed her to her daughter's bedroom suite: Bridget was feminine and romantic. Tessa felt as if she were on the set of a Merchant Ivory film. The furnishings and decor were unabashedly Victorian. A nest of gossamer pillows piled doubly high on a lace-trimmed counterpane graced a mahogany bed with a carved headboard and posts. Embroidered sheers at the windows filtered the afternoon light into a space with stark white walls. A collection of pale straw hats hung from pegs along one wall.

Photographs of Bridget, chronicling her life from infant to womanhood, along with photos of her brothers, parents, sisters-in-law, nephews and nieces, crowded the fireplace mantel. She stared at one of a younger Micah in his regulation NYPD uniform; her gaze shifted to an updated photograph of him with Edgar and Rosalind in front of Brooklyn Law School. There was no mistaking Rosalind's pride when she smiled up at her son resplendent in a gown, hood and velvet tam.

Cognizant that the Sanborns were waiting for her, she left the bedroom and made her way down the long hallway to the staircase. She'd just placed her foot on the first stair when she saw Micah standing at the bottom, waiting for her. A sweatshirt had replaced his sweater, and as she came closer she saw Columbia University stamped across the front.

She stopped on a stair that brought her head level with his. Eyes narrowing, she glared at him. "I owe you one for tricking me," she threatened softly.

He stared, unblinking. "What are you talking about?"

"You didn't tell me that I'd become a participant in a football game."

He flashed a smile, his eyelids lowering slightly, and she held her breath for several seconds. The expression was sensual enough to be X-rated.

"Touch football, Tessa."

"Touch, flag or regulation football," she drawled. "It's still involves tackling, rolling around on the ground and possible injuries. I can't afford to break something."

Whenever the members of her family got together for anything physical, Tessa was always the one who sat on the sidelines. She harbored a fear that she would break a bone and she hated to sweat. She was the complete opposite of Simone, who loved rolling around on the grass, digging for worms and climbing trees.

Reaching for her hand, Micah assisted her off the staircase and toward the rear of the house; he slowed his pace to accommodate her shorter legs. "We've been playing football for more than ten years, and so far no one has ever been injured or broken anything. There's an unspoken rule that the guys have to be gentle with the ladies."

"So if it's separate but unequal, then where's the competition?"

"It's a competition between partners. You, my dad, Will and Ruby will be on one team, and I'll be with Lindy, Bram and my mother. Now if Bridget and Seth were here, they'd be on opposing teams."

Tessa gave Micah a sidelong glance. "I'm not your girlfriend or your partner."

"Not in the literal sense, but today we'll make an exception." He gave her a quick glance. "Is that okay with you?"

She nodded. "Okay, only for today. What do you do after the game?"

"The kids usually relax with a movie while the

adults cook, but there're times when we all go out for Sunday dinner."

"So Sunday is family day for the Sanborns."

"It is whenever all of us show up. Sundays in the summer are always iffy because when the kids are out of school Will and Bram hang out together on Cape May. They have condos in the same vacation community. Seth's folks own property in the Berkshires, so we didn't get to see too much of Bridget this past summer."

"How long have Bridget and Seth been dating?" Tessa asked.

"Not long. They met at a party hosted by a mutual friend over the Memorial Day weekend, and since that time they've been inseparable."

"It's a whirlwind romance that will culminate in a fairy-tale wedding."

Micah nodded. "Bridget shocked all of us when she got engaged, because even though she's dated off and on over the years, she's never been serious about any one guy. She claims when she saw Seth it was love at first sight. I find that more shocking than her getting engaged."

"You sound like a cynic, Micah."

He laughed under his breath. "Of course you would think that. After all, you're in the happily-ever-after business."

"One of these days love is going to jump up and bite you so hard you won't have time to react," she predicted. "And if you decide you want Signature Bridals to coordinate your wedding, then I'll offer you a family discount because of Bridget."

"Never happen," he drawled confidently.

"Never say never, Micah," Tessa teased. Raising her head, she inhaled deeply as they passed the kitchen. "I smell turkey."

Smiling, Micah gave her a sidelong glance. "You've got a good nose. Dad decided on turkey today instead of his usual standing rib roast."

"Your father is a fabulous cook." Edgar Sanborn had prepared a brunch with pancakes, omelets, bacon, sausage, eggs cooked to order and home fries.

"He couldn't boil water before he married my mother and now he cooks better than she does."

"Do you cook?"

"I do okay."

Micah opened a side door and they stepped out into bright sunlight. The sun was hot, but the heat was tempered by a cool breeze. The afternoon weather was perfect for a football game.

Tessa looked around, but she didn't see anyone. "Where is everybody?"

Micah pointed to his right. "They're over that rise. Perhaps you want to stretch before we get there."

She rolled her eyes at him. "Stretch, Micah? Are you saying I might pull a muscle?" A swollen silence followed her query. "If I hurt myself, I'm going to sue the hell out of you."

Throwing back his head, Micah laughed, the sound warm, deep and rich. "That's not going to be so easy."

"Why?"

"I'll have to decide whether to represent myself or retain my parents as legal counsel."

"Your parents are attorneys?"

"Dad is a law professor at Princeton Law School, and my mother is a retired family court judge."

Tessa wanted to ask Micah if his brothers were also lawyers, but her query died on her lips when she saw the Sanborns in an open grassy meadow, all wearing college sweatshirts, stretching and warming up, while the younger members of the family had become cheerleaders, waving white T-shirts and towels and dancing to the music coming from a boom box sitting under a tree. It'd become an impromptu pep rally.

She felt her features become more animated. Just as the bimonthly Monday dinners with her sister and cousin reinforced their bond as members of the same family, the Sanborn Sunday brunch and subsequent football game served the same purpose. It probably would be another decade before the role of the younger children would go from spectator to participator, and they no doubt would exhibit the same enthusiasm and competitiveness as their parents and grandparents.

Bending from the waist, Tessa shook her arms and hands, then went through a ritual that stretched her biceps, triceps and quadriceps. She felt a rush of adrenaline as she raised her arms and kicked up her legs in time to the cheerleading music.

Will pumped his fist in the air. "Hot damn, Dad, we got a live one on our team!"

Maybe if I tire myself out during the warm-up, then I can plead exhaustion and can sit out the game, Tessa mused. She wasn't about to let Micah or Abram—especially Abram—tackle her. The man was built like a Hummer.

Edgar motioned for Marisol to lower the volume on the boom box as he got all of the players together in a huddle to go over the rules and restrictions: no gauging or clothesline moves. He identified the trees that were goal lines for each team, then tossed a coin. Abram, who'd chosen to play the quarterback position, called tails, winning the coin toss.

The first two plays occurred so quickly that Tessa felt

as if she'd had her eyes closed. Micah had caught the ball and run halfway up the imaginary field before he was tackled by Will.

Isaac and Jacob did the happy dance, chanting, "Go, Daddy! Go, Daddy!" Marisol screamed at the top of her lungs, executed a back flip and followed it with a full split.

Tessa huddled with Edgar, Will and Ruby as they planned their next strategic play. Edgar's dark eyes were serious. "Tessa, you're going to become our secret weapon. When Bram releases the ball, I want you to run downfield and cover Micah."

"Are you sure he's going to throw it to Micah?" she asked Edgar. "What if he elects to run the ball?"

Ruby shook her head. "I doubt if he's going to run," she said. "Bram's strong and fast, but he's not as fast as Micah."

"Who's going to cover me?" Tessa asked.

"I'll cover you," said Will.

Edgar clapped his hands. "Let's do it!"

Tessa took her position, her gaze meeting and fusing with Micah's. There was no mistaking the challenge in the eyes that communicated that whenever he played it was to win. Well, she thought, whenever she played it wasn't to come in second but in first place.

Instead of the passing the football, Abram tucked it under his arm and took off running. His wife was right— he was fast; however, his size proved a disadvantage. Reacting quickly, Tessa took off after him. She focused on the broad back wearing a Brown University T-shirt as she forced herself to run faster. Half a dozen more steps and she'd catch up with him.

Tessa heard the pounding footsteps behind her at the same time she felt the hot breath on the nape of her neck. One moment she was on her feet, then seconds later she was lifted high in the air. She couldn't stop the scream exploding from the back of her throat as she fell, landing on a hard body before the ground came up at her.

Gritting her teeth against the impact, Tessa peered up at Micah grinning at her in a supremely masculine cockiness that fired her temper. He pressed his chest to hers. His heat and scent swept through her like a sirocco, making her feel things she didn't want to feel.

"Let me up," she whispered. He was much too close, and his potent virility threatened to overwhelm and embarrass her in front of his family.

Lowering his head, Micah pressed his mouth to the side of her neck. "You smell delicious," he crooned seconds before rolling off her body and pulling her to her feet.

"Flirt on your own time, Micah," Edgar shouted. "The clock's running and I have a turkey to check on."

All gazes were fixed on Micah holding Tessa's hands. It wasn't the physical contact that had them mesmerized but the longing expression softening his features. He released her, turned and rejoined his team.

"Is there something wrong, Micah?" Rosalind asked quietly as she moved closer to her eldest child.

He forced a smile. "No. Come on, let's win this game."

Micah's attempt to concentrate on the game was short-lived. The next play resulted in a turnover, Tessa pouncing on the football like a cat. He watched, stunned, as she danced in triumph, her lithe body moving sensuously in tempo to the blaring hip-hop music.

What was it about Tessa that had him reacting like a deer caught in the headlights *and* a randy adolescent boy? He couldn't stop the smile parting his lips. She'd just demonstrated that she could loosen up, that she'd literally and figuratively let down her hair: the curls pinned on the nape of her neck had escaped the neat chignon and lifted slightly with the warm breeze.

Tessa sat in the formal dining room with the Sanborns, passing serving dishes around a table with enough room for sixteen. The chairs that would've been occupied by Bridget and Seth were vacant, and another chair had been replaced with a high chair for Kimika.

She'd found herself energized instead of exhausted from the strenuous football game. The competition ended in a tie as time ran out. Everyone had retreated to the house to shower and change while the younger Sanborns had gathered in the family room to view *Pirates of the Caribbean: Dead Man's Chest.*

The gourmet kitchen was filled with activity, with Edgar basting a large, fresh turkey, and Melinda chopping the ingredients for potato salad and couscous. Ruby poured out a creamy mixture of filling for several sweet-potato pies. Tessa helped Rosalind snap the ends off fresh green beans before she retreated to the dining room to set the table.

She welcomed the hustle and bustle of preparing Sunday dinner because it served to distract her from the man whose nearness made her senses spin, whose very presence wrapped her in an invisible warmth she hadn't felt in a very long time.

Tessa took a second helping of green beans cooked with fork-tender pieces of smoked neck bones and a delicious black-eyed-pea salad tossed with arugula and piquant vinaigrette. She met Micah's gaze across the table; he lifted his wineglass in a mock salute. Raising her glass filled with a fruity Zinfandel, she peered at him over the rim, smiled, then took a sip, her gaze fusing with his.

She was aware of the open invitation, the blatant realization that she was more than curious about Micah
Sanborn, that she couldn't remember the last time she'd
truly enjoyed herself with a man. Her lids lowered slowly,
demurely, hiding her innermost feelings.

Micah was stunned, the awakening emotion of staring
at Tessa Whitfield across the table in his parents' house
leaving him reeling from sensations he'd never known.

He'd met a lot of women, yet none had managed to
ensnare him in a web of desire and longing like Tessa.
He didn't know her, and he wanted to know her not as
the brother of her client but as a man would a woman.

She'd showered after the football game and changed
back into her clothes but hadn't styled her hair in the
severe style she'd affected earlier that morning. Damp
curls framed her face, making her look softer, more ap-
proachable. He winked at Tessa, then turned to Isaac
when he tapped his shoulder to get his attention.

Rosalind watched the surreptitious and sensual visual
interchange between Micah and the young woman sitting
to her right. Picking up a damask napkin, she touched it
to the corners of her mouth, hiding a smug grin behind
the square of cloth. She'd seen her eldest son with other
women, but this was the first time she recognized tenderness in his gaze rather than boredom and indifference.

She wanted to tell Tessa that she'd enthralled her son
but held her tongue. Both were adults, and she suspected
they—Micah in particular—would resent her interference.

Rosalind loved all of her children, but Micah was
special—what she'd thought of as her golden child.
Adopting Micah had changed her life; he'd made her a

mother for the first time, while she'd learned to be patient, tolerant. And, more importantly, he'd taught her how to love selflessly.

Dinner ended more than two hours later, everyone pushing back from the table and complaining they'd eaten too much. Marisol, Isaac and Jacob were recruited to clear the table, Melinda and Ruby put away leftovers, while William, Abram and Micah stacked dishes in dual dishwashers.

Tessa sat with Rosalind, discussing the seating arrangements for the reception dinner. The formal dining room in the Franklin Lakes home had pocket doors that opened out to the expansive living room and adjoining area that doubled as a small ballroom, an area where the younger Sanborns had entertained their friends as teenagers.

"Most of the parents in this community thought Edgar and I were insane to have their children over for birthday parties and sleepovers, but I preferred knowing where my children were—and they were close enough for me to monitor their behavior rather than staying on my knees praying they'd make it home in one piece."

Tessa nodded, recalling her parents' angst when their children got their driver's licenses and asked to use the car. Driving had permitted them more mobility but less freedom when the elder Whitfields imposed curfews. And, if broken, subsequent sanctions were unspeakable.

"You've done very well, Rosalind. Your sons are perfect gentlemen."

Rosalind lifted her eyebrows. "Are you referring to Micah?"

Tessa nodded. "Yes. You've raised him well."

A smile of enchantment touched Rosalind's lips.

"Micah's my pride and joy. I may not have carried him within my body, but he *is* my son in every sense of the word. The first time I saw him I felt something here." She rested a hand over her heart. "And that something was an instantaneous love that's never wavered or waned. I know you don't want to hear the ramblings of a self-absorbed, narcissistic old woman—"

"You're not old," Tessa interrupted.

Rosalind snorted delicately. "I'm a sixty-six-year-old mother of four adult children, grandmother of four, I'm collecting social security and have a Medicare card—and you claim I'm not old. I'm not ancient or relegated to relic status, but I'm secure enough to admit that I am a senior citizen."

Tessa and Rosalind talked about everything but Bridget's wedding because both knew they couldn't plan any further without Bridget's input. When Micah returned to the dining room to inform Tessa that he was ready to drive back to New York, she bid everyone goodbye, feeling as if she were leaving friends instead of the family of her client.

Tessa stood in the foyer of her home with Micah. The soft light coming from the lamp on a table turned him into a statue of gold. She smiled up at him staring down at her.

"What time should I be ready Saturday?"

"Are you opposed to leaving at sunrise?"

Her eyebrows lifted. "No. Why?"

"I like watching the sun come up and eating breakfast on the road."

"How far upstate is your place?"

"It's about three hundred and fifty miles from here. If it's not going to be a problem for you, I'll pick you up around six."

Tessa offered him her right hand. "I'll see you Saturday morning at six. And thank you for a wonderful afternoon."

Ignoring her hand, Micah leaned over and kissed her cheek. "No, Tessa, thank you for being a good sport."

She wagged a finger at him. "You know I owe you one for tricking me into playing football."

He straightened, smiling. "Did you have fun?"

She returned his smile. "Yes, I did."

"Good. Perhaps we can do it again. But, of course, after Bridget's no longer your client," he added quickly.

Tessa stared up at Micah through her lashes. "I'm willing to do it again even if Bridget is still my client." A grin deepened the slashes in Micah's lean, stubbly jaw, making him so devastatingly virile that she was forced to hold her breath for several seconds.

"Let me know when you're available and I'll make it happen," Micah said softly. "Thank you again, and I'll see you Saturday morning."

"Saturday morning," she repeated as Micah turned, opened the door and walked out of Signature Bridals.

Tessa stood there staring at the door before she slid the dead bolt in place and activated the security system. She checked her voice mail for messages, then climbed the staircase to the third floor. When she touched a wall switch, bright light flooded the room where she designed wedding gowns. Opening the doors to a built-in wardrobe that took up an entire wall, she selected several in Bridget Sanborn's size.

And as she hung the garments that resembled frothy concoctions on a rack she wondered which one would she choose if she were planning her own wedding?

As soon as the thought came to mind she banished it.

She'd coordinated hundreds of weddings and not once had she ever imagined herself a bride.

Why now? she asked, praying that it wasn't because of Micah. Tessa shook her head. She couldn't afford to get involved with him, could not afford to mix business with pleasure. It'd happened once before and she'd sworn an oath it would not happen again.

Something told her that Micah Sanborn was not Bryce Hill, but could she afford to take the risk?

Yes, the silent voice inside her head whispered.

"Yes!" she said aloud. And she'd continue to tell herself yes until she actually believed it.

Chapter 7

Streaks of orange feathered the darkening sky as dusk descended on Westchester County, the waning light throwing the swaying skeletal branches of trees in stark relief. The fall foliage had peaked, and an overnight thunderstorm with wind gusting in excess of fifty miles an hour had stripped many leaves from the trees; they littered the roadway and the lawns like colorful confetti.

Tessa maneuvered into the driveway leading to Simone's modest farmhouse-style home and cut off the engine to her late-model SUV. A knowing smile parted her lips as she got out of the vehicle. Her sister's mantra—*Let there be light*—was evident from the warm golden glow ablaze from every window in the two-story structure.

Her sister had been diagnosed with seasonal affective disorder, and the Whitfields were forced to endure Simone's mercurial moods from late fall through mid spring; however, with the onset of daylight saving time and the return of warmer weather Simone once again became the free-spirited woman with the infectious smile and bubbly personality.

Mounting the three steps that led to an expansive wrap-around porch, Tessa rang the doorbell. Less than a minute later she came face-to-face with her cousin. Faith was a Whitfield, but she hadn't inherited the distinctive genes that gave them reddish curly hair and glowing catlike eyes. Tall, naturally slender and claiming dark gold-brown coloring, the renown pâtissier was usually mistaken for a model. Her close-cropped black hair, large, slanting dark eyes and even, delicate features always turned heads—especially those of the opposite sex—whenever she entered a room.

She hugged Faith. "Welcome home, gypsy."

Faith kissed Tessa's cheek. "It's good to be home."

"How long are you staying?"

"I don't have anything on the West Coast until the end of the month," Faith said, pulling her cousin gently into the house and closing the door.

Tessa took off her three-quarter coat, hanging it on a wooden coat tree. "What's happening then?" Tessa asked as she followed Faith through the living room, down a hallway and into the kitchen, where Simone had just taken a clear bowl filled with salad greens from a stainless-steel refrigerator/freezer.

"Tristan Symons is giving his wife a surprise thirtieth birthday party and he wants me to bake a cake with replicas of her favorite shoes and handbags."

Tessa smiled. A collective groan from single women all over the country went up when the Major League Baseball heartthrob superstar announced that he'd secretly married a girl from his Oakland neighborhood.

"Is he as gorgeous in person as he is on camera?"

Faith moaned softly. "I know he thought I was crazy when I couldn't stop staring at him. He's luscious, Tessa."

"Who's luscious?" Simone asked.

"Tris Symons," Faith and Tessa chorused.

Simone fluttered her lashes. "Please, baby, please. I'm not into athletes, but I'd make an exception with Mr. Symons. Tessa, I'm glad you're here because I need you to make a pesto dressing."

Rolling her eyes and resting her hands on her hips at the same time, Tessa gave her sister a blank stare. "Why is it whenever we eat at your house Faith and I end up cooking?"

Simone Whitfield's hazel eyes widened, giving her the appearance of a startled child. At five-three and one hundred twelve pounds with a mop of red-tinged curls framing her oval face and falling halfway down her back, the thirty-three-year-old floral decorator complained incessantly because she was still carded whenever she ordered anything alcoholic.

"You and Faith don't have to eat at my place."

"And where we would eat every other Monday?" Faith asked as she placed metal skewers with cubes of marinated chicken, olives and lemon, seasoned with ground cumin, turmeric and cinnamon, on a heated grill. The tantalizing aromas of the Moroccan dish filled the kitchen.

"Why, at your place or Tessa's," Simone said as placed the salad bowl on the table in the kitchen's dining area set with fine bone china, silver and crystal. A delicate bouquet of white Akito roses, Mexican orange blossoms and Weber parrot tulips, all grown in the greenhouse on her White Plains property, served as the table's centerpiece.

Faith shook her head. "Just because you set a pretty table that doesn't preclude you from cooking. We all agreed last year that we'd meet twice a month and whoever hosts cooks. I'm suffering from jet lag, tired as hell, and here I am cooking, Simone Whitfield, cooking at *your* house."

Tessa washed her hands, then gathered the ingredients for the salad dressing as she half listened to her sister and her first cousin verbally spar with each other. Nothing had changed from their childhood. Tessa got along better with her first cousin than she did her sister, and Faith and Simone were like oil and water—they couldn't find anything on which to agree.

"Ladies, in case you've forgotten," Tessa said, hoping to act as mediator when the argument between Faith and Simone became more heated, "we have to discuss a formal wedding."

Faith removed a pot of couscous from the heat and covered it with a matching lid. "When's the wedding?"

"New Year's Eve."

Faith blinked once. "A formal wedding *this* New Year's Eve?"

Tessa nodded. "Yes."

Simone sucked her teeth. "I hope you're charging them through the nose for the short notice."

"The problem isn't money but time," Tessa said as she chopped leaves of fresh basil and garlic cloves. "The Sanborns are prepared to pay whatever we charge for their daughter to become a Signature bride."

Simone moved closer to her sister, watching as Tessa put the ingredients for the pesto salad dressing into a food processor, slowly adding virgin olive to the mixture that took on a bright green color. The advantage to having a greenhouse on the property was ready access to fresh fruits, vegetables, herbs and flowers year-round.

Tessa and Faith complained about coming to her house and having to cook, but Simone wasn't ashamed to admit that they were better cooks. Her culinary skills were adequate, but Faith's were unequal, and Tessa, although not a trained chef, ran a close second.

"What are we working with, Tessa?" Faith asked.

"It's going to be an interfaith wedding that will take place at the bride's home. The guest list is projected at eighty——"

"Eighty," Faith said, interrupting Tessa. "How large is the house?"

A mysterious smile played at the corners of Tessa's mouth. "Try eighteen thousand square feet."

"Damn!" Simone drawled.

"How many rooms do they have?" Faith asked Tessa.

"Six bedrooms, six full baths, two half baths, two kitchens, five fireplaces, formal living and dining rooms, ballroom, full theater, pool and pool house set on six and a half acres."

"I guess money wouldn't be a problem with a house that large," Simone said in a quiet voice. "Has the bride decided on a color scheme?"

"Her mother said she wanted silver and black with red accents, to coincide with the holiday season."

Simone nodded. "I like that. The colors would reflect somewhat of an Art Deco look."

Faith picked up a quilted pot holder and removed the top to the pot; she fluffed up the couscous and ladled it onto the middle of a serving platter. She tested the kabobs for doneness, then placed them on the platter around the couscous.

"Let's eat."

The three women sat down at the table and talked while they ate. Retrieving their PDAs, they entered a timeline for the Sanborn-Cohen wedding: final dress fittings, approval of a cake design and filling, bridal bouquet and floral arrangements, musical play list, the band, photographer and souvenirs.

Tessa's gaze shifted from Faith to Simone. "It's not as bad as I originally thought it would be. We don't have to concern ourselves with a place to hold the reception or get a caterer to prepare food for one of the busiest nights of the year. And there's only the bride's gown and her maid-of-honor dress, so that eliminates a lot of diva attitudes from bridesmaids."

"What about the mothers?" Simone asked as she tapped the keys on her PDA. "Are you going to supply their dresses, too?"

"No. I don't have the time to alter four dresses."

"You're going to have to let us know when you're going to meet with baby girl," Simone teased.

Tessa nodded. "As soon as I know, I'll let you know."

Faith turned off her PDA. "E-mail, call or page me as soon as you set a date to meet with baby girl." Smiling, she reached across the table and affected a high-five with Simone.

Faith, like Simone, had little use for spoiled, self-centered brides, while Tessa appeared to have the patience of a saint when dealing with their mood swings, virulent outbursts and tearful apologies.

Raising her water goblet to her lips, she took a long swallow. "I'm going to be busier than usual."

"Don't tell me you got a boyfriend," Tessa said, smiling.

"I told you before that I've sworn off men."

Tessa waved her hand. "We're your cousins, Faith. You can…" Her words trailed off when the telephone rang.

"Excuse me," Simone said as she pushed back her chair and stood up. "I'm expecting a call from a customer." She picked up the receiver on the wall phone before the third ring.

Tessa and Faith exchanged a knowing glance when they heard Simone refer to her caller by name. "I thought she'd stopped speaking to *him*," Faith whispered.

"I don't want to even get into that," Tessa whispered back. "Only Simone will know when enough is enough." She'd tired of her sister's on-again, off-again relationship with her ex-husband.

Faith stood up. "I don't know about you, cuz, but I'm ready to roll out." She pantomimed that she was leaving to Simone, who was so engrossed in her telephone conversation that she hadn't noticed her cousin and sister leaving. Normally they would've stayed to help clean the kitchen, but not tonight.

Tessa double-parked along a cobblestone street in front of a landmark building in Greenwich Village. Shifting, she glanced at Faith, who'd fallen asleep during the ride from White Plains to Manhattan. She shook her gently.

"You're home, Faith," she said in a quiet voice so as not to startle her.

Faith opened her eyes, blinking and trying to get her bearings. She placed her hand over her mouth to smother a yawn. "I haven't felt this tired in a long time."

"You'll be all right in a couple of days if you don't go online, turn off your phone and don't answer your doorbell."

"That would be all right if I didn't have to go into the shop tomorrow."

"No, you don't have to go in, Faith Vinna Whitfield. Did you forget that you pay people to run Let Them Eat Cake when you're not there?"

"No, you didn't go there and call me by my born name," Faith teased, smiling.

"I'll call you more if you don't get some rest. You look as if a strong wind will blow you away."

"You know I don't eat when I'm working," Faith countered defensively.

"Then stop working so hard and eat."

Unsnapping her seat belt, Faith leaned over and kissed Tessa's cheek. "You sound like Aunt Lucinda."

Tessa gave her a cheeky grin. "That's because I'm my mama's child." She pressed a lever, releasing the hatch on the SUV so Faith could retrieve her luggage. She waited until Faith opened the door to her building and disappeared inside before shifting into gear and driving toward Brooklyn.

Vehicular traffic on the Brooklyn Bridge was lighter than usual, and within half an hour of dropping off Faith and parking her vehicle in an indoor garage Tessa walked the three blocks to her home.

She opened the door and was met with light from a table lamp, heat coming from the baseboard heating and the ringing of the telephone. Quickening her steps, she made it into her office, flicked on a wall switch and reached for the receiver before it switched over to the voice-mail feature.

"Hello." Her greeting had come out as a breathless whisper.

"Did I wake you?"

A dreamy smile crossed Tessa's face as she sat down at her desk. Why, she thought, did Micah's voice sound so sexy on the telephone? "No. I had to run to answer the phone. Did you call to cancel this weekend?" she asked when there was a moment of silence from the other end of the line.

"No. We're still on. I called to tell you that Bridget is finished with jury duty. She says they stayed up all night and finally agreed on a verdict this afternoon. She's going to take a few days off before she meets with you."

"Tell her I'm free all day Wednesday. Micah, please try to stress to your sister that we're working with a very small time frame."

"I'll make certain she shows up."

Tessa smiled. "Thank you."

"You're quite welcome."

Her smile widened when she heard his sensual laugh. "Then I'll look for you and Bridget Wednesday."

"Good night, Tessa."

"Good night, Micah."

Tessa was still smiling when she ended the call. The reality that she would see Micah again filled her with an unexpected anticipation she'd never thought she'd experience again. The truth was she felt more comfortable with him than with any other man with whom she'd become involved.

Micah found himself squinting as he read what seemed like the umpteenth file from the stack in a cabinet behind his desk. Although an incoming A.D.A., he'd been assigned to Gang Busters because as a rookie police officer he'd successfully gone undercover to bust several members of a violent street gang. In Brooklyn, cases involving violent gang activity were given the highest priority, and the senior prosecutors assigned to the Gang Bureau Rackets Division tried the cases so that they received the attention they deserved. The prosecutors sought out the highest bail possible to ensure the defendant's availability for trial.

A tapping on the door shattered Micah's concentration. "Hey, Sanborn, you have a visitor."

"Who is it, Townsend?" he asked without looking up. Vaughn Townsend, a senior prosecutor, had also graduated Brooklyn Law School, but at the bottom of his class, and had had to take the bar exam twice before finally passing. In the short time Micah had been with the D.A.'s office Vaughn had become the bane of his existence. Although quite knowledgeable, the never-married middle-aged man talked incessantly.

"Someone who claims she's your sister."

Micah put down the file and stood up. He ignored Vaughn's reference to Bridget's *claim* that she was his sister. "Where is she?"

"I told her to wait in the waiting area."

"Thanks." Micah put away the file, tightened his tie and reached for his suit jacket. Bridget had called to tell him that she would come to Brooklyn to meet him rather than have him drive to the Bronx only to return once they concluded their meeting with Tessa Whitfield.

Vaughn glanced at his watch. There was another hour before quitting time. "Leaving already?"

Staring at the rotund man with thinning brown hair and a sallow complexion, Micah met his questioning stare. "Yes, I am."

He wanted to tell Vaughn that he'd worked until ten the night before and had come in at seven, but because

Vaughn Townsend wasn't his supervisor he didn't want to establish a precedent reporting to him.

"Have a good evening, Townsend," he said instead.

"Uh…uh, you, too, Sanborn." Vaughn nervously cleared his throat. "I hope you don't think I'm out of line, but you and your sister don't look anything alike."

Micah smiled and angled his head. "You're right. But let me assure you that she *is* my sister."

A slow flush crept up Vaughn's neck. "She's very pretty."

"I'm certain her fiancé would agree with you."

Vaughn turned even redder. "I guess I'd better quit while I'm ahead."

Suddenly Micah felt sorry for the man who hadn't had a date in years. In a moment of compassion he thought of calling one or two single female police officers who were looking for a "nice friend" but thought better of it. He'd tried matchmaking once, and when the relationship ended badly, he'd blamed himself and in the end lost two friends.

He left his office and made his way to the waiting area. Bridget sat on a wooden bench, flipping through a magazine. He hadn't seen her in weeks. Her hair was pulled back in a ponytail and her scrubbed face enhanced her youthful, fragile look.

"Bridget." Her head came up and her shimmering green eyes grew wide. There was no doubt he'd startled her.

Rising to her feet, a grinning Bridget Sanborn approached her eldest brother, arms outstretched. "You look wonderful."

"Thanks." Micah hugged his sister before he kissed her cheek. A slight frown furrowed his forehead when he saw the dark smudges under her eyes. She looked tired. "How are you feeling?"

"I'm good."

Reaching for her hand, he cradled it gently. "Have you eaten?"

Bridget nodded. "Seth came over early this morning and brought me breakfast."

"That's only one meal, Bridget. And don't look at me like that," Micah warned when she glared at him.

"You should be the one getting married and starting a family, because you sure sound like you're rehearsing to be a daddy."

A swift shadow of annoyance swept over Micah's face before he schooled his features into an expression of indifference. He'd replayed his conversation with Tessa about his reluctance to marry, realizing his rationale for remaining single wasn't as meaningful as it'd been.

He'd told women he wanted to put in his twenty years as a cop, go to law school and, instead of arresting the bad guys, wanted to prosecute them before he thought about settling down to become a husband and father.

Professionally Micah had accomplished everything on his wish list, yet his personal life hadn't changed. He dated and had a couple of relationships that ended amicably. He'd never told a woman that he loved her because he feared her professing the same. The one woman that he'd loved unconditionally had told him that she loved him before abandoning him. The loss had scared him for an eternity.

His brothers were happily married fathers, and now his sister was planning to share her life with a man with whom she'd fallen in love. Would he, he mused, love and trust a woman enough to share his future?

"Are you all right, Micah?"

His gaze shifted to Bridget. "Yes. Why?"

Bridget looped her arm over the sleeve of his suit jacket. "You had this look on your face as if you'd just zoned out."

Micah winked at her. "I have a few things on my mind."

"Are they PG-13 or R?"

"X-rated."

Bridget wrinkled her nose. "Ouch."

"It serves you right for trying to get into my business."

She stuck her tongue out at him. "You don't have any business, Micah Sanborn. Mom says all you do is work."

Bridget waited until she was seated in the low-slung car, then told her brother about the trial that had dominated her life for the past two weeks. She fell silent when Micah maneuvered into an empty space with a No Parking sign and placed placards bearing insignias of the NYPD and the Kings County district attorney's office in the windshield.

"I should hang out with you more often," she teased as he opened the passenger-side door for her.

Reaching for Bridget's hand, Micah pulled her gently to her feet. He closed the door and set the alarm with the remote device. He held up his hand when Bridget opened her mouth to say something. "Not another word, Bridget," he warned in a soft tone. "You've kept Ms. Whitfield waiting long enough."

Chapter 8

Tessa opened the door, and within seconds of seeing Micah with his sister twin feelings of warmth surged through her. The emotion was one she always felt when meeting a prospective bride for the first time, and the other was one she couldn't explain except that she was glad to see Micah again.

She'd spent the past three days trying to remember everything about him, from the way he angled his head when listening to something she'd said to when his expressive eyebrows lifted or lowered, indicating surprise or disapproval. Tessa also remembered the deep-set dark eyes that seemed to photograph everything he saw within seconds.

Opening the door wider, she smiled. "Please come in."

Bridget preceded Micah, her green eyes taking in the tasteful furnishings in the foyer. She waved her left hand,

and the overhead light shimmered off a large emerald-cut engagement ring with baguettes. "This place is beautiful." There was no mistaking the awe in her voice.

Tessa closed the door and turned slowly to find Micah staring intently at her. "Thank you, Bridget." She extended her hand to his sister. "Tessa Whitfield."

Bridget shook her hand, smiling. "We finally meet. I'm Bridget."

Tessa nodded, and the curls falling over her forehead shook as if buffeted by a soft breeze. "Yes, we do finally meet."

Her professional eye cataloged Bridget in one sweeping glance. She was prettier in person. Her thick dark brown hair was the perfect complement to a flawless complexion with pink undertones. Her wide-set emerald-green eyes, straight nose and full pink mouth made for an arresting face. She estimated Bridget stood about five-four and weighed between one hundred fifteen and one hundred twenty pounds; the book editor was probably a six in the hips and an eight in the bodice.

Her gaze shifted to Micah. "Hello."

He angled his head and smiled. Tessa had affected the flyaway hairstyle he preferred. She looked different from the time he'd first come to her home. Today she wore a tailored white blouse with a pair of black cropped slacks that flattered her slender figure and a pair of low-heeled leather slip-ons.

"Hello, Tessa." Leaning down and resting a hand in the small of Bridget's back covered by a tan barn jacket, he said, "Call me on my cell when you're finished here."

"You don't have to leave," Tessa said quickly.

Micah shook his head. "I don't need to hang out here and listen to you ladies talk about—"

"Please, Micah," Tessa crooned softly, cutting him off. "I've been in this business long enough to know that most men don't want to become an observer or a participant in planning a wedding." She and Bridget exchanged a knowing glance. "If you follow me, I'll show you where you can hang out while your sister and I talk."

Turning on her heels, she made her way down the hallway, coming to a stop at the room she referred to as her parlor. It was where those other than the prospective bride or groom waited while she conducted her orientation.

"Please make yourself comfortable," she said to Micah as he stared mutely into the space where he would spend the next couple of hours.

"Very nice," he crooned, smiling, the warmth of his smile echoing in his voice. The inviting room beckoned him.

The fire blazing in a fireplace behind a decorative screen countered the chill of the autumn afternoon. Plush armchairs and love seats covered in pale hues, a flat-screen television resting on its own stand on a table, muted and tuned to ESPN, and a credenza filled with china, silver, crystal, bottles of water, soft drinks, crystal decanters of wines and spirits and warming trays from which wafted tantalizing smells was the perfect setting to dine and relax.

He walked in, slipping out of his suit jacket. "This is better than nice."

Tessa stared at his broad shoulders under a white shirt. "Enjoy, and please make yourself at home."

Bridget laughed softly. "You may come to regret that invitation. All you have to do is put a Sanborn man in front of a television with a sporting event, offer him some food and drink, and he'll never leave."

"We'd better get started," Tessa told Bridget as she led her down the hall to the room where she'd taken Micah seconds before the lights had gone out. It hadn't been a week, yet she felt as if she'd known him much longer than that.

"Hey-y-y," Bridget sang when she saw the setup Tessa had prepared for her: a table filled with an assortment of crudités, petits fours, herbal teas, sliced seasonal fruit, cheese, crackers, a crunchy vegetable salad with chopped chicken and bottled water.

"You're incredible, Tessa, and definitely top-shelf. I've been to quite a few weddings, but the one you coordinated for Jadya was truly spectacular. I told Seth that I just had to have Signature Bridals do ours. Daddy gave me a blank check, so I can pay for whatever I like or what you suggest."

She is a baby girl, Tessa mused. Bridget Sanborn was pampered *and* spoiled. She held out her hand, palm up. "May I see your ring?"

Bridget complied, grinning smugly as Tessa examined the three-carat flawless diamond in a platinum mounting. "I had no idea that Seth was going to give me a ring when he said he wanted to surprise me with a special gift for my birthday."

"It's beautiful, Bridget. I wish you and your fiancé the very best life has to offer."

Tears filled Bridget's eyes. "Thank you so much."

"We'll eat and talk at the same time."

Tessa entered the information on the Sanborn-Cohen nuptials into her notebook computer. Bridget had selected her wedding stationery, flowers for her bouquet and her maid of honor's, boutonnieres and floral decorations. She'd also brought her play list of the songs she wanted the band to play. The musical selections ranged from big band for Seth's grandmother to hip-hop for the younger crowd.

"You're going to have to set aside time to see Simone Whitfield so she can customize a cake. You'll have to let her know the design, the icing and the flavor for the filling."

Bridget set down her cup of tea. "We're having a formal wedding, so wouldn't the cake also have to be a classic multitiered white cake?"

"It's your wedding and you can have anything you want," Tessa said to Bridget. "Just as the bride stands out amidst the assemblage of all at a wedding ceremony, the wedding cake, which is a work of art, becomes the center of attention at the reception. You can have a three- or four-tiered cake with a classic white frosting that may conceal delectable different flavors for the cake and filling within each tier. I recommend you bring your fiancé with you when you meet with Simone. She designed Jadya and Ashton's cake, so you've seen—and hopefully tasted— her creation."

Jadya had requested that replicas of the covers of her children's books adorn each layer of a towering eight-tiered edible architecture with white and chocolate roses perched around the base of each layer. The wedding guests were given individual servings as souvenirs, each with a cover of the sixteen bestselling books written by the bride.

An attractive blush colored Bridget's cheeks. "Jadya gave me an individual cake with the cover of the book I'd edited for her."

"Do you want individual servings for your guests?"

"I don't know. I'll have to ask Seth."

Dabbing the corners of her mouth with her napkin, Tessa placed it on the table and pushed to her feet. "Now it's time we see about your dress. I've selected a few I believe you would like and would fit you without too many alterations. However, if you want a custom-made gown, then I'm going to recommend that you secure the services of a wedding gown designer with a staff who will be able to devote the time to completing it before the holiday."

Bridget stood up. "Did you design Jadya's dress?"

"No. That's was my mother's creation. Come with me upstairs and I'll show you what I have." She'd learned how to sew as a child when Lucinda Whitfield gave her scraps of leftover fabric from the beautiful wedding gowns she'd been commissioned to sew for any bride lucky enough to wear an LCW creation.

Tessa took a back staircase up to the third floor. When she'd purchased the brownstone five years before, it'd taken the contractor more than six months to renovate the three-story structure to her specifications. She'd had all of the walls on the third floor removed to create a loft effect. A black-and-white vinyl floor, redbrick walls, skylights and track lighting provided a setting conducive for her whenever she spent hours in her studio designing and piecing wedding gowns.

Bridget gasped, then covered her mouth with her hand as she moved into the space as if propelled by an invisible wire. Her hand trembled noticeably when she lowered it.

Tessa was hard pressed not to smile. "Do you see something you like?"

Blinking back tears, Bridget nodded like a bobblehead doll. "Yes," she whispered, recovering her voice. She touched a silvery silk-satin *peau de soire* ball gown with a halter neckline, a dropped waistline, inverted pleats and a chapel train.

Tessa moved closer. "I selected this gown because even though you're having a winter wedding you won't have to travel from your home to a church, then a catering hall for your reception. It should show off the lines of your body to their best advantage.

"The halter neckline is elegant, cut to flatter your shoulders and back, while the tightly fitted bodice and dropped waistline will emphasize your midriff. The skirt is cut so there's no bulkiness at the front, yet the two deep inverted pleats add dimension, giving the illusion of added fullness and formality. I recommend you get a back facial a week before your wedding to make certain the skin on your back is smooth and blemish-free."

Bridget took a deep breath. "Can I try it on, Tessa?"

"Sure. You can change behind that screen." Tessa pointed to a decorative four-panel screen in a far corner. "I want you to try on a few others before you make a final decision."

Bridget gathered the gown off the padded hanger. "If this fits, then I want it."

Tessa placed her hand on her client's shoulder. "May I make a suggestion?" Bridget nodded. "Try on more than one gown, because later on you may decide you don't like it. And once I alter the dress to fit you, then it's yours. Remember—all eyes will be on you, so if you don't like what you're wearing, then that will show through when you force yourself to smile when you don't feel like smiling."

Running a hand over the delicate fabric, Bridget bit down on her lower lip. "I should've asked my mother to come with me. I always trust her judgment."

"Perhaps, in the interest of time, I can help you out."

"How?"

"Try on several dresses, then select the ones you'd

want your mother to see. I'll FedEx them to New Jersey. Make your final selection, enclose a note, then FedEx them back to me in the same carton with the prepaid mailing label."

Bridget reached out and hugged Tessa with her free arm. "Thank you so much."

Patting Bridget's shoulder—the gesture purely maternal even though she and her client were the same age—Tessa smiled. "You're welcome. Now please go and try on your gowns."

Sitting on a comfortable armchair, she waited for Bridget to model the gowns she'd chosen for her. A smug smile tugged at the corners of her mouth. The gowns she'd selected were perfect for the bride-to-be. Bridget had slim, firm arms, good shoulders and a smooth back. Most of the garments accentuated her small waist and firm breasts.

Simone had referred to Bridget as "ditzy," but Tessa thought of her as impulsive. Ditzy, impulsive, spoiled and pampered Bridget Sanborn was sly as a fox, because she'd snagged one of New York City's most eligible bachelors. Seth Cohen and two of his college buddies had founded a Google-type Internet company, and the net worth of the trio had exceeded a billion dollars before they'd celebrated their thirtieth birthdays.

Bridget had confided to Tessa that Seth wanted to pay for the wedding but his future father-in-law wouldn't hear of it. Edgar claimed he wasn't going to be cheated out of the honor of giving his only daughter whatever she wanted for her very special day.

Four hours after Tessa opened the door to Signature Bridals for Bridget and Micah Sanborn, she closed it behind them. Bridget had quickly changed her mind about her first choice once she'd tried on several other gowns.

Tessa had suggested she try on the gowns with the heel height she wanted for her wedding and with jewelry, especially if she wanted to wear earrings and a necklace, and decide whether she wanted to wear her hair loose or up off her neck and shoulders. She'd looked confused until Tessa had given her a printout of her recommendations. The maid of honor's dress would not become an issue until after Bridget selected her gown.

Returning to her office, she picked up the telephone and dialed the number to the graphic designer who handled all of Signature Bridals' wedding stationery. Juan Cruz operated a very successful graphic design enterprise out of his loft in DuMBo, an area of Brooklyn undergoing gentrification.

"This is Juan. Speak to me, beautiful. I hope you called to tell me that you're going to be my bride."

Tessa smothered a laugh as she shook her head. "No, I didn't. I need you for a rush job."

"Juan no make love fast," he crooned, affecting an accent. "I do it real slow and make you scream, *'Ay, ay, papi.'*"

"Juan, please be serious for once."

"I am serious, *mami*. When are you going to stop playing hard to get and say yes? You know we work well together."

"You're right, Juan, because I pay you very, very well."

"Ouch, *mami!* Why you have to go there?"

"I went there because all we have between us is business."

"You really know how to hurt a guy, Tessa. What do you need?"

"I need a wedding stationery trousseau for one

hundred invitations for a formal New Year's Eve wedding."

"Give me the specs," Juan said.

She gave him the color, paper stock and type of print for the invitations, reception and reply cards. "As soon as I hang up I'm going to scan the names and addresses of the guests. You'll get them as an e-mail attachment." Having Juan address the envelopes would save the Sanborns having to handwrite each address. He had a software program with calligraphy so refined that it mimicked handwriting. "I'm also going to include the food and cocktail menu. My client also wants place and seating cards and a map with directions."

"The silver with the black trim and ribbon is going to be pricey, but it'll look spectacular, Tessa."

She ignored his reference to money. "How soon can you get them to me?"

"How soon do you want them?"

"Can you do it in a week?"

"For you, *mami,* I will have them done *mañana.*"

Tessa tried to suppress a giggle. "A week will do. I'm going to messenger over a check tomorrow as a deposit. Please give him an invoice for the job when he gets there."

"Okay."

"Thanks, Juan."

"I should be the one thanking you. If you hadn't used me for the Fyles-Cooper wedding, I would've been forced to go back to a nine-to-five."

"I used you instead of my regular guy because you're a perfectionist."

"And you're not?"

"I'm not as finicky as you, Juan. I'm going to ring off

and e-mail you that information. Call me if you have any questions."

"Talk to you later, *mami*."

"Later, *papi*," she teased, then disconnected the call.

She met Juan when both were graduate students at the Parsons School of Design. They'd earned MFA degrees in graphic design, but it was Juan who'd made graphic design his career, while Tessa's love of fashion design had lured her back into the family's wedding business.

She sent Juan the information he needed to begin the Sanborn-Cohen job, then cleaned up the remains of the repast she'd put out for her client. A copy of the contract and the check Bridget had given her lay on her desk. Tomorrow she would call her favorite band to find out whether they were available for New Year's Eve.

Her mind was reeling with ideas, but she decided not to jot them down or she wouldn't get any sleep. Bridget's formal wedding would provide the perfect ending to what had become Signature Bridals' most successful and profitable year in its very short history.

She climbed the staircase to the second floor. Within minutes of showering and getting into bed Tessa fell asleep. However, she slept restlessly. Images of Micah Sanborn came and went, leaving her breathing heavily.

What, she thought as she lay in the dark, was there about him that kept her from a peaceful night's sleep? The question bombarded her and she wasn't able to come up with an answer.

Hopefully she would find the answer to her question when she saw him again.

Chapter 9

Micah maneuvered into a parking space in front of Tessa's brownstone. Leaving his sheepskin-lined jacket in the space behind the seats, he opened the door, got out and left the engine running. Using a remote device, he locked the doors. Bounding up the stairs, he rang the bell.

"The door's open," came Tessa's voice through the intercom.

He pushed opened the door and stepped into the foyer. Light and warmth enveloped him like a blanket. The vase on the table filled with wildflowers in autumnal colors added a homey touch to the space.

"Tessa!"

"Come on back to the kitchen."

He found her in the kitchen drinking coffee. His gaze lingered on her curvy hips in a pair of fitted jeans she'd tucked into a pair of low-heeled black suede lace-up boots. A cashmere pullover in a soft peach shade complemented the yellow-orange undertones in her complexion. She'd brushed her hair off her face and secured it in a curly ponytail.

"You're taking a chance leaving your door unlocked."

Lowering her cup, Tessa smiled at Micah. "And where is your coat, Micah Sanborn?" He stood in the middle of her kitchen wearing a pair of black wide-wale cords, a matching chunky turtleneck and Timberland boots.

"It's in the car. And don't try to change the subject, Tessa Whitfield."

"I opened it minutes before you rang the bell."

"Why didn't you wait for me to ring the bell?"

Tessa took a long swallow of coffee as she massaged the back of her neck. "I wanted to finish my coffee."

Crossing his arms over his chest, Micah approached her. "I thought I told you we would eat breakfast on the road."

Tilting her chin, Tessa met his penetrating stare. "I couldn't wait. I didn't sleep very well last night, so the caffeine is what I need to keep my eyes open."

Micah reached out and took the cup from her hand, placing it on the countertop. "Turn around," he said softly.

"What?"

He crooked a finger. "Come closer and turn around, Tessa."

She gave him a sidelong glance. "Should I be afraid of you?"

"No. Who you should be afraid of are perps looking for an easy score. And you're like a glaring bull's-eye when you leave your door open."

Smiling, she turned and presented him with her back. "Is *perp* the same as a perpetrator?"

Micah nodded. "It's hard to lose the police jargon after twenty years." He rested his hands on her shoulders, massaging the muscles in her back and neck. Lowering his head, he pressed his mouth to the nape of her neck. "Gosh, you're tight."

Tessa closed her eyes, moaning softly under the soothing ministrations. "How much do you charge for a massage?"

"There's no charge. By the way, why are you so tense?"

"I've got a lot on my mind."

"Is Bridget giving you a hard time?"

She moaned again when he kneaded a knot under her shoulder blade. "No, but Bridget's brother is." Tessa's eyes flew open when she realized she'd spoken her thoughts aloud.

Micah's hands stilled. "What have I done to give you hard time? If you don't want to go upstate with me this morning, then you don't have to go."

"It's not that, Micah."

He turned her to face him. His gaze lingered on her parted lips before moving up to her eyes—eyes that mesmerized, held him spellbound. "What is it?"

Tessa's lids fluttered wildly as she struggled to bring her thoughts in some semblance of order. How could she explain to a man she'd known a week that he'd made her reassess her stance when it came to interacting with a man? That going out with him went against her own rule for becoming involved with a man associated with a client?

"I'm uneasy because I've broken my promise to myself."

Micah's eyebrows lifted. "Which is?"

"Not to get involved with a man."

"We're not involved, Tessa. Not yet, anyway," he added as a hint of a smile parted his lips.

"Do you want to become involved?"

Attractive lines fanned out around his eyes when his smile grew wider. "Do you want a lie or the truth?"

Her smile matched his. "I want the truth, the whole truth and nothing but the truth."

Angling his head, Micah brushed a light kiss over her parted lips. "Then the answer is an unequivocal yes."

Rising on tiptoe, Tessa pressed her mouth to his. "Can you promise me that it won't get too serious or complicated," she whispered, "and that we can still be friends once it's over?"

Looping his arms around Tessa's waist, he pulled her closer. "I don't make promises."

"Why not?"

"There is no guarantee that I'll be able to keep them. The only thing I'll attest to is an absolute." He lowered his head to kiss Tessa again, but her hand came up, stopping him.

Easing back in his embrace, Tessa studied his impassive expression. "Are you still on friendly terms with your ex-girlfriends?"

"No."

"Was it because you didn't want to be friends?"

"Just say it was by mutual agreement." His expression changed, softening. "Why are we talking about breaking up when we haven't begun dating?"

There was a beat of silence. "You're right, Micah. I've been known to obsess about things that don't need obsessing over."

"Now that we've solved your dilemma, can we go?"

"Yes. If you let me go, I'll get my coat."

Micah wanted to tell Tessa that he didn't want to let her go, that he liked holding her, that he wanted to really kiss her and communicate wordlessly how he actually felt about her.

She'd confessed to not sleeping well at night when it'd been the same with him. He went to work early and stayed late, hoping that when he returned home he would be so exhausted that he would fall asleep as soon as his head touched the pillow.

Lately he'd found himself sitting up in bed watching late-night and late-late-night TV shows. At first he thought he'd become an insomniac, but when he backtracked as to when his sleeplessness began, the evidence pointed to the night of the blackout, the night he'd slept with Tessa Whitfield, the night he'd felt a rush of desire for a woman whose face he couldn't remember. What he did remember was her sultry voice and her perfume.

And when he did see her again—this time in the full sunlight—it was as if someone had punched him in the gut, knocking the breath out of him and rendering him speechless for several seconds. Unknowingly Tessa Whitfield had charmed him as no other woman had.

He released Tessa, watching as she rinsed her cup and placed it in the dishwasher. He picked up a camel-hair swing coat off the back of a stool and held it for her as she slipped her arms into the sleeves.

Reaching for her keys and handbag, she winked at him. "I'm ready."

Tessa was ready, but was he ready for her? He was no schoolboy when it came to women, yet there was something about the wedding planner that made him feel like a gawky adolescent. He'd found her a chameleon. There was Ms. Whitfield, wedding planner extraordinaire who was formal and the consummate professional, and there was Tessa, smiling, teasing, soft and undeniably feminine.

What Micah had to decide was which one he liked or wanted. He respected her as a businesswoman but wanted the woman without with the professional attitude and trappings that surfaced when he least expected.

He hadn't asked Tessa to go upstate with him on impulse, because Micah Sanborn had never made an impulsive move in his entire life. He'd asked her because spending the day together away from all that was familiar would tell him whether he should pursue her or retreat honorably.

He waited for her to activate the alarm and lock the door, then, reaching for her hand, he led her down the stairs of the brownstone to where he'd parked his car. Using the remote device, he unlocked the vehicle and waited until she settled on the seat. He closed the door with a solid slam and rounded the sports car and got in beside her. They exchanged a smile before he put the vehicle in gear and maneuvered away from the curb in a smooth burst of power.

"Thanks for keeping the car warm," Tessa said, pressing her head against the headrest and closing her eyes. The heat from the vents and the soft jazz coming from the speakers lulled her into a state of total relaxation.

Micah gave her a quick glance. "If it gets too warm, let me know."

She shook her head but didn't open her eyes. "It's good."

"Why don't you try and take a nap. I'll wake you up when we stop for breakfast."

A dreamy smile crossed her delicate features. "Thanks."

"Tessa, wake up. We're stopping here to eat."

She heard the deep voice but was loath to open her

eyes. She was past being tired—she was exhausted. Her lids fluttered wildly as she struggled to surface from what had become the best sleep she'd had in days.

When they'd left Brooklyn, the sun hadn't come up, but now light came in through the windshield. Rolling her head from side to side, she let out a soft exhalation of breath.

"How long have I been asleep?"

Resting his right arm over the back of Tessa's seat, Micah stared at her enchanting profile. "Not long."

"How long is not long?"

"You zonked out before we left Brooklyn. You weren't kidding when you said you were tired."

Tessa glanced at the clock on the dashboard. It was ten o'clock. She'd been asleep for four hours. "I feel better now."

"Are you ready to eat?"

"Bring it on," she said, grinning. She was rested *and* hungry.

Micah had stopped at a diner that resembled a railroad boxcar and had been appropriately named The Boxcar. The family-owned restaurant had achieved landmark status in the tiny hamlet boasting a population of less than three thousand. The ongoing joke was that the census would be less than two thousand if the residents didn't count the dogs, chickens, sheep, cows and goats and horses, all of whom they considered family.

Cornstalks tied to lampposts, pumpkins carved with happy and macabre faces and inflatable ghosts and skeletons decorating the area surrounding the historic eating establishment were a constant reminder that Halloween was only days away.

He helped Tessa out of the car, wrapping an arm

around her waist. "It feels like snow up here." His breath was visible in the colder air.

Tessa looked up at him. "Will I still be able to go apple picking?"

"Not in the snow. Even though it is close to the end of the season for apple picking, you can always buy them from farm stands."

"I'd like to pick up some Granny Smiths. They're perfect for pies and cobblers."

"After we eat breakfast, I'll stop at a farm stand that's not too far from my place."

Micah opened the door to the diner, and the distinctive smell of coffee, bacon and eggs wafted to Tessa's nose. "Oh, that smells divine."

The diner was crowded with the usual locals, and Micah managed to find an empty booth that'd just been vacated by an elderly couple. Waitresses in flower-sprigged pink uniforms hoisted trays laden with dishes, while a busboy worked feverishly to clear away the remains of meals and set the tables for waiting customers.

The teenage boy came over to the booth, his blue eyes widening before crinkling in a smile. He extended his hand, giving Micah a loud, slapping handshake before snapping his fingers.

"How've you been, Lt. Sanborn?"

Micah waved his hand. "I'm no longer a lieutenant, Bobby. I retired this past spring."

"My dad says he's retiring next year." Bobby glanced up at the clock. "He should be getting off in a couple of hours, so he'll be in later on. I'd better clean up this table before Grandpa yells at me."

"Hey, Bobby, you're needed over here!" shouted a male voice above the din of rattling dishes, waitresses calling out orders to the short-order cooks and the blare of music coming from a colorful jukebox.

Bobby rolled his eyes. "See what I mean."

Tessa exchanged a smile with Micah as Bobby quickly cleaned off the table, put out place settings and gave each a plastic-covered menu. Her gaze lingered on Micah's lean face, noticing the flecks of gray in his close-cropped hair. Light from an overhead fixture slanted over the ridge of his prominent cheekbones, giving him the appearance of a carved African mask. He lifted his expressive eyebrows questioningly, and she lowered her gaze, pretending interest in the menu in front of her.

A knowing smile tilted the corners of Micah's mouth as he stared at the length of lashes casting a shadow on Tessa's cheeks. She hadn't worn any makeup other than a soft rose color on her lips, and he found himself enchanted with the freckles dotting her satiny face.

"You're gorgeous."

Her head jerked up. "What!"

Leaning forward in his seat, he whispered, "I said you are gorgeous. I can't be the first man who's told you that."

Tessa stared at Micah through her lashes, unable to meet his penetrating gaze or stop the rush of heat flooding her face. "No, you're not," she said truthfully, "but men have said things to me for different reasons."

"What would they be?"

Resting her arms on the table, she gave him a direct look. "Most of them wanted to get into my panties."

Micah's jaw slightly dropped before he recovered enough to say, "Are you always so blunt?"

She lifted a shoulder. "Why shouldn't I be? Some of them just came out and said they wanted to sleep with me.

A few others tried to cloak it with an offer of friendship, but after a few dates I had to fight them off or threaten to dial 911 if they didn't leave."

"It sounds as if you've been dealing with losers."

She affected a cynical smile. "I've had more losers than winners."

Resting his elbow on the table, he cradled his chin in his hand. "It isn't that much different with men and women. I've had more losers than winners." Tessa's eyes widened until he could see pinpoints of gold in the soft brown depths. "You think women have a monopoly on picking up losers or crazies?"

"You don't hear men complain about there's not enough good women the way we do. And if we do find a good man, then he's afraid to commit."

"How are you interpreting the word *good,* Tessa?"

"One who's faithful, truthful, loyal, respectful and ethical."

"Are you saying that if he's unwilling to commit, then he's not good?"

"I'm not talking about committing to marriage, because not everyone is suited for marriage. What I'm saying is that if he's in a relationship, then he should be committed to his woman *and* their relationship. Some men claim they love a woman even when she's his baby mama, but they continue to sleep with other women because as long as he's not married to his baby mama, then he's not cheating. That's a load of BS."

"I agree with you."

"You do?"

Reaching out, he captured her hands. "Yes. Why is that so hard for you to believe?"

"I don't know, Micah. I'm not used to a man agreeing with me on the topic of relationships." She glanced over his shoulder. "Have you ever been in a committed relationship?"

He nodded. "I've been in a few. You?"

Tessa closed her eyes and the image of Bryce Hill came to mind. "I've had one."

"Only one?"

She opened her eyes. "Yes."

Tessa tried to pull her hands away, but Micah tightened his grip on her slender fingers. "What happened?"

"I ended it because it was based on lies and deception."

"That'll do it every time."

A waitress wearing a champagne-pink bouffant-style wig and blinking skeleton earrings approached the table carrying a coffee carafe. She nodded to Tessa. "Mornin', missy. Long time no see, Micah. Bobby, I need mugs over here!" she shouted, not pausing to take a breath.

Releasing Tessa's hands, Micah straightened against the back of the lipstick-red booth. "How's the family, Helen?"

"Fair to middling. I can't wait until my youngest leaves home. He's driving me batty. Bobby! I need mugs!" she screamed again.

Tessa brought up her hand to cover a cough, concealing the laugh struggling to erupt, before she picked up her menu, pretending interest in the typed selections. More than a dozen varieties of muffins were listed under breakfast favorites.

Bobby jogged over with two large mugs. "Sorry about that, Miss Helen." He set them on the table, then scurried away to pick up a plastic bin overflowing with dirty dishes.

"Do you know what you want or should I give you a few minutes?" the waitress asked.

"We're going to need a few minutes," Micah said, reaching for his menu.

Waiting until Helen walked away to wait on another table, Tessa glanced up to find Micah staring at her. "What?" she whispered.

He blinked as if coming out of a trance. "Nothing." His gaze shifted to the menu. "May I make a suggestion?"

"Yes."

"Try the blueberry-cream-cheese streusel coffee cake."

"What are you going to have?"

Micah perused the menu he knew like the back of his hand. "I think I'm going to try the carrot cake loaf with pistachios."

Tessa smiled. "That sounds yummy."

Micah wanted to tell her that she looked and smelled yummy—yummy and good enough to eat. He wanted to sample her lips, then work his way down her body to her toes before reversing his exploration to return to her luscious mouth. Brushing his mouth over hers just served to whet his appetite for more, much more.

The erotic musings exploded in his head like lightning bolts, leaving him shaking from the aftermath of the realization that he was no different from the other men who'd found themselves enthralled with Tessa Whitfield.

Did he want to sleep with her?

Yes, said a silent voice.

But did he want more than a physical relationship?

Yes, it said again.

However, old doubts and trepidation lingered. Could he, Micah wondered, put aside his dread of trusting a woman completely to experience the joy and satisfaction of a normal relationship for the first time in his life?

He closed his eyes and whispered a silent prayer for

strength, and when he opened his eyes and stared across the table at Tessa Whitfield he believed that she was the one—the one woman who would help to overcome his fear of abandonment.

She wanted what he wanted—a relationship based on friendship and honesty and free of encumbrances. She was beautiful and intelligent, and he enjoyed talking to her, unlike other women with whom he'd found himself involved.

His sister would marry in eight weeks, and eight weeks was more than enough time for him to ascertain whether whatever he would share with Tessa would continue beyond the new year.

Chapter 10

Fortified with a sumptuous breakfast that included a spinach-and-feta-cheese omelet with a rasher of crispy bacon and a cream-cheese-and-blueberry muffin, all washed down with two cups of steaming coffee, Tessa could barely get out of the car when Micah stopped at an enclosed farm stand several miles from what he'd referred to as his vacation retreat.

The patrons at The Boxcar had been as memorable as the food. Micah told her that The Boxcar offered family discounts for Saturday- and Sunday-morning breakfasts in an attempt to reinforce the family-ties motto adopted by the local school district. Young children had come in wearing Halloween costumes for the various all-day parties hosted by local churches and civic organizations.

"I'm so full I can't walk, Micah," she groaned as he

tucked her hand into the crook of his elbow. Bending slightly, he swept her up in his arms and made his way from the parking area toward the clapboard building. Tessa pounded his solid shoulder. "Put me down."

He stopped, grinning at her. "You said you couldn't walk."

"Don't be silly. It was only a figure of speech because I'd eaten too much."

Micah took a step. "You hardly ate anything. You left half your omelet and I finished up your muffin."

"That's because I'm not used to eating that much in the morning."

He smiled as he continued walking. "Well, I am. Didn't your mother teach you that breakfast is the most important meal of the day?"

"Yes, she did. But that has nothing to do with overeating."

"Don't tell me you're dieting?"

"No!"

"Well, I had to ask because nowadays it seems as if every woman is on one diet or another."

Tessa pushed against his shoulder. "Put me down, Micah!" He complied, setting her on her feet. "I'd thought you'd be different from the other men I've met."

"Different how, Tessa?"

"You lump all women into one category, then you come out of your face with some stereotypical—"

"Stop it, Tessa," he said, cutting her off. "Don't say another word." His voice, though low, dared her to refute him. "I'm neither a sexist nor a misogynist. Statistics show that if you ask ten women from any racial group if they've ever dieted or are currently on a diet, nine of ten will say yes. I don't know anything about you other than what little you've told me, and because I'm not a mind reader I had to ask. Will you forgive me?"

Tessa and Micah stared at each other in what had become a stalemate. Neither was willing to concede. It was only their first date and they realized they shared an obvious negative personality trait: stubbornness.

She nodded "What do you want to know about me?" she asked, ending the impasse.

"Everything you're willing to tell me."

She nodded again. "Okay."

The tense lines in Micah's face eased. "And I'll tell you about me, but first let's go and buy your apples."

"If they're going to be *my* apples, then I suppose that means I don't have to share the pie with you," she teased.

Reaching for Tessa's hand, he gave her fingers a gentle squeeze. "I *will* throw down for some pie."

A hint of a smile found its way across Tessa's upturned face. "I suppose I'll have to make the pie and see who..." Her words trailed off when particles of ice pelted her forehead. "It's sleeting."

Micah led her toward the farm stand. "We better buy what we need and get up to the house before the roads get icy. I'm going to stop at another store to pick up something to eat for later on, because if the sleet turns into snow we're going to be stuck until the roads are plowed."

Tessa stopped short, causing Micah to stumble, but he regained his footing quickly. "What if we're snowed in?"

He saw the wariness in her eyes. "Do you have anything planned for tomorrow?"

"No. But when I agreed to come up here with you I hadn't expected it to snow before the end of October."

He eased her forward. The sleet was falling faster, the

icy pellets slashing exposed skin like tiny razors. "Some years there's hardly a trace of snow, and others accumulations can go as high as sixty inches."

"I agreed to have dinner with you, Micah Sanborn, not spend the weekend snowbound."

Reaching over her head, Micah pushed open a solid oak door. "If I had to get snowed in with someone, I'd pray she looked like you."

Tessa rolled her eyes at him. "Flattery will get you nowhere."

"I know one thing I'm going to get from you," he whispered close to her ear.

Going completely still, her heart pounding a runaway rhythm, Tessa turned and stared up at Micah as if she'd never seen him before. *Please don't let him be like all of the others,* a silent voice pleaded.

"What's that, Micah?"

Dipping his head and pressing his mouth her ear, he whispered, "Some apple pie."

A wave of relief bubbled up in her chest and came out like a schoolgirl giggle, causing several people close enough to hear her titter smile. His low chuckle joined hers.

"You thought I was going to say your panties, didn't you?" She sobered quickly, her mouth forming a perfect *O*. "Yeah, you did," he said, teasing her. "Why, I believe you're blushing."

"I don't blush."

He pulled her gently along with him to the rear of the large clapboard building. "Come on, beautiful, and pick out what you want."

Micah waited patiently, a large wicker basket filled with ears of bread-and-butter corn, carrots, snow peas, lemons, limes, Vidalia onions and Granny Smith apples on the floor next to his feet, watching Tessa as she examined every fruit and vegetable in every basket and bin. He wanted to warn her that if they lingered too long, the bridge along the road leading to his house would freeze, making driving hazardous. But the enraptured expression on her face when she'd discovered lesser-known varieties of squash and melons forced him to remain silent.

Tessa picked up a small, round, seedless watermelon. Turning, she smiled at Micah. "Do you like watermelon?"

"I like and eat everything," he said in a patronizing tone.

Tessa's gaze narrowed when she noticed he'd crossed his arms over his chest and his expression was undeniably boredom.

"I'm almost finished here. Give me a few more minutes to get some herbs, then we can go."

Micah bowed from the waist. "Thank you, madam."

She'd affected an attractive moue. "You're welcome, sir."

The sky had turned a slate gray and the sleet changed over into snow, quickly blanketing the road, trees and dry surfaces. Micah downshifted and flipped a switch to increase the wiper speed as he maneuvered over the steel bridge that always froze before the roadway. The first time he'd driven over the bridge in an ice storm he'd spun out, his car stopping within inches of a steel girder. Only his tactical-driving training and quick reaction time had saved him from injury and/or totaling out his car.

"We're almost there," he said to Tessa. She'd gasped audibly when the tires began slipping on the bridge's icy roadway.

"What made you decide to buy property up here?"

His hands tightened on the steering wheel as he attempted to keep the car steady. "I bought it from a friend who was going through a divorce. Neither he nor his wife wanted it because they said it held too many memories. Unfortunately I bought it sight unseen, and when I came up here the first time the only thing I thought about was dousing it with gasoline and lighting a match. But when I hired an architect to look at it, he said it had a lot of potential."

Tessa stared at Micah's profile, admiring his strong, masculine features. "Did it?"

He smiled without taking his gaze off the roadway. "You'll see."

A quarter of an hour later Tessa saw for herself the potential the architect had espoused when Micah touched a panel on the wall near the front door and lights from table lamps, high hats and hanging fixtures flooded the first floor with a warm golden glow. Leaving her boots on a thick straw mat, she walked into the dark gray-and-white-trimmed house that originally had been constructed as a barn, while Micah unloaded their purchases from the car's trunk.

She was astounded by an enormous stone fireplace that rose to the height of the second-story loft and that the entire first floor was constructed without walls. The living/dining/family rooms blended into an enormous kitchen with top-of-the-line stainless-steel appliances. A bathroom, a pantry, a laundry and a mudroom with a snowblower, rakes and a lawn mower were tucked away in an alcove at the back of the expansive structure. All of the furniture was covered with dustcovers, but the pale oak floors gleamed as if someone had recently dusted them. She opened the side-by-side refrigerator/freezer. It was running, clean and fresh-smelling.

Micah walked into the kitchen area carrying several bags. Tessa took one from him and set it on the countertop. "I still have to get a few more." They'd stopped at a supermarket to buy what she needed for the pie, dairy products and meat and poultry from the butcher section.

She smiled at him. "I'm going to wash the fruit before I put them in the fridge."

He headed toward the rear of the house. "Don't take your coat off until I push up the thermostat." The indoor temperature registered a chilly forty-eight degrees.

Tessa followed him. "I'm okay." She took off her coat and hung it on a wall hook in the mudroom while Micah opened a door to where the heating/cooling system was installed.

"Who cleaned the house?" she asked.

"I've contracted with a landscaping company to do the grounds, and a cleaning service comes once a month to dust and check for creatures."

Tessa halted placing lemons, limes and the apples in one of two stainless-steel sinks. "What kind of creatures are you talking about?"

Micah stuck his head out of the boiler room and winked at her. "Little furry things."

She cut her eyes at him. "I'm not staying here if I have to share the space with anything that's furry, crawls or slithers."

"Don't worry, Tessa. I'll protect you from all creatures—big and small."

But who's going to protect me from you? she thought. Micah Sanborn was too masculine and much too virile to ignore for long periods of time. She'd only seen him three times, and recalling his image played havoc with her sleep pattern. They'd shared a bed without making love and he'd only kissed her cheek, yet she still found herself thinking about him at the most inopportune times, and on one occasion craving him.

She'd complained to him about men wanting to get into her panties when that was exactly what she wanted Micah to do. She wanted him in her panties, in her bed and inside her.

Her lascivious thoughts left her shaking like a sapling in a storm. It was storming outside and inside the house, the latter leaving Tessa weak in the knees. She wanted to dismiss Micah from her head like one erasing a chalkboard or hitting the delete button on a keyboard, but it wasn't that easy when he stood only feet from her. How, she thought, was she going to get through the weekend without communicating to the man that she wanted him, all of him?

Twenty minutes later, the sounds coming from the heating vents competed with the crackle and popping of burning wood in the gluttonous fireplace. Micah retreated to the bathroom to wash his hands, but when he returned to the kitchen he came to a complete stop when he saw Tessa placing large, bright green apples into a glass bowl. She was the first woman, other than family members, he'd invited to his vacation retreat, and seeing the domestic scene evoked an unexpected longing.

There were times when he'd asked himself whether he wanted to duplicate his brothers' lives. Did he want to marry and father children? And the answer was always a resounding no. But now he wasn't that certain. Was it because he was no longer a police officer, required and authorized to carry a firearm? Or was it because at forty-one he realized that half his life was behind him? Or was it because he'd never met the woman who, just being who she was, made him reassess whether he could continue to live out the rest of his life as a bachelor.

What surprised him most of all was that he didn't know Tessa Whitfield, hadn't made love with her, yet there was something about her that drew him to her like moths to a flame, bees to flowers and sunflowers facing the sun.

Slowly he came up behind her, wrapping his arms around her waist while easing her back against his chest. "Come upstairs with me. I'm going to give you something to change into so you won't soil your sweater."

Smiling at Micah over her shoulder, Tessa wrinkled her nose. "Is *she* my size?"

Micah caught her meaning immediately. "I don't think *I* was your size when I was ten," he said with a wide grin. Tessa sobered as heat flooded her cheeks. "What's the matter? Cat got your tongue?" he teased.

She lowered her gaze in a demure gesture. "Okay, Micah, you got me this time."

Turning her around in his embrace, he smiled down at her. "If it counts for anything, you're the first woman I've invited here."

"What about your mother and sister?"

"They don't count," he said in a dangerously soft voice.

"And why don't they count?"

Slowly lowering his head, his warm breath sweeping over her mouth, he whispered, "Because I can't do this to them." Micah did what he'd wanted to do earlier. He kissed Tessa with all of the passion he could summon for a woman. He placed soft, feathery kisses at the corners of her mouth, increasing the pressure at the same time his hands came up and cradled her face. The pads of his thumbs traced the curve of her cheekbones, delicate jaw and chin. His fingers committed the shape and hollows of her face to memory. Even in the dark, with his eyes closed, he'd be able to identify Tessa Whitfield in a room with hundreds of other women.

Her lips parted, and he sampled and tasted the sugary, frothy confection of her mouth. Her mouth was sweet. She smelled sweet and the softness of her body molded to his was luscious. He wanted to put Tessa inside him as much as he wanted to be in her. Within seconds the dictates of his brain were communicated to his body and he was helpless to control the hardening flesh between his legs. Slowly he lifted his head, studying Tessa's expression for a reaction to his rising desire. He didn't know what to expect, but he was prepared for whatever would follow. Either she would accept or reject his overture.

Tessa stared wordlessly, her thoroughly kissed lips parting as she struggled to bring her dizzying emotions into some semblance of order. A slow smile slipped through her expression of uncertainty. She hadn't expected Micah to kiss her—and she hadn't expected herself to react to the drugging effects of his mouth, his masculine scent and his warmth.

"You've just proven your case, Counselor."

Throwing back his head, Micah laughed loudly in relief. He'd thought he was moving too quickly and that he wouldn't be given a second chance to prove to Tessa that she could trust him. After all, they were alone at his house in the Adirondack Mountains and more than quarter of a mile from his nearest neighbor. The falling snow, like the unexpected blackout, had changed their plans. And if they weren't able to leave until after the snow stopped, then he wanted to replicate their first night together.

Reaching for her hand, he gave her fingers a soft squeeze. A gentle smile ruffled his mouth. "Come upstairs and I'll show you where you can change."

Chapter 11

Wearing Micah's T-shirt and a pair of sweatpants that she'd rolled over twice at the waist and hem, Tessa slipped easily into domesticity mode as she peeled, cored and sliced apples for a ready-made crust. She would've preferred rolling out her own crust, but when Micah revealed he didn't have a rolling pin she opted for the frozen variety. He'd also changed out of his cords and sweater and into a pair of sweatpants and a white T-shirt. A pair of tattered leather moccasins had replaced his boots, while she'd elected to walk around in her socks.

The voice of the newscaster coming from the small television under a kitchen cabinet predicted at least three inches of snow would blanket the region before tapering off to flurries throughout the night and into the morning hours.

Micah returned from stoking the fire in the fireplace

in time to hear the weather report. "Three inches isn't much of an accumulation, but what do you say we sleep over? In separate bedrooms, of course," he added quickly when Tessa shot him a look. He'd said separate bedrooms when actually he wanted to share a bed with her again.

Tessa saw the smoldering invitation in the dark eyes staring at her in a waiting silence. Did he feel what she was feeling or beginning to feel? Was Micah aware of the invisible thread pulling them together against her will?

"I hadn't planned on spending the night with you, but I suppose it could be fun."

Micah exhaled an audible breath. "What do you usually do on a sleepover?"

She went back to selecting spices for the pie filling, adding them to the bowl of sliced apples. "Talk about men."

His eyebrows shot up. "You talk about men with a man?"

"No. I've only had sleepovers with my sister and my cousin, and invariably the topic of men is always at the top of our agenda."

He exhaled again, this time inaudibly. It was apparent Tessa didn't make it a practice to sleep with men. After all, she'd admitted to having one serious relationship.

"Well, I assure you that I don't want to talk about men with you," he said.

"Tell me about Micah Sanborn."

He went completely still. "What do you want to know about me?"

"Why were you adopted?"

"It's a long story."

"We're stuck with each other until tomorrow morning, so don't forget that you have a captive audience," she reminded him.

Leaning over the countertop, his elbows resting on the granite surface, Micah closed his eyes for several seconds to compose his thoughts. "I never knew the man who fathered me and I was abandoned by my biological mother in a hospital clinic in Newark, New Jersey. I'd sat there for hours before a nurse noticed I was alone and called the police. When they questioned me I gave them my name and address, but when they sent someone to check out the address there was no sign of my mother. I'd just turned four, so a social worker placed me in a group home while the police tried to locate my missing parent."

"Didn't you have any relatives who could take care of you?"

He shook his head. "No. My mother never spoke of her parents, sisters or brothers, and I remember her telling me once that it was just the two of us. The little I do recall about her is that she liked sitting in the dark. Whenever I asked her if she wanted me to turn on the light she'd say, 'No, baby, I like the dark.' Once when I tried turning on the light I discovered it wouldn't come on. I figured she'd done something to the switch, but when I think back I believe it was because she hadn't paid the bill and the utility company had turned off the electricity."

"The police never found her?"

Micah's expression hardened, becoming a mask of stone. "No. I went from a group home to various foster homes for three years until I was adopted by Edgar and Rosalind Sanborn. Rosalind, who at that time had become New Jersey's youngest family court judge, couldn't have any children, so she decided to adopt."

"Did your parents decide in advance that they wanted to adopt a child of color?"

"Not at first. The waiting list for white babies some-time took years, and Rosalind Sanborn may be many things, but patience is not one of her virtues. I'd been assigned to a social worker charged with failing to remove a battered child from a family who'd been inves-tigated for physically and sexually abusing several other children.

"Rosalind did something that was unprecedented at the time—she ordered an investigation and interviewed every child on the social worker's caseload. She asked me if I'd ever been hit or denied food and I told her no. Then she asked me if I were granted one wish, what would it be? I just stared at her for a long time, thinking about a bicycle I saw in a toy store window, but changed my mind when I said I wanted a real family.

"She smiled and told me that she would make certain my one wish would be granted. Three days before I cele-brated my seventh birthday my adoption was legalized and I became Micah Edgar Sanborn, son of Edgar and Rosalind Sanborn."

Tessa's eyes shimmered with excitement. "Had you known Rosalind wanted to adopt you?"

"Not at first. She'd come over to see my foster parents and we'd spend Sundays going to church, then either to the zoo or an amusement park. Even though we looked nothing alike, something told me she would become my mother. I was ten when I became an older brother. William was born with a deformed left foot, and when his unmarried teenage mother was discharged from the hospital she left him behind. Although most childless couples want infants, they weren't willing to accept those with special needs. Rosalind and Edgar became the ex-ception."

"Your brother's foot appeared normal to me," Tessa said as she squeezed fresh lemon into the bowl. The aroma of the lemon mingling with the scent of cinnamon, nutmeg and brown sugar filled the kitchen.

"That's because Mom and Dad took him to every pediatric orthopedic specialist in the country until they found one willing to perform a series of operations that would enable him to walk without a pronounced limp. Will went to physical rehab several times a week and wore a special shoe on his left foot until he was about fifteen. Most girls didn't know about his foot because he'd practiced walking in a way that gave him a slight swagger, so they referred to him as the brother with the sexy walk."

Picking up a large wooden spoon, Tessa stirred the pie filling as Micah talked about Abram and Bridget's adoptions. Again, as with Micah and William, Abram and Bridget, who were born to drug-addicted mothers, were older children, left to languish in the foster care system until the Sanborns adopted them. With four children, two of them teenage boys, Rosalind finally decided to give up her career to become a stay-at-home mother.

Reaching into the bowl, Micah pilfered an apple slice and popped it into his mouth before Tessa could react. "That's really good," he mumbled, chewing the slightly tart sweetened fruit.

She slapped at his hand. "Why don't you wait for me to fill the pie shell, and if there's any left over you can eat them."

He reached for another piece. "I can't wait. I'm hungry."

"How can you be hungry? You just ate breakfast."

He kissed her cheek. "I'm still a growing boy."

Tessa rolled her eyes at him. "I'm sure you're over forty—and I don't believe you're still growing."

Micah sobered, frowning under lowered brows. "Why do you have to say it like that?"

"What are you talking about?" she countered.

"You said my age like it was an expletive. And for your information, I'm only forty-one."

Tessa patted his shoulder. "Don't get bent out of shape, because I'm only ten years behind you."

Tugging gently on her ponytail, he eased her head back. "It looks as if I'm going to have to teach you to respect your elders," he said teasingly.

She gave him a sassy smile before blowing an air kiss. "Promises, promises," she chanted.

"Remember, I don't make promises," Micah said, reminding her of what he'd told her earlier that morning in her kitchen.

"Yeah, I know, because you don't know if you can keep them."

Moving around until they stood face-to-face, Micah rested his hands on Tessa's hips, and in that brief, fleeting moment everything he was seeped into her like early-morning dew covering freshly turned earth.

Going on tiptoe, she cradled his lean face between her palms and gently pressed her lips to his. "Please get out of the kitchen until I finish making the pie."

He smiled. "But I want to help."

"You can help me season the chicken."

Micah winked at her. "You promise?"

She returned his wink. "Yes, Micah, I promise."

"I just thought of an idea."

"What is it?"

"Why don't we have a picnic in front of the fireplace?

After that we can take a nap together, then get up and watch a movie."

Tessa lowered her hands. "Now that sounds like a plan."

"I aim to please, madam."

Releasing Tessa, Micah walked back into the living room, removed the cloths from the sofas and chairs, then opened a massive oak wardrobe and gathered a quartet of rugs made from the skins of llamas from a lower shelf. Shaking them out to fluff up the fur, he placed them on the floor in front of the fireplace.

Dimming the overhead lights and turning off the lamps, he lit several candles lining the mantelpieces. The overall effect was cloaking, comforting and sensual.

Tessa picked up a goblet of chilled watermelon-and-citrus *agua fresca* and took a sip, as a hint of a smile crinkled her eyes when she met Micah's amused gaze across the space of the coffee table. His idea of having a picnic on the floor in front of a blazing fire was perfect—as perfect as the man sharing the meal with her.

And the roast chicken infused with the flavor of fresh rosemary, lemon and garlic, roasted asparagus with sun-dried-tomato vinaigrette and bread-and-butter corn grilled in their husks on the stove-top grill and flavored with herb-and-spice butter was nothing short of perfection.

Micah set down his fork and dabbed at the corners of his mouth. "I'd pay you to cook for me every night."

Tessa swallowed a mouthful of the tartly sweet pureed watermelon-orange-lime-lemon juice beverage, her eyes widening in shock. "You're kidding, aren't you?" she asked in a quiet voice.

His expression grew serious. "No, I'm not kidding."

She shook her head. "No, Micah, I can't cook for you because I'm a wedding planner and dress designer, not a chef. And besides, I don't cook every night."

"I'd take every other night."

She wrinkled her nose. "You're really pushing it, playa."

Micah rose and came around the table to sit next to Tessa, his left arm looping around her waist. "You really think I'm a playa?"

She met his steady gaze. "I don't know. Why don't you tell me?"

There came a moment of silence before he said, "No, I'm not. I've never been one to mess over a woman."

Lowering her lashes, Tessa stared up at him, totally unaware of the seductiveness of the gesture. "That's good to know."

Micah leaned closer, his moist breath sweeping over her face, then eased Tessa down to the softness of the rug beneath them. A hint of a smile tilted the corners of his mouth as he saw her eyes widen in surprise before a knowing smile parted her lips.

"I'm glad you approve," he whispered seconds before his mouth covered hers in a slow, drugging kiss that communicated everything he felt for her at that moment.

Tessa's fingers caught in the cotton T-shirt covering Micah's back, pulling it up until she bared flesh. The heat, smell and hardness of the body pressing her down to the floor shattered the vestiges of the hurdles she'd erected since the man she'd believed she loved enough to share her love and life with had forever betrayed her. All and everything that'd been Bryce Hill vanished, leaving in its place a healing that was a long time coming. Her arms moved up of their own volition and circled Micah's strong neck, pulling him closer.

She'd felt the invisible pull of attraction the instant Micah Sanborn had walked into her home, and it had continued to intensify each time they came face-to-face. And it was the second time an incident that was beyond their control had conspired to bring them together where they were unable to escape each other.

A familiar shiver—one long forgotten—rippled through her as his hand searched under her shirt to cradle her heaving breast. She couldn't stop the soft sigh that came of its own accord when his fingers worked their magic, slipping under her lace bra. Tessa never knew when the clasp on her bra came undone, nor could she remember when Micah had relieved her of her shirt. She lay on the rug, the soft fur pressed to her bare back and the man who made her feel things she'd long forgotten straddling her.

Breathing heavily through parted lips, she stared up at him as he relieved himself of his shirt, appearing larger and darker in the flickering lights coming from the many candles. Muscles knotted in his biceps as he supported his upper body on his hands before he lowered himself again over her prone figure.

Although Micah's gaze was riveted on Tessa, he was aware of everything going on around him: the smoldering flame in the fireplace, the distinctive voice of Dave Matthews coming through stereo speakers, singing "Dreamgirl," the steady tapping against the windows that indicated the snow had changed back over to sleet and the scent of vanilla-infused candles mingling with burning wood permeating the space.

He pressed his face against the side of Tessa's neck and closed his eyes, still seeing the perfection of her full, firm breasts rising and falling above a rib cage he could span with two hands. Her clothes had concealed a slender, curvy body that sent his libido into instant overdrive.

The seconds ticked off, him drowning in the sensual femininity of the woman that he found himself drawn to despite the inner voice warning him that emotionally he was in too deep.

"I need you to trust me."

Closing her eyes, Tessa curved her arms under Micah's shoulders and held on to him as if he'd become her lifeline. "What are you going to do?"

He kissed her ear. "Nothing you don't want me to do."

A secret smile softened Tessa's mouth. "There are things I want you to do, but it's too soon."

"Why is it too soon, baby?"

"We hardly know each other, Micah."

His mouth moved from her ear to her hair. "We'll never know each other *that* well. Even if we make love a thousand times I'll never know the real Tessa, nor will you know the real Micah."

"What are you hiding from me?"

He chuckled, the sound coming from deep within his chest. "What makes you think I'm hiding something?"

"The last man I was involved with was living a double life, and when I found out, to say I was devastated was putting it mildly."

Micah went still, then without warning reversed their position, Tessa lying between his outstretched legs. She snuggled closer like a trusting child, her cheek resting on his bare shoulder. "What did he do to you?"

Despite the seriousness of what she was going to tell Micah, Tessa smiled. "What are you going to do, Micah? Go look for him and give him a beat-down?"

"Do you want me to?"

Lifting her head, Tessa met the dark eyes filled with a lethal expression that unnerved her for several seconds. "No, Micah. I detest violence."

"I won't hit him, Tessa. I'll just tell a few of my buddies to ticket his car or, better yet, have it towed to the impound."

"That's not going to happen because I'm not going to tell you his name." She returned her head to his shoulder, feeling the steady pumping of his heart against her breasts keeping time with her own. It was odd that she felt comfortable enough with Micah not to attempt to cover her naked breasts.

Running his fingertips up and down her back, Micah smiled. "Even if you tell me his name I promise I won't go after him."

"No fair. Weren't you the one who said you don't make promises?" Not waiting for his reply, Tessa said, "I met this guy, who will remain nameless, when I was contracted to coordinate his sister's wedding. He was not only the bride's brother but also the best man, so we got to see each other quite often. He worked as a sales rep for a software company, and I hadn't realized he'd been living a double life until he got a call on his cell phone from a Buffalo hospital informing him that his wife was injured in an auto accident and they needed to know if she had any drug allergies."

"What about his sister, Tessa? Didn't she know her brother was married?"

"No. He confessed to me that although he'd married this girl because he'd gotten her pregnant, she wasn't the type whom he could introduce to his family."

"And what type is that?"

"She'd been arrested several times for loitering."

Micah's eyebrows lifted. "In other words, she'd been a prostitute."

Tessa nodded. She told Micah that Bryce's wife had picked him up in a bar. "A week later she'd called him to ask for money. She'd been arrested again and needed bail money. He gave her the money, then convinced her to go into rehab to kick her drug habit. After she was clean, he got her an apartment and they lived together whenever he was in town."

"Do you hate him, Tessa?"

Again there was a pregnant silence before she said, "No. I can't. I was forced to admire him because he'd gotten a woman to give up her self-destructive lifestyle. What I'm unable to accept is his duplicity. If he'd told me that he was married, we would've been friends."

What Tessa couldn't and didn't want to tell Micah was that she'd fallen inexorably in love with Bryce Hill and he'd been the first and only man who'd made her consider marriage.

Vertical frown lines appeared between his eyes. "What's with you and this friendship thing? Once we make love, what we'll share will be more than friendship."

Tessa went completely still, holding her breath until she felt her lungs laboring for air and forcing a smile she didn't feel. "You are a cocky somebody, Micah Sanborn. What makes you so certain that we will make love?"

He gave her an incredulous look. "We're lying here half-naked—"

"I'm half-naked because you took off my shirt," she said, interrupting him.

"Why didn't you stop me, Tessa?" he asked, his voice calm, his gaze steady and resolute.

Even though Bryce had lied to her whenever she'd questioned the depth of his love for her, she knew she couldn't do to Micah what had been done to her. She'd always been honest and up front with every man she'd known and she didn't want it to be any different with the one in whose arms she lay.

She closed her eyes. "I didn't want to stop you."

Micah's eyes brimmed with tenderness *and* passion. "Look at me, darling." The lashes that shielded her gaze from his came up, and what he saw in the catlike depths rocked him to the core. He recognized pain and a silent pleading for understanding. She'd fallen in love once, and instead of experiencing joy it had brought her pain.

"I haven't lied to you, Tessa, and I will never lie to you. I knew there was something special about you the moment I walked into Signature Bridals. I still don't know what it is, but I can't stay away from you." A gentle smile crinkled the skin around his eyes. "I'm like a cat after a piece of catnip."

Her smile matched his. "You're pretty potent your-self, playboy."

"Isn't this where it all started—when you called me a playa?"

"There is a difference between a playboy and a playa."

"I'm neither," he whispered, lowering his head and slanting his mouth over Tessa's. "Sometimes you talk a little too much," he said softly against her moist parted lips.

She opened her mouth to come back at him, but whatever she'd planned to say was locked away in her throat when he fastened his mouth over a breast and suckled her as if he were starving. The sucking motion elicited a swirling sensation that raced down her body, settling between her thighs. The swirling grew into flutters, then a long-forgotten pulsing that held her captive as she struggled not to climax.

Micah moved down the length of Tessa's body, his fingers and mouth mapping every inch of her bared flesh. He kissed her breasts, the distended nipples and the velvety skin on her flat belly. He removed her sweatpants, and seconds later her panties lay in a heap with the other discarded articles of clothing.

Then he did what he'd wanted to do the first time he'd shared a bed with Tessa Whitfield. He buried his face between her trembling thighs and tasted the essence of her femininity. He'd fantasized making love to her, but nothing in his imagination came close to what he was feeling at that moment. The sweet-smelling, sexy woman writhing beneath him had the power to make him forget any other woman he'd known or made love with.

"Micah!" Tessa said, gasping, his name a strangled cry.

He heard the desperation in her voice, felt her trembling limbs and knew it was only moments before both would pass the point of no return.

Cradling her face between his palms, he placed light kisses over her eyelids. "What do you want, darling?"

Tears trailed down her cheeks, dotting his fingers. "Love me, Micah," she pleaded softly, shamelessly. "Please make love to me."

"And I will," he said, gathering her in his arms and coming to his feet. Cradling Tessa against his chest, Micah turned in the direction of the stairs and made his way up the staircase to the loft.

Chapter 12

Tessa buried her face in the hollow between Micah's neck and shoulder and looped her arms around his strong neck. Seconds after she'd asked Micah to make love to her she'd wished that she could retract her plea. What was wrong with her? Begging a man she didn't know to take her to bed with him.

Perhaps, she mused, she'd taken her promise to swear off all men too far, that not all men were lying, duplicitous dogs like Bryce Hill, that perhaps she could have a normal, intimate relationship with Micah Sanborn without the unnecessary drama that she'd experienced with the men in her past.

She knew all of the answers to her silent queries because she'd always been the Whitfield who wasn't willing to take chances, to act spontaneously. Simone and Faith had teased and sometimes harassed her because of her unwritten rule to date at least for three months before going to bed with a man.

Her sister and her cousin enjoyed countless laughs at her expense because none of her dates surpassed the three-month milestone. The only exception was Bryce Hill. He didn't need to sleep with her when he was also sleeping with his *wife,* which meant Tessa had become an additional bonus for him.

She closed her eyes, letting her senses take over when she counted the number of steps it took for Micah to walk into his bedroom and place her on the bed. Her eyelids fluttered wildly when she felt the side of the mattress dip as he kicked off his shoes and lay down beside her.

Reaching for Tessa's hand, Micah threaded his fingers through hers, feeling the runaway beating of her pulse. "Are you afraid of me, baby?"

"No."

He smiled. "That's good, because I don't ever want you to fear me."

Tessa's eyes opened, and she tried to make out objects in the semidark room. The only light coming into the room was from the light Micah had left on in an adjoining bathroom. "Why would I be afraid of you?"

Her query sent a shiver of awareness up Micah's back. He loved her voice, its sensual timbre and husky quality. "You're trembling, darling."

There came a beat of silence. "It's been a while."

It was his turn to close his eyes. "How long has it been?"

"Too long," she said cryptically.

Shifting to his right side, he brushed a kiss across her parted lips. "I'll try not to hurt you. If you want me to stop, I'll stop. And if I do something you don't like, then

I want you to tell me. And you don't have to worry about protection, baby. I'll take care of that."

Tessa couldn't stop the tears pricking the back of her eyelids. Never, ever had a man given her a choice when it came to making love with each other. She'd always permitted them to take the lead. This time it would different.

She moved closer, pressing her breasts to his chest. "Now I know why you became a lawyer."

"Why is that?"

"You sure like to run off at the mouth."

He chuckled softly. "Are you telling me that I talk too much?"

"Yes…I…am, Counselor," she whispered between small nibbling kisses she placed at the corners of his soft, strong mouth.

Micah met Tessa's steady gaze. "I'll stop talking on one condition."

She blinked once. "What's that?"

"Undress me." There was no mistaking her surprise at his directive, but his impassive expression didn't change. "I'm asking you to take off my clothes."

"Why?"

"I want you to feel as comfortable with me as I am with you."

"Are you comfortable with me, Micah?"

"Yes."

Tessa moved over Micah, her hands going to the hem of his T-shirt, easing it up his belly, chest and over his head to reveal an incredible upper body with rock-hard abdominals and defined pectorals. His body was perfect, magnificent. She faltered slightly when removing his sweatpants and boxer-briefs. Seconds later she found herself on her back with him looming over her, his gaze slowly moving from her head to her legs, then back again.

"You are so beautiful," Micah whispered reverently.

For the second time within minutes Tessa felt like crying. If she'd never felt beautiful, she did now. Extending her arms, she welcomed him into her embrace. Everything outside the bedroom ceased to exist as she lost herself in the touch and smell of her soon-to-be lover.

Micah kissed her—everywhere. Touched her—everywhere. There wasn't an inch of her flesh his mouth hadn't tasted or explored. Rising slightly off the bed, her hips moving of their own volition, she gritted her teeth when she felt the long-forgotten pulsing in her core.

Her mouth was swollen from his kisses, her breasts full, the nipples hard from his suckling and the folds between her legs moist from his rapacious tongue. She was on fire and only he could extinguish the flames of desire that threatened to incinerate her into millions of infinite pieces.

Micah felt as if he were drowning in a riptide of sensual pleasure that he'd never experienced before. He wanted to be inside the woman in his bed but knew if he did penetrate Tessa, then it would result in the end even before he'd gotten enough of her. Cupping her breasts, he trailed kisses over her satiny belly. Her stomach muscles contracted as he moved up her writhing body. He took possession of her mouth, swallowing her hot, moist breath before she compressed her lips.

Tessa gritted her teeth rather than shame herself again and beg Micah to take her. She wanted him deep inside her, filling her with his hardness and assuaging the rising passion that had no place to go.

Her right hand trailed down his ribs, searching

between their bodies until she found the source of her frustration. Her fingers closed around his straining, throbbing erection, eliciting a deep groan that came from deep within Micah's chest.

Her hand worked its magic, moving up and down, around and around. A small smile softened her mouth and relaxed the muscles in her face as his breath came in quick pants. He was as close to exploding as she was.

She wasn't given time to react when he twisted out of her grasp and reached into the drawer in the nightstand. It took only seconds for him to roll a condom down the length of his erection. Time seemed to stand completely still when he pushed into the hot flesh beckoning like a beacon on a stormy night, both gasping audibly when flesh joined flesh, making them one with the other.

It was Tessa's turn to drown in the sensations that reminded her of why she'd been born female. Everything ceased to exist except the man taking her to a place where she'd never been. She bit down on her lower lip, but it wasn't enough to stem the whimpers that escalated to soft moans of unabashed pleasure. Her former apprehension that she was sharing a bed with a stranger waned with Micah's first thrust and vanished completely when he established a slow, measured rhythm that sent shivers up and down her spine. Every man she'd ever met or known was forgotten as she surrendered to the passion that pounded the blood racing through her heart, chest and head.

First there was fire, then ice and fire again. And when she couldn't take it anymore she cried out as waves of ecstasy washed over her again and again. She'd just breathed out the last of her passion when Micah buried his face between her face and shoulder, shuddered violently and collapsed on her, his weight pressing her down to the mattress.

They lay together for several seconds until Micah rolled over, removed the condom, then pulled Tessa to his chest. No words were necessary. What they'd offered each other went beyond dialogue, beyond description. The steady tapping of icy pellets against the shuttered windows drowned out the sounds of measured breathing. Their moist bodies entwined, both found a peace and comfort that made them one with the other.

His eyes opened as Tessa groaned softly, attempting to find a more comfortable position.

"Are you all right?" he asked her.

"I'm good," she said.

"That's not what I asked you, Tessa." Pulling back, he tried making out her expression in the eerie light coming through the windows. "Did I hurt you?"

"No," Tessa said truthfully. She was tight because she hadn't had sex in a long time, but once Micah had penetrated her there hadn't been any pain.

Leaning on an elbow, he stared down at her. "Why did you moan, baby?"

"Sleeping with you reminded me of muscles I hadn't used in quite some time."

Running his hand through her mussed hair, he smoothed down her wayward curls. "We won't make love again until you're feeling better."

"I'm not in pain, Micah," Tessa countered waspishly.

"We'll see about that."

"What are you doing?" she shrieked when he sat up and straddled her, resting his hands on her inner thighs.

"I'm going to massage your legs."

She sucked in a breath when his fingers kneaded the

tender flesh. The tightness eased as Micah's hands became magical. Her former moans became soft erotic groans when she felt herself becoming aroused again. Her nipples had hardened and her core had grown moist.

"Stop, Micah." His fingers stilled. "Please, no more."

"What's the matter?"

Tessa heard the concern in his voice. "You don't want to know."

Leaning closer, he nuzzled the side of her neck. The heat that had flared between her thighs swept upward, burning her face. "Are you blushing, darling?"

"Why would you ask me that?"

"Because your cheek is hot." His right hand moved between their bodies. "That's not the only place that's hot," he crooned.

"That's because you're making me hot."

Micah laughed. The sensuous sound increased the heat coursing throughout her body. "I make you hot and you're making me hard." Reaching for her left hand, he placed it on his swelling organ.

Tessa felt the warmth and heaviness against her palm before her fingers closed around his sex and stroked him in a measured up-and-down motion as his breath came in deep shuddering gasps that excited her even more. Slowing, she eased her grip when she felt him straining for release, then increased the pressure and quickened her motions.

Micah felt as if his heart would explode if he didn't climax. But he didn't want to release his passions in Tessa's hand but inside her. His attempt to reach for the drawer with the condoms was thwarted when he surrendered completely to her exquisite seduction. He bellowed as if impaled on an iron stake as a flood of uncontrolled and unrestrained passion shook him from head to toe. Unintelligible and guttural noises came from his throat when he opened his mouth to plead with Tessa to let him go, but she continued to stroke him until he ejaculated again.

Pressing her breasts to Micah's chest, Tessa kissed him tenderly. "Are you all right, sweetheart?"

Still shaking from the aftermath of the raw act of her masterful persuasion, he reversed their positions. "You're going to pay for that little stunt."

"How?" she asked with a wide grin.

"I'm going to tie you to the bed and make love to you until you pass out."

Tessa traced one of his expressive eyebrows with a forefinger. "You promise?"

His grin matched hers. "Yes. And that's one promise I intend to keep." He kissed her to seal his vow. "I'm going to have to change the sheets before we take a nap."

"While you change the sheets, I'm going to take a shower, then clean up the kitchen."

He shook his head. "The kitchen can wait until later." Sitting up, he scooped Tessa up into his arms and moved off the bed. "We can save water by sharing a shower."

Wrapping her arms around his neck, she rested her head on his shoulder. "No funny stuff."

"Look who's talking about acting up. You almost gave me a heart attack."

"Are you complaining that you didn't enjoy it?"

"I plead the Fifth."

"I rest my case, Counselor."

Micah carried Tessa out of the bedroom and into the adjoining bath, unable to believe the very straight-laced Tessa Whitfield would be so uninhibited in bed. He liked everything about her—in and out of bed.

* * *

As she brushed her teeth, Tessa thought about the man whose bed she'd just left, still puzzled as to why she'd found it so easy to forget her requisite three-month time limit for getting to know Micah well enough to consider sleeping with him.

She rinsed her mouth, patting it dry with a towel from a stack on a marble-topped table in a corner; she stared at her reflection in the mirror as a knowing smile parted her lips. I like him. And she did. There was something about Micah that made it very easy to fall in love with him.

Love!

With eyes wide, she froze. What was she thinking about? There was no way she wanted to or could fall in love with Micah Sanborn. If that were to happen, then she would expect a commitment—and he'd already admitted, *Marriage is just not for me.*

Her shock fading quickly, she shook her head, headed for the shower stall and joined the object of her musings.

Micah stood in Tessa's foyer cradling her to his chest, knowing he had to leave but not wanting to let her go. She was a chameleon, unlike any other woman he'd met or known. One minute she would withdraw from him, leaving him to believe that the passion she'd offered was all for show. Then she would come on to him like a cat, soft and purring, adorable and affectionate. He never would've imagined that her sexual repertoire would've included such sensual foreplay. Was he shocked? Yes! Did he enjoy it? Oh, hell yeah!

"I'll call you," he said in a quiet voice.

Tilting her head back in order to see his expression, Tessa smiled. "What if I call you?"

Micah's jaw tightened as he clenched his teeth. *Uh-oh,* he thought, *here it goes.* The don't-call-me-I'll-call-you scenario. Was it his turn to pay the piper for the few times he'd slept with a woman, then told her that he would call her and didn't?

"You don't want me to call you, Tessa?"

Her gaze narrowed slightly. "Did I say you couldn't call me, Micah? Is there a reason why you don't want to give me your number? Are you afraid a woman will answer your phone? Don't concern yourself about my feelings, because you know we're both in this for sex."

He recoiled as if she'd struck him across the face. "Is that what you believe? That it's all about sex?"

She pulled away from him. "Isn't it? You made yourself very clear when you said you're not the marrying kind. And I am a grown-ass woman, Micah, so don't you treat me like a girl. So if we're going to continue to see each other, then it can only be for friendship with a fringe benefit."

His eyebrows lifted slightly. "What is the fringe benefit?"

There was a profound silence until Tessa said, "We get to sleep together."

"All you want is friendship and sex?"

She nodded. "Yes." *That's all I expect because that's all you want, Micah,* she added silently.

It was Micah's turn to nod. "Okay. There'll be nothing more." He extended his hand. "Give me your cell phone and I'll program in my numbers." Tessa reached into her handbag and handed him her cell phone. "I'm going to give you my cell, home and my direct line at the D.A.'s office. I'll also give you my parents' number—"

"I have your parents' number," Tessa said, interrupting him.

Micah continued to punch in his numbers. "If you call

my cell during the day and I don't answer, then leave a message on my office voice mail, because I may be in court or at one of the correctional facilities." He handed her back her phone.

Going on tiptoe, Tessa pressed her mouth to his. "I will call you." She gave him a wink. "That's a promise."

His former annoyance vanished quickly. Looping an arm around her waist, he deepened the kiss. "Good."

"I want to thank you for a wonderful weekend. We must do it again."

"And we will, baby." Lowering his head, Micah kissed her again with a passion he hadn't known he possessed. He ended it, dropped his arms and opened the door. He walked out of Signature Bridals and made his way down the stairs to where he'd parked his car.

Two words assaulted him during the drive back to Staten Island: *friendship* and *sex*. It was the first time a woman had openly demanded what she wanted from him, because he usually established the ground rules whenever he went into a relationship. He'd never concealed the fact that he wasn't looking for a wife or that he didn't want to become a father. Those were not options, nor were they debatable.

He dated women because he enjoyed their company, and if they did advance to the bedroom, it would be for sex. He'd navigated the dating game unscathed; however, now at forty-one he'd discovered the tables turned.

He'd been forthcoming when he'd told Tessa that he wouldn't change his marital status, but she'd gotten the better of him when she'd tipped the scales in her favor when she'd stated that they would be friends who would sleep together.

"Damn!" he whispered under his breath. It was a blow to his male ego to have a woman tell him exactly what

he meant to her—but his ego wasn't so bruised that he
wouldn't go along with what she proposed.

He would continue to see Miss Whitfield. And as she'd
said, when it ended, it would end as all of his other relationships had—without threats or hostility.

Tessa had to replay the voice-mail message twice
before registering her mother's words. Lucinda wanted
her to come to Mount Vernon for Sunday dinner and see
a new gown she'd designed. Picking up the telephone, she
dialed the number to the house where she'd grown up.
She told her father that she would see him later that afternoon, and Malcolm Whitfield informed her not pick
up Faith because she was already in Mount Vernon.

She ended the call feeling as if she were losing her
mind, that she was having an out-of-body experience.
She'd known Micah Sanborn just over a week, had sex
with him twice—three times if she were to count her
shocking impromptu masturbation scenario—and she
had set down the parameters for their relationship. In the
past, loving a man with all of her heart had wounded her
deeply—and she'd vowed it would not happen again.

As long as Micah knew where she was coming from,
then she would be able to protect her heart.

Chapter 13

Tessa maneuvered into the driveway behind her father's car and cut off the engine. When she was younger, the entire Westchester County Whitfield clan got together the first Sunday in each month after church to eat together while catching up with the latest family gossip. But as the younger children became adults and started their own families, the ritual changed to holidays and milestone birthdays.

This Sunday wasn't a holiday or a milestone birthday, so Tessa wondered why her mother had called a family gathering. And, for that fact, she could've come to Mount Vernon at any time to see Lucinda's latest design.

She got out of her vehicle and turned up her collar to ward off the above-freezing temperature. Quickening her pace, she mounted the steps to the three-story farmhouse and unlocked the front door. Warmth and mouthwatering aromas greeted her as soon as she opened the door.

Slipping out of her coat, she hung it on the coat tree in the entryway and placed her handbag on a cushioned bench.

She made her way through the living room, past the formal dining room, with a table set with china, silver and an elaborate floral centerpiece, and into an enormous kitchen bustling with activity. Her mother and her aunt stood opposite each other at a cooking island, ladling food into serving dishes.

Simone, resting a hip against one of two dishwashers, observed the activity with an expression of bored amusement. A roar of deep voices came from the enclosed back porch, where the Whitfield men were watching their favorite sport. In the spring and summer it was baseball, and in the fall and winter football and basketball.

Tessa smiled. Faith was decorating a marbled jelly roll cake with curls of dark and white chocolate. Another cake, this one decorated with coconut, sat on a countertop along with a baked ham, a stuffed pork crown roast and a platter piled high with fried chicken.

"What are we celebrating?"

Lucinda Whitfield stopped stirring a large pot of collard greens and glanced up. A bright smile crinkled the attractive lines around her dark eyes. Petite, with a rounded body, Lucinda wore her salt-and-pepper hair in a close-cropped natural style that complemented her delicate features and nut-brown complexion. Wiping her hands on a towel, she went over to her youngest daughter and kissed her cheek.

"You'll know soon enough," she said cryptically.

Simone straightened from her leaning position. "She told me the same thing."

"Same here," Faith added.

"What is it with the younger generation," Edith Whitfield said, "that they're so impatient? Everything is about instant gratification."

Faith rolled her eyes at her mother. "It's not about instant gratification, Mother." Edith flinched visibly when she registered Faith addressing her as "Mother." "You call and tell us to show up, but you don't want to tell us why. I've been offered a contract to complete a coffee-table book with my designer cakes and—"

"When did this happen?" Simone asked, interrupting her cousin.

"It hasn't happened. I'm still thinking about it," Faith countered.

"What is there to think about, darling?" Edith crooned. Tall, slender and incredibly beautiful, former showroom model Edith Harris Whitfield had passed her good looks onto her daughter Faith, who'd briefly gone into modeling but gave it up when she decided she wanted to be a chef. "It sounds like an opportunity of a lifetime," Edith continued, smiling.

"It is," Faith confirmed. She didn't want to talk about her literary project with her family, especially her mother, until she discussed it with Tessa and Simone. "I'll let you know more once I get all of the details."

"Why are we here, Mama?" Tessa asked her mother, giving her a penetrating stare. She was aware that Lucinda Whitfield had a flare for the dramatic, and the longer she held everyone's attention, the better.

Lucinda stopped ladling spoonfuls of collard greens cooked with smoked turkey wings into a large tureen. She glanced at her daughters, then her niece. "Your fathers and uncle have decided to close down the catering hall."

"No!" gasped Tessa.

What!" Faith and Simone chorused.

"Why?" Tessa asked, stunned that her father and uncle had decided to sell what had become somewhat of a historic landmark in Westchester County. She'd lost count of the number of weddings, birthdays, political fund-raisers, graduation parties and church functions that had been held in the two-story Revival Regency-style mansion with stone-colored brick, a bowed entry and a portico constructed on sloping lawns that overlooked an English garden and a pond filled with water lilies and a family of magnificent graceful swans.

Edith waved a delicate hand. "It's not as bad as it sounds."

"But, Mom," Faith wailed, the pain of losing a multi-generational business so apparent in her voice. "They can't."

The two sisters-in-law exchanged a glance. "They can if a developer is willing to offer them nearly four times what the property appraises for," Lucinda announced smugly. "Y'all know that business hasn't been what it was before those hotels went up right off the interstate—"

"That's true, Aunt Lucy," Faith said, stopping her aunt, "but they're still showing a profit."

"Right now they're barely breaking even," Lucinda said. "This year's functions booked for the months of January, February and March get special low-rate advantage packages, but that still didn't spur business our way."

"Why didn't you say something before now?" Simone asked.

"Because you have your own businesses to worry about," her mother retorted. "Whitfield Caterers sits on prime property, and Malcolm and Henry would be fools not to sell."

"If they sell it, then what would they do?" Tessa asked.

"Daddy and Uncle Henry are too young to retire." Her identical-twin father and uncle had celebrated their fifty-eighth birthdays in April.

"They've decided to open an upscale bilevel bowling alley with a game room for kids and a jazz club for adults."

"Hot da-*amn!*" drawled Simone with more enthusiasm anyone had seen her exhibit in a very long time.

Tessa smiled. "I like the idea."

"So do I," Faith concurred. "When is all of this going down?"

"Hopefully by the beginning of the year," Edith said. "And I don't see a reason why the zoning board won't approve it, especially since they're trying to revitalize the downtown business district."

Tessa felt the enthusiasm of her mother and her aunt as they talked excitedly about the architect's proposal for the abandoned building that would be converted to a modern, state-of-the art bowling alley. She washed her hands and helped carry platters and serving bowls into the dining room as her father and uncle walked in grinning from ear to ear. It was apparent their team had won.

"Hello, Daddy. How are you, Uncle Henry?"

Tessa endured the bear hugs and kisses until she begged the bookend brothers to let her go. Her father and her uncle had grown up switching identities at will, fooling everyone. The only exception was their mother. They stood an inch under the six-foot mark, and the year they turned fifty both men had affected trim mustaches and goatees. The facial hair added character to their khaki-brown faces, and with their close-cropped curly graying hair and hazel eyes they still garnered stares from the opposite sex, much to the consternation of their wives.

Releasing and winking at his younger daughter,

Malcolm walked out of the dining room to see if his wife needed his help.

"I heard about your new venture," Tessa said to her uncle.

"What do you think, Tessa?" asked Henry.

"I think it's wonderful. But what's going to happen to the clients who've booked with you through next year?"

Henry ran a hand over his graying hair. "We're going to honor their contracts. Mal and I decided not to book anyone beyond next August."

Resting her arms on the back of one of a dozen dining room chairs, Tessa listened as Henry told her that he and his brother had gotten a loan from their bank to cover the start-up cost of renovating an abandoned factory building, and as soon as the sale of the catering hall was finalized they would repay the bank at a very low interest rate. What surprised her most was that her brother Vernon planned to resign his teaching position at a Winston-Salem, North Carolina, high school at the end of the school year and return to New York to go into business with his father and his uncle.

Vernon Whitfield married a fellow college student, and they'd made North Carolina their home when both were offered teaching positions in neighboring cities. Vernon, Yolie and their young sons came to New York for the summer break and every other year during the Christmas recess. Tessa smiled. Now she knew why Lucinda was so in favor of the new business. There was no doubt she would agree to anything if it meant having her only son close by.

Tessa followed her mother into her sewing room, her breath stopping and catching in her throat when Lucinda flicked the wall switch. The bright glow from recessed lights shimmered on a quartet of Asian-inspired wedding gowns draped over dress forms. All were made in silvery fabrics that glowed like polished platinum. A kimono-style bronze-hued sash provided a chic clinching at the waist and bodice of a silk-satin strapless gown. Another had an obi-inspired bow in smoky gray that lent a sophisticated effect on a satin A-line dress with narrow straps tucked into the bow. The third backless gown with the folded artistry of a large satin bow attached on the left at the waist made a major Asian statement. The last but definitely not the least was a folded detachable train that gave the A-line satin dress a Japanese feel.

Tessa shifted her gaze from the gowns to her mother and then back again. "You've outdone yourself, Mama. They are exquisite. What made you go with an Asian look?"

Lucinda affected a mysterious smile. "When I saw *Memoirs of a Geisha,* my mind started working overtime. Once I began sketching the gowns I knew I didn't want any jewels or beadwork, just simplicity and sleek elegance."

Running her fingertips over the large fanlike bow, Tessa nodded her approval. "How long did it take you to finish them?"

Lucinda slipped on a pair of reading glasses and peered closely at the folds in the kimono-style sash. "It took me about six weeks for each one."

"How much do you want for them?" Tessa asked.

"Which one do you want?"

"I want all of them, Mama."

"When do want them, Theresa?"

Tessa was hard-pressed not to glare at her mother. Lucinda Whitfield was like a dog with a bone. Once she designed a dress she held on to it just to admire her exquisite handiwork. "If you can bear to part with them before the end of the year, then I'll include them in my spring lineup."

She spent ten minutes negotiating prices that were commensurate with the time, labor and materials that it took for Lucinda to design and sew her much-sought-after creations. "I'll send you a check tomorrow," Tessa promised.

Unlike Whitfield Caterers, which was experiencing a decline in business, Signature Bridals was booked solid for the coming year's spring and summer months. Tessa was booked for as many Friday weddings as she did Saturdays and Sundays. In early April she was scheduled to go to Daufuskie Island, South Carolina, to oversee the wedding of the daughter of a preeminent Palm Beach plastic surgeon.

She glanced at her watch. It was after eight. "I'm going to leave now, otherwise I'll be stuck in traffic."

Lucinda removed her glasses and placed them on a table with bolts of off-white satin. "Why don't you stay over and leave after the morning rush hour."

"I'd love to, Mama, but I'm expecting a delivery of wedding stationery tomorrow morning. Why don't you come into the city and spend a few days with me?"

A knowing smile softened Lucinda's mouth. "I'll come only if we can eat in that wonderful Caribbean restaurant in Manhattan."

Looping an arm around her mother's neck, Tessa kissed her. "You drive a hard bargain, Mrs. Whitfield." It wasn't often Lucinda left what she considered the sane environs of Westchester County for New York City's nonstop pulsing energy.

"How else am I going to see my baby girl?"

"Either get on the railroad or drive to Brooklyn."

"When have you known me to ride the railroad?"

"You're spoiled, Mama."

"No, I'm not," Lucinda countered. "I just don't take public transportation."

Tessa wasn't about to argue with her mother because she would just come out on the losing end. And it wasn't the first time she believed Lucinda had gone into the wrong profession. She should've been an attorney, because her debating skills were legendary.

Leaving Lucinda in the sewing room, she returned to the kitchen to ask Faith if she was ready to go back to Manhattan.

Tessa gave her cousin a quick glance before returning her gaze to the roadway. "Why all the secrecy about your book deal?"

Faith pressed the back of her head against the leather headrest and closed her eyes. "I didn't want to say anything until I get the go-ahead from my agent to sign the contract. And knowing my mother, she'd have the news blasted all over Mount Vernon before the contract is executed."

"Ah, sookie, sookie," Tessa drawled. "My cousin's going to become a celebrity chef like Paula Deen and Bobby Flay."

A rush of heat stung Faith's dark brown cheeks. "Not quite, Tessa. Don't forget I still have to kitchen-test the recipes, bake and then decorate the cakes. The publisher wants me to use one of their contract photographers, but I'm not too crazy about his work."

"Will they permit you to use your own photographer?"

"That's something my agent is negotiating. Do you

have someone in mind? Because I need someone with an exquisite eye for detail."

"Remember the photos from the Gilbert-Angelo wedding?" The A-list Hollywood couple had arranged a private wedding ceremony on a sparsely populated Caribbean island, but a resourceful ex-still photographer posing as a waiter had managed to snap photos of the couple who'd managed to keep their liaison under wraps.

Faith nodded. "Who could forget them? Is it true the photographer sold the photos to the tabloids for half a million?"

"Try one million," Tessa corrected.

"Who's your contact?"

"Paul Demetrios."

"Didn't he also photograph the Fyles-Cooper wedding?"

"Yes!"

Faith's dark eyes sparkled like polished onyx. "If you can get Paul Demetrios to photograph my book, I'll owe you forever."

Tessa laughed softly. "If you can convince your publisher to use him, then all I want is an autographed copy."

Faith sobered as she gave her cousin a lingering stare. In just a few short years Signature Bridals had become one of the most sought-after wedding consultants in the northeast. Tessa ran her one-woman operation with the ease and skill of a company with dozens of employees. Since the Fyles-Cooper wedding, requests for her services had doubled, most coming from A-list actors and fiancées of athletes and musicians.

"Are you seeing anyone?"

Tessa's fingers tightened on the steering wheel, but her expression did not change. "Why would you ask me that, Faith?"

"Well, I…I find it hard to believe that you come into contact with so many eligible men yet you're still single."

"The same can be said for you," Tessa retorted.

"At least I date. Or I did date," Faith said, correcting herself. "I'm serious when I say that I've sworn off men. I've kissed so many frogs in my life that it's amazing I don't have warts."

A soft laugh filled the closed space as Tessa slowed down to avoid rear-ending the car in front of her that'd stopped suddenly. Her smile faded when she thought of Micah. "I think I found a prince."

Shifting on her seat, Faith stared at Tessa. "Who is he?"

Tessa was forthcoming when she admitted to Faith that she'd broken her vow not to become involved with a client's family member. "His name is Micah and he's Bridget Sanborn's brother."

"Good for you. I always thought that was an asinine vow," Faith drawled. "You've put up so many roadblocks and have so many dos and don'ts that it's no wonder you're not married."

"I'm really not looking to get married," Tessa said truthfully. "What I want and need is a relationship that's open, honest and uncomplicated."

"It'll remain uncomplicated until you and your Micah start sleeping together. I just hope you're luckier than me, because the minute I sleep with a man, that's when he turns into a jealous, possessive monster," Faith admitted wistfully.

"We're already sleeping together."

Faith's beautifully arched eyebrows lifted. "How long have you known him, Tessa?"

"Not long."

"How long is not long?"

"Just over a week."

Faith couldn't halt a soft gasp of surprise that escaped her parted lips. "What happened to your three-month waiting period?"

Tessa gave her cousin a quick glance, smiling. "I don't know. At first I thought it was because after so many years of not sleeping with anyone I'd finally come into heat. But then I realized my attraction to Micah wasn't solely physical but also intellectual. He's the first man with whom I'm able to have an intelligent conversation without having to defend or justify my opinions."

"What does he do for a living?"

"He's a lawyer."

"What type of law does he practice?"

"Criminal. He works out of the Brooklyn D.A.'s office."

"Do you see him as a potential husband?"

Tessa shook her head. "No." She told Faith about the conversation she'd had with Micah about his views toward marriage. "I respect him because at least I know exactly what type of relationship I'll have with him."

"It doesn't bother you that he's not willing to commit to a future together?"

She shook her head again. "Not in the least. I still have time before I think about getting married and having children. Don't tell me you're getting the wedding-bell blues?"

"No, but my mother has been on my case because she wants grandchildren. When I told her I could have a baby without getting married, she went into a rant that she didn't raise her only child to become a baby mama."

Tessa blew out her breath. Her aunt was known for her histrionics when she didn't get her way. "What did you tell her?"

Faith affected a smug grin. "I told her that if she continued to nag me, I was going to sleep with Lying Leon." Leon Jamison had earned a reputation as the neighborhood wino.

"No, you didn't tell her that."

"Yes, I did. Of course, she wouldn't talk to me for several weeks, but at least I didn't have to hear her beat her gums about grandbabies."

Faith talked incessantly about her book as bridge traffic slowed to a crawl before Tessa was able to maneuver into an E-ZPass lane. Her excitement was evident in her voice when she talked about decorating cakes for children with animal shapes and theme cakes using shoes, ties, hats, tools, books, fruits and bows as accessories.

"Do you want to come up?" she asked Tessa three-quarters of an hour later when she miraculously found a parking space in front of her building.

"Not tonight, Faith. Perhaps we can get together one night this week."

"This week isn't too good for me. I have several parties in the tristate area and then I'm going to D.C. for a senator's daughter's sweet sixteen celebration over the weekend."

"When are you coming back?"

"I should return Sunday morning."

"Remember, we meet at my house next Monday," Tessa reminded her.

Leaning over, Faith kissed Tessa's cheek. "Do you want me to bring dessert?"

"But of course."

"What do you want?"

"Surprise me," Tessa drawled.

Smiling, Faith pushed open the door. "You may come to regret those words."

Tessa waited until Faith disappeared into her apartment building before she maneuvered away from the curb and headed for Brooklyn.

An hour after leaving Mount Vernon she walked into her brownstone. She sorted through the mail that had been delivered on Saturday. There was nothing that required her immediate attention. Leaving the envelopes on the table in the foyer, she made her way up the staircase to her bedroom to prepare for bed.

Tessa turned out the bedside lamp and slid down to the pillows cradling her back. The weekend had been filled with surprises: sleeping with Micah, the news that her father and her uncle were shutting down their catering hall business to open a bowling alley and her cousin writing a coffee-table book about cakes.

A shiver of excitement and awareness eddied through her when she recalled the aftermath of her body's reaction to Micah's lovemaking. Sitting up, she turned on the lamp and reached for her cell phone. Scrolling through the directory, she punched a button and listened for a break in the connection.

"Hello."

She froze for several seconds when hearing the deep, resonant voice. "Unlike you, I make promises—and I've kept my promise and called."

"If you didn't call me, then I was going to call you."

"Are you free any night this week?"

"Why?"

"I'd like to take you out to dinner."

Micah's sensual laugh came through the earpiece. "Are you asking me out on a date, Tessa Whitfield?"

A bright smile curved her mouth. "Yes, I am."

"I just happen to be available Tuesday—that is, if that's a good day for you."

"It is," she said.

"What time should I come by?"

"Can you get here by seven?"

"That's not a problem."

"Then I'll see you Tuesday. Good night, Micah."

"Don't hang up yet."

"Why?"

"I have something to tell you."

Tessa held her breath before letting it out slowly. There was something in Micah's voice that gave it an ominous tone. "What is it?"

"I miss you."

Her heart lurched against her ribs before settling back to a normal rhythm. She opened her mouth, closed and opened it again, but no words came out.

"Did you hear me, Tessa?"

"Yes…yes, I heard you." Her voice was quivering. He'd verbalized what she was feeling. They'd slept together one night, and Tessa couldn't believe how much she wanted to be with him at that very moment.

"Good night, Micah."

There came another silence before he said, "Good night, Tessa."

Tessa ended the call and turned off the lamp. Even though she was tired, sleep was slow in coming. She tossed and turned for what seemed like hours before she relaxed enough to fall asleep, albeit restlessly. Her dreams were filled with erotic images of Micah making love to her, and when she finally awoke she was more exhausted than she'd been before going to bed.

Chapter 14

Micah sat in chambers in a Brooklyn community court, going over a defendant's file with the judge, a social worker from a community-based drug treatment program and a public defender. He'd spent a restless Sunday night mentally beating up on himself for admitting to Tessa that he'd missed when he'd only left her hours before. Once the words were out, he'd been unable to retract them because that was how he'd felt at the time.

But when he lay in bed hours later recalling everything about Tessa—the silken feel of her skin against his, her begging him to make love to her, her smell, the sensual moans she was helpless to control during lovemaking and the aftermath of her trembling body after she'd climaxed—he knew he'd told her the truth.

Tessa Whitfield had called, as she'd promised, to ask him out to dinner, while he, in a moment of weakness, had confessed to missing a woman he'd known a week. He knew he had to be careful—very, very careful—otherwise he'd find himself in over his head emotionally. In the past, he'd always been the one to control where he wanted his relationship with a woman to go. He'd call if he promised to call and he'd made it a practice never to date more than one woman at a time.

Although he'd had his share of one-night stands, none of his liaisons ever made the one-year mark. There was something about seeing a woman for more than a year that frightened him. Edgar Sanborn had preached to his sons that if they dated a woman exclusively for a year, then she was worth marrying. What Micah's father didn't know was that he wasn't like his other sons because he didn't want to marry or father children.

Forcing his attention back to the discussion circulating around the table, Micah focused on the printout in the file. "My recommendation is that he's to be mandated to a substance-abuse treatment program with close monitoring by probation. If he turns up dirty, then he'll be violated and he'll have to serve the remainder of his sentence."

The judge peered over his reading glasses at the Legal Aid attorney busy entering notes on a legal pad. "I think the D.A.'s office is quite generous this morning, Miss McDonald, wouldn't you say?"

Jill McDonald's closed expression did not change with Judge Andrew Carr's query. With straight salt-and-pepper hair secured in a tight bun, light blue eyes, a pale face and mouth and an omnipresent dour expression, Jill was perceived as a bumbling, stuttering and insecure jurist until she took center stage in the courtroom.

"I believe the A.D.A. is being a bit hard-nosed, Judge Carr," Jill countered.

Micah's eyebrows lifted. "If I were truly hard-nosed, then we wouldn't be sitting here discussing an alternative to your client's incarceration."

Jill pulled her lower lip between her teeth. She knew when she was bested, but her dogged determination wouldn't let her concede that easily. "Mr. Sanborn, are you aware that my client has no priors?"

"Yes. And the reason your client is being seen in the community justice center is because he has no prior criminal record. He's charged with misdemeanor assault and possession with intent to sell and he tested positive for cannabis. He's admitted to having ties with a local street gang, so if you don't accept my office's recommendation, then his case will be turned over to the Gang Bureau Rackets Division. Miss McDonald, you should know that most gang members who live the thug life wind up in two places—dead or in jail. It's your choice. Community justice court or criminal court?"

Jill emitted a long, audible sigh. There was no way she wanted to put a frightened seventeen-year-old through a court trial where he was certain to spend a minimum of eighteen months in jail. "I'll accept community justice court."

Judge Carr smiled at the taciturn public defender. "Thank you, Miss McDonald."

Micah spent the next half hour conferencing the cases on the morning's calendar. He asked the judge to hear the case of a defendant who hadn't attended his treatment sessions for the past week before the others listed on the docket.

If the judge remanded a defendant to spend several nights in jail, it usually got the attention of everyone sitting in the courtroom, especially defendants new to community court.

"Do you have any objections, Mr. Kinsella?" Judge Carr asked the social worker.

The young man shook his head. "No, Judge."

The quartet filed out of the judge's office, down a narrow hallway and into the courtroom.

The doorbell rang as Tessa made her way down the staircase, at the same time slipping her arms into the sleeves of a black cashmere coat. Dressed in the ubiquitous black that most New Yorkers affected year-round, she was more than ready for her date with Micah, if for no other reason than to relax and unwind from two days of frenetic activity.

It'd begun early Monday morning with the delivery of wedding stationery for the Sanborn-Cohen nuptials. Juan Cruz had designed the invitations, response and seating cards and the menu on silver parchment with black satin ribbon, and the result was a stunning sophistication. It took more than two hours for her to check and double-check the accuracy of the addresses of the wedding guests.

She stepped off the last stair, walked to the door and peered through a panel of glass. Her heart rate accelerated. As usual, Micah was on time. She opened the door to find him glaring down at her. Stunned by his scowling expression, she missed the expert cut of his dark gray tailored suit he'd paired with a stark white shirt and gray-and-white houndstooth patterned silk tie.

"Please come in. I just have to get my handbag."

Micah stalked into the foyer and caught Tessa's upper arm. "Didn't I warn you about opening your door without knowing who's on the other side?"

It was her turn to frown. "I knew it was you, Micah."

He tightened his grip. "Do you have X-ray vision where you can see through doors?"

Tessa tried extricating her arm, but she was no match for his superior strength. "Let me go." He dropped his hand. "First of all, you were the only one I expected to show up here at this time. Secondly, if it had been anyone else, my very vigilant neighbor with a pair of powerful binoculars who lives across the street would've been able to give the police a very accurate description of a perpetrator if something had happened to me."

Micah's expression softened as he took a step and cradled Tessa's face in his hands. "But what I don't want is for anything to happen to you."

Her hands came up to grasp his strong wrists. "Nothing is going to happen to me."

"It better not," he said softly. He lowered his hands.

Tessa fixed her gaze on his firm mouth. "And why is that?"

His lips parted in a slow, sensual smile. "I didn't give the NYPD twenty years to spend my pension hiring someone to guard you."

"You wouldn't!"

"I would, Tessa. So don't test me."

"What is this all about, Micah? Is this because I live in Brooklyn? Or is this—"

"It has nothing to do with where you live," he said, cutting her off. He ran a hand over his face. Closing his eyes, he inhaled a deep breath before letting it out. He opened his eyes. "It's about you, Tessa."

"What about me?"

"I like you."

"And I like you, too."

Anchoring a hand under her chin, Micah leaned closer.

"Liking you means I don't want anything to happen to you. Promise me that you'll be more careful."

Leaning into his warmth and strength, Tessa looped her arms under his shoulders. Not only did he look good but he smelled and felt good, too. "I promise." She pulled back. "I'd love to stay and chat with you, but if we don't get going, we're going to be late for our reservation."

"Where are we going?"

"You'll see."

Micah's gaze moved slowly from Tessa's flyaway curly hairdo and down to her lips outlined in a seductive raspberry hue that matched the color on her lids and her graceful cheekbones. Reaching out, he buttoned up her coat, then lowered his head and brushed his mouth over hers. "I'm ready."

Tessa retrieved her handbag and activated the alarm system while he waited on the stoop to wait for her to lock up. "I'm parked around the corner."

"There's no need for you to get your car. The restaurant is within walking distance."

He escorted her down the stoop, his gaze narrowing when he noticed the curtains hanging at the front window of the brownstone across the street move slightly. "I think your neighborhood security guard is on duty."

Tessa smiled. "Mrs. Burgess is an insomniac. I ran into her the other day and she told me she was going to call the police to have your car towed because it was illegally parked. But when she came out to check your license plate she noticed your NYPD and D.A. placards in the windshield."

"Damn!" Micah drawled. "She's nosey like that?"

"She's lonely, Micah. She was widowed a couple of years back, and with her children and grandchildren living on the West Coast, she spends most of her time staring out the window and patrolling the block."

"Do you ever invite her over for coffee?"

"No, but she's invited me."

"Have you taken her up on her offer?"

"I did a few times."

Micah tucked Tessa's hand into the bend of his elbow. "You're a good neighbor, Tessa Whitfield."

They walked for several blocks in silence, each lost in their own thoughts. It was an almost perfect fall night with a near-full moon in a clear sky littered with millions of stars. The autumnal decorations festooning front doors would soon be replaced with Christmas wreaths with the approaching holiday season.

"The restaurant is down this street."

Micah was surprised to discover that the tiny restaurant was tucked inside a narrow cobblestone alleyway. They were greeted by the owner of The Bijoux—a tall, thin man dressed entirely in black, with a shaved head and a goatee.

Jason Riley kissed Tessa on both cheeks. "Where on earth have you been, stranger?"

Tessa gave him a tender smile. "I've been busy, JR."

Jason winked at her, his dark eyes sparkling like onyx. "So busy that you couldn't stop by and let a friend know that you were still alive."

Wrapping her arm around Micah's trim waist inside his suit jacket, she smiled up at him. "Micah, this is my very good friend, Jason Riley. JR and I went to the same high school. Jason—Micah Sanborn."

The two men exchanged handshakes as a waitress wearing a cancan outfit came over and took Tessa's coat. She guided them to their table, where Micah seated Tessa before rounding the table to sit opposite her. The dining establishment was an exact replica of a Parisian café. Prerecorded music playing a soft bluesy number added to the subdued laid-back ambience. The Bijoux, with a seating capacity of fifty was half-filled, with more patrons steadily streaming into the cozy dining establishment.

Micah stared at Tessa, transfixed. The glow from a lighted votive bathed her face in a shimmer of gold. It highlighted the tawny gold-tipped curls framing her face, and with her black off-the-shoulder cashmere sweater and wool pencil skirt, dark stockings and suede pumps, Tessa Whitfield was the epitome of Bohemian chic.

Tessa registered the strange look on her dining partner's face. "What's wrong?"

There came a swollen silence. "There's nothing wrong except that…" His words trailed off.

Her eyebrows flickered slightly. "If you don't want to eat here, then we can go to another restaurant."

The tense lines in Micah's face relaxed. He, who was never at a loss for words, found that he was unable to tell Tessa what he was feeling at that moment. He'd admitted to her that he liked her; however, the liking was more intense than any he'd ever felt for a woman. "It's not the restaurant."

Tessa couldn't stop the frown forming between her eyes. "Why," she said softly, "do I get the impression that you're uncomfortable because I asked you out on a date?"

Micah stared across the small space, complete surprise freezing his features. "You think I'm upset because you asked me out?" She nodded. "Wrong, Tessa. Despite what you might believe about me, I'm not a chauvinist."

"What's with all of the talk about paying someone to keep an eye on me?"

Lowering his head, he bit back a grin. "Once you get to know me better you'll realize I'm just a blowhard." His head came up. "But I am serious about you being more careful as to who you open your door to. You have an alarm, but have you considered putting in a close-circuit camera?"

Reaching across the table, Tessa rested her right hand atop Micah's left one. "Yes, I have. In fact, I called a company last week and I have an appointment with one of their salespeople Thursday morning." The attractive slashes in his lean jaw appeared when he smiled, the gesture making the breath catch in her chest. "Now will you stop sweatin' me?"

"I'll think about it."

She gripped his fingers, her nails biting into the flesh on the back of his hand. "Micah!"

"Okay, baby," he conceded, gritting his teeth against the pain. She removed her hand when a waiter approached the table and handed them menus. "Speaking of dating—are you free this weekend?"

"I'm free Friday night. Why?"

"I'd like you to go with me to a scholarship dinner-dance hosted by the National Latino Officers Association."

She smiled. "I'd love to go."

"What about Saturday?"

"I can't commit to Saturday because I'm meeting with the parents of a young girl who's having a quinceañera. It's a Spanish equivalent to a sweet sixteen," she explained when seeing Micah's puzzled expression. "Sunday is also out because I'm meeting with Bridget at your parents' house. Will you be there?"

"I hadn't planned on going. But if you want, I'll drive you."

"It can't be in your car. There's not enough room to store a box of wedding gowns."

"Then I'll drive your car."

"Okay. But I'm not playing football."

"Aw, baby. Be a sport."

She leaned over the table. "I don't play sports, sport. My reason for going to New Jersey is business, not fun and games."

Micah picked up his menu, pretending interest in the selections. "Dress casually, baby."

"Dream on, mister." Tessa picked up her own menu. JR had added several new dishes since her last visit to The Bijoux.

"If you finish up early Saturday, then I'd like you to spend the night with me."

A slow smile crinkled her eyes. "Are you inviting me to a sleepover?"

"Yes. And we'll top it off with a very special Sunday brunch before leaving for Jersey."

She saw the tenderness in Micah's gaze, felt the sexual magnetism that permitted him to be so self-confident. "You are full of surprises, aren't you?"

"I just don't want you to regret breaking your vow to go out with me."

"There's not going to be any regrets. What we have is a special friendship with fringe benefits."

Micah rolled his eyes upward while slapping his forehead. "Yup. How could I forget that?"

What he wanted to tell Tessa was where she could stick her so-called special-friendship-with-the-fringe-benefits gobbledygook. What he felt for her went beyond friendship, and sleeping together was hardly a fringe benefit. Her sharing her body with him was an honor, a privilege.

"Tessa? Is that you?"

Her head came up, and Tessa saw her sister and ex-brother-in-law standing several feet away. Pushing back her chair, she came to her feet, hugging Simone at the same time Micah stood up. "What are you doing here?"

"I had an appointment in Crown Heights, so I called Tony and told him to meet me here."

Tessa didn't want to get into it with Simone about sharing dinner with Tony, because there was no doubt she would end up sharing his bed, too. Forcing a facetious smile, she extended her hand to Anthony Kendrick. "It's nice seeing you again."

Tony ignored her hand, leaned over and kissed her cheek. "How long has it been?"

She wanted to tell him not long enough but didn't want to hurt her sister, who appeared unable to keep away from a man who'd disappointed her over and over.

"It has been a while." She saw Simone staring at Micah. "This is Micah Sanborn, Bridget Sanborn's brother. Micah, this is my sister Simone and my brother-in-law Anthony Kendrick."

As much as she disliked the man, she didn't want to embarrass him by introducing him as an ex. Other than his Billy Dee Williams good looks, she never knew what Simone saw in him. An only child of a well-to-do widowed mother, he'd been spoiled. He'd earned a college degree yet always complained about not finding the right position for his intelligence. He'd changed jobs so often that Tessa lost count of where and whom he'd worked for. Once Simone divorced him, he moved back home with his mother, who gave him a monthly allowance whenever he was unemployed.

Micah shook Tony's hand, then nodded to Simone. "It's nice meeting you."

Simone's hazel eyes shimmered like precious gems. "I'm really looking forward to doing the floral decorations for your sister's wedding. Do you guys mind if Tony and I join you?"

Tessa stared at Micah, who nodded. "Please do," she said when she wanted to say, *Oh, hell, no.*

She loved her sister unconditionally, yet tonight she didn't want Simone or her deadbeat ex-brother-in-law to intrude on her time with Micah because she needed time with him—alone. What she'd shared with him had gone against everything she'd professed to when interacting with a man. He was related to her client, she'd slept with him within a week of meeting him for the first time and her feelings for him went beyond what she'd openly admit.

Micah beckoned to a waiter to bring two more chairs. He waited until Simone and Tessa were seated before sitting down again. Once Simone and Tony were given menus, he ordered a bottle of wine for the table.

Simone exhibited the lighter side of her personality, laughing, joking and entertaining everyone with stories about some of her more quirky clients. Tony, enraptured with his ex-wife's beauty and carefree attitude, shed his normally grim expression and joined in when he and Micah got into a heated discussion about various sports teams.

Tessa's annoyance with Simone and Tony's unexpected intrusion vanished quickly after her first sip of wine while sampling an assortment of appetizers that included a traditional French foie gras served with celery salad and walnuts and carpaccio—thinly sliced beef tenderloin with shavings of *reggiano* parmesan.

The two couples shared main courses of grilled black tiger jumbo shrimps, pasta linguini tossed with lobster meat, fresh tomato, thyme, basil with a touch of light red chili and a salad of julienne of hearts of palm and carrots on a bed of crisp lettuce.

Micah pretended he didn't see Tessa scowling when he settled the bill. Helping her into her coat, he leaned down and pressed his mouth close to her ear. "We'll talk about it later," he whispered.

Tessa compressed her lips tightly, if only to keep the curses building up on her tongue from exploding. She'd asked him out, not the reverse. And she hadn't wanted him to pick up the tab for her sister and Tony.

"Later," she said between clenched teeth.

Looping an arm around Tessa's waist, Micah escorted her out of the restaurant and into the narrow alley. He smiled at Simone as she huddled closer to Tony to share his body's warmth.

"We have to do this again."

"Most definitely," Simone said cheerfully. "There's no doubt I'll see you again before your sister's wedding."

"Have you seen the house?" he asked.

Simone shook her head. "Not yet."

"Tessa and I are going Sunday. You're welcome to join us."

"I can't. I have to set up the floral arrangement for a birthday brunch."

Micah angled his head, his gaze shifting from Simone to Tessa. There was no doubt the two women were related, their natural beauty startling, but there was something about the woman pressed to his side that held him spellbound, ensnared in a web of sensual delight. The seconds ticked off as he visually searched her face in the glow of the lanterns affixed along the walls of the alley.

"I hate to break up what has been a very enjoyable get-together, but I have to make a stop before I go home," Simone said softly. She smiled at Tessa. "I'll see you Monday." Extending her hand to Micah, she gave him a bright smile. "Again, it's a pleasure meeting you. And thank you for dinner. The next time it'll be my treat."

Tessa hugged her sister and pressed a light kiss to Tony's cheek, shocking him with the affectionate gesture. "Take care of yourself."

The two couples walked out of the alley, parting at the corner. Cold air stung Tessa's cheeks as she turned her face into Micah's shoulder. "Where's your topcoat?"

He pulled her closer to his length. "It's not cold enough for a coat."

"If you get sick, then don't expect me to play Florence Nightingale." Cupping a hand to his mouth, Micah affected a hacking cough before dissolving into laughter when she landed a soft punch to his ribs.

"I'm rarely sick." He'd given the NYPD twenty years, and over the two decades he hadn't taken more than ten days of sick leave. His admission that he was rarely sick was because he refused to acknowledge when he wasn't feeling well. Aside from the times he'd run a high fever, he could be found on duty or in class.

His mother on occasion accused him of being too driven and anal. Rosalind didn't know that her oldest child had blamed himself for his biological mother abandoning him in a hospital. Perhaps if he hadn't been so sickly, perhaps if he hadn't been born, then his mother wouldn't have had the responsibility of taking care of a child when she could hardly take care of herself. The perhaps, perchances and maybes haunted him for years— and continued to haunt him. The questions and doubts had come back with a vengeance two years ago, the episodes forcing him to seek the assistance of a psychologist.

Talking about his childhood, his feelings of loss and abandonment, had temporarily put his fears at bay. But Micah knew they would never disappear completely. That was something he'd come to acknowledge and accept.

"Mrs. Burgess is at her post," he said when noticing movement at the window in the house across the street from Tessa's.

Tessa unlocked the front door and deactivated the alarm. Turning around, she smiled up at him. "Maybe I'll invite her over for dinner tomorrow."

Lowering his head, Micah pressed a kiss to the side of her neck. "That would be nice."

"What time do you want me to be ready Friday?"

"Six-thirty," he whispered seconds before his mouth covered hers in an explosive kiss that left both fighting for breath. He had to leave before he did something he hadn't planned to do—make love to Tessa when he didn't have protection with him. "Good night, baby."

There came a swollen silence as Tessa met Micah's unwavering gaze. "Good night."

He was there, then he was gone, melting into the darkness of the cold autumn night. Tessa closed and locked the door behind him, set the alarm and slowly made her way up the staircase to her bedroom.

Her unease that Simone and Tony had intruded on her time with Micah faded, replaced with a fearful likelihood that her sister might reconcile with her deadbeat ex. And she knew Anthony Kendrick would sweet-talk his way into Simone's bed and then into her life again.

Please, don't let it happen again, she said in silent prayer.

Chapter 15

Tessa awoke feeling more tired than she had before retiring for bed. Again she'd spent the night tossing and turning, erotic dreams assaulting her mind and body relentlessly. Each time she managed to go back to sleep she was jolted awake again, her body awash with perspiration and an intense pulsing between her thighs that threatened to make her scream aloud. Realizing that sleeping throughout the night was futile, she'd left her bed and showered three hours before dawn.

By eleven that morning she'd called to reserve a tent for a neighbor who was throwing a surprise birthday party for her husband's thirty-seventh birthday. Even though it wasn't a milestone birthday, the event would be significant because he'd been given a clean bill of health once he'd completed his chemotherapy treatment. The heated tent would be erected in the backyard of their brownstone, and the invited guests would share a six-course sit-down gourmet dinner under artificial lights and candles. Tessa had called one of her favorite DJ's to provide the music for what promised to be a momentous celebration.

A delivery of fresh flowers arrived from Simone's greenhouse, the bouquet of red, orange and dark pink orchids and roses adding warmth and color to the foyer. The doorbell rang again, and this time the mail carrier handed her a stack of envelopes and a certified letter. Sorting through the envelopes, she breathed a sigh of relief. If she'd gotten her invitation to Bridget and Seth's wedding, then there was no doubt those on the guest list had received theirs. After a hastily eaten lunch she retreated to the third floor and lost herself in sewing.

One day blended into the next, and Friday morning Micah called to remind her that he would pick her up later that evening to take her to the dinner-dance. She'd already selected an outfit for the affair and made appointments with her hairstylist and nail technician.

Micah didn't know what to expect when Tessa opened the door to his ring; he stood motionless, staring at her hair falling above her bared shoulders. The curls were missing, and in their place was a shiny mane of red-streaked waves. His gaze moved lower to a fitted strapless black dress that ended inches above her knees and lower still to her slender, shapely legs encased in sheer black nylon. A pair of matching silk-covered stilettos put the top of her head at his nose. Reversing itself, his gaze lingered on a swell of brown flesh rising and falling above the dress's revealing pleated bodice whenever she inhaled.

Without warning—and shockingly—the flesh between his thighs hardened instantaneously, as if he were experiencing the stirring of physical desire for the first time. He stood motionless, stunned at the rush of passion that made it impossible for him to move, talk.

"I don't believe it," Micah whispered when he found his voice.

Taking a step, Tessa moved closer until her breasts touched the crisp front of his white shirt. "What don't you believe?" Her query was a whisper.

He ran a hand through the heavy waves gracing the nape of her neck. "You are absolutely, amazingly and incredibly beautiful." Pulling her flush against his body, he trailed soft kisses along the column of her neck and permitted her to feel his surging hardness. "I've just changed my mind."

Vertical lines appeared between Tessa's eyes. "What are you talking about?"

"Let's stay home tonight."

"You're kidding, aren't you?"

"No, I'm not."

Tessa's lashes fluttered as she struggled to understand the enigmatic man holding her to his heart. She'd endured the heat from a blow-dryer when she'd had her curly hair blown out—something she rarely did. And she'd chosen a pair of four-inch stilettos—a height she seldom wore—because of Micah's towering height.

Resting her hands on her hips, she smiled up at him. "We stay home and do what?"

Micah tightened his hold on her waist. "We'll have our own tea party," he drawled deadpan in a very proper British accent.

Her hands went to the lapels of his exquisitely tailored

dark blue suit. "We can't make love for at least another three days."

A slight frown creased his smooth forehead. He wanted to shake Tessa. Did she not know? When would she realize that what he felt—what they shared—wasn't all about sleeping together?

"It's not about sex, Tessa. That's something I can get from any woman." One of her eyebrows lifted with his disclosure. "I'd want to be with you even if we didn't sleep together."

She flashed an attractive moue, drawing his gaze to the vermilion color on her mouth. "Perhaps I should put you to the test. If I don't give you any, then we'll see how long you'll hang out with me."

His fingers looped around the nape of her neck. "I'm not going to lie and say I don't enjoy making love with you, but if you choose not to give me *any* then that doesn't mean that I'll want to stop seeing you." Lowering his head, he brushed his mouth over hers, careful not to smear her lipstick. "What do you say we have our own private party after we leave the fund-raiser?"

She smiled. "That sounds wonderful."

"Why don't you go upstairs and pack an overnight bag. We'll hang out at my place tonight."

Disengaging herself from his comforting embrace, Tessa made her way up the staircase, feeling the heat of Micah's gaze on her back. What she didn't tell him was that she'd looked forward to going to the dinner-dance, that she wanted to spend time with him. She'd taken him to The Bijoux because she'd wanted to share a quiet, intimate dinner; however, that was thwarted when Simone and Tony joined them. Micah Sanborn seemed so sure of himself and his rightful place in the world. But what he didn't know was that as charming as he was, she had no intention of permitting herself to fall under his intoxicatingly virile spell.

Tessa stood in the middle of the ballroom of an opulent catering establishment that overlooked Flushing Meadows Park. She smiled and mouthed the appropriate responses whenever Micah introduced her to politicians and law-enforcement officials. Prisms of light from chandeliers competed with the sparkle of precious baubles in earlobes, around necks and wrists of the beautifully attired women in attendance who clung possessively to the arms of their dark-suited escorts. She gave Micah a surreptitious glance as he chatted comfortably with the police commissioner, who chastised him about retiring before reaching his potential with the NYPD.

The commissioner gave her a friendly smile. "Your boyfriend scored at the top of the captain's test but retired before he was to be promoted. Our loss is the Brooklyn D.A.'s gain, but what's encouraging is that we're still on the same side."

Micah lost count of the number of people who'd told him that he'd made a mistake to leave the NYPD. As soon as he received notification that he'd passed the bar on his first attempt he'd put in for retirement.

Lowering his head, he met Tessa's amused gaze. She'd come to the fund-raiser as his date, but it was apparent that those who knew him believed they were a couple. They'd seen him over the years with other women, but their reaction had always been indifference. What, he mused, was there about Tessa, other than her beauty and intelligence, that had them believing she was *that* special?

But what Micah had to admit was that Tessa *was*

special—special in every way he could've imagined a woman to be. And he hadn't lied to her when he'd told her that he'd changed his mind about taking her out, preferring instead to remain at home. As a retired police officer and past vice president of 100 Blacks in Law Enforcement Who Care, his appearance at this event was merely symbolic. The greetings and introductions continued until he steered Tessa to their reserved table before he made his way to an open bar.

Introductions, speeches and an invocation from a police department chaplain, sumptuous dinner selections of prime rib, roast chicken and tender, grilled flaky salmon with the accompanying steamed vegetables preceded a live band playing upbeat Latin rhythms that had everyone up on their feet. Micah found himself cornered by several community leaders while Tessa danced nonstop. He half listened to the conversations going on around him as he managed to keep his date within his line of vision as she was spun around and dipped, her hips swaying seductively to the pulsating music.

He experienced an emotion so foreign that it squeezed his heart for several seconds before permitting him to draw a normal breath. Jealousy! It should've been him dancing with Tessa. He should've been the one holding her to his chest, pressing his mouth to her ear, whispering what he was feeling and what he wanted to do with her. The seething escalated, burning his mind and his chest, and for the first time in his life Micah Sanborn felt as if he were losing control. Why, he mused as he stared at Tessa smiling up at her dancing partner, did he feel like punching the cheesy-grinning man who held her a tad too close for social respectability?

Resting a hand on the shoulder of an assistant deputy warden from the Department of Corrections, he forced a polite smile. "Please excuse me, Qadir, but I have to take care of something."

"Is that *something* you're talking about wearing a black dress and dancing with one of my captains?"

Micah froze. "Is it that obvious?"

Qadir Sherman smiled. "You haven't taken your eyes off her. Go get your woman before some vulture swoops down and carries her off."

"Never happen," he countered confidently as he turned on his heels and headed toward his date. He tapped the man on his shoulder before clamping a hand around his neck. "Excuse me, my man, but I need my girlfriend." His tone was soft, yet his words were edged with steel. He gave Tessa a smile that was as intimate as a kiss. "Are you ready to leave, darling?"

A slight frown touched Tessa's smooth forehead before fading quickly. She couldn't remember the last time she'd danced so much. "You're right, *darling*. It is time we leave."

Micah's expression was a mask of stone as he retrieved Tessa's fur shawl, then instructed her to wait until he brought the car around. Minutes later, he started up the engine and shifted into gear.

"What's with you allowing that clown to slow-grind with you?"

Her delicate jaw dropped. "Is that what this is all about? You're jealous because some man was dancing with me?"

"He was bumping and grinding with you, Tessa."

Tessa didn't know whether to laugh or scream at Micah for behaving like a mistrustful junior high school boy. She sucked her teeth. "For your information, he wasn't grinding with me. In fact, our bodies weren't even touching."

"It didn't look that way to me."

"You saw what you wanted to see." She rested her left hand on his right over the gearshift. "If we're going to continue seeing each other, then you're going to have to learn to trust me. If not, then we should end what we have right now—tonight."

There came a long pause. "I don't want what we have to end," Micah said in a hushed tone.

"Then you must trust me," Tessa countered.

"I do trust you," he insisted.

"No, you don't, Micah. If you did, then we'd still be at the dinner-dance and I'd be dancing with you."

A hint of a smile found itself through his expression of uncertainty. "I'll make it up to you, darling, once we get to my place." He stopped for a red light, angled his head and nuzzled the side of her neck.

Tessa giggled like a little girl. "You're using that word rather glibly."

"What word?"

"Darling."

The light changed and Micah shifted into gear and sped off. "Darling, dear, sweetheart or dearest. They're all the same."

She stared out the windshield. Micah calling her "darling" meant absolutely nothing to him, while if he were any other man, it would've signified a deeper, more meaningful emotion. Tessa had to ask herself if she wanted more from him. Did she want him to love her? Could she afford to fall in love with him? The questions nagged at her as she settled back to enjoy the ride and the comforting presence of the man beside her.

* * *

"You like living in the woods, don't you?"

Micah gave Tessa a quick glance. "Staten Island isn't the woods," he countered, maneuvering into the enclave with sprawling single-family dwellings claiming two- and three-car garages.

"How did you find this place?"

"It found me."

"Explain, Micah."

"I bought a two-bedroom condo in the Bronx overlooking the Throgs Neck Bridge a couple of years ago. When Bridget starting complaining about the amount of time it took for her to commute between Franklin Lakes and Manhattan, I told her that she could stay at my place several nights a week. It worked out well until she met Seth."

"Did he move in?" Tessa asked.

"No. But there were times when he spent more nights with Bridget than at his own place. I didn't mind the weekdays because I was up and out early and there were times when I didn't come home until after they'd gone to bed. It was the weekends that bothered me, because after dealing with BS all week I wanted to kick back and relax without bumping into my sister or future brother-in-law, their friends and colleagues.

"I didn't want to tell Bridget to leave, so I left. I heard through the station grapevine that the grandmother of a cop who'd lost his life on 9/11 was looking for someone to rent a room in her house, so I took her up on her offer. Living in Staten Island works out well for me because I'm closer to Brooklyn than I'd be living in the Bronx."

"Does Bridget like living in the Bronx?"

"She and Seth love the location and the views of the water and bridge. That was the reason I bought the place."

"Are you going to move back after Bridget's married?"

Reaching up, Micah pressed a button on one of the devices attached to his car's visor. The door to a three-car garage lifted silently. "No. She and Seth have offered to buy it from me."

"Where are you going to live?"

"I'm thinking of buying a house around here. Don't move," he ordered in a soft tone.

He parked beside the tarpaulin-covered race car that had belonged to his landlady's late grandson, got out and came around the car to assist Tessa. He retrieved her overnight calfskin bag from the space behind her seat. One second she was standing before he swept her up in his arms and headed for the steps that led up to his apartment.

Tessa pounded his shoulder. "Put me down, Micah."

"Hush, darling. You're going to wake up the neighborhood."

With eyes wide, she clamped a hand over her mouth. "I can walk," she said between her fingers.

Punching in a code on a keypad beside the door, Micah waited for the light to change from red to green. "I know you can walk, Miss Whitfield. In fact, I watched you execute some very fancy footwork tonight."

She sucked her teeth. "Don't tell me you're back to that. The band was incredible, and it's been a while since I'd had the opportunity to dance mambo and merengue, so there was no way I was going to sit out dancing while you were running your mouth."

"I was networking, Tessa."

She rolled her eyes again as he pushed open the door. "Is that what you call it? Well, I was also networking, because I managed to exchange business cards with the bandleader."

"Damn, Tessa, are you ever not working?"

"Not when an opportunity presents itself. Remember, I'm coordinating a quinceañera. I need a versatile band that can play mambo, merengue and hopefully flamenco and mariachi."

Bending slightly, Micah set Tessa on her feet. He turned on the lamp on the table behind the sleeper sofa, and the soft golden glow warmed the space. He'd complained to Tessa that his studio apartment was small but only when compared to his Bronx condo. There he had enough room to move around comfortably even after Bridget had moved in with him. What he couldn't abide were the hordes who invaded his home on the weekends. There was no doubt his sister and brother-in-law would do a lot of entertaining.

Tessa stood in the doorway, a slow smile parting her lips. "I love it."

Micah shook his head in amazement. "You like it?"

She took several steps and stood in the middle of what was Micah's living room. His studio apartment, constructed above the garage, was more spacious than he'd proposed it to be. A utility kitchen with Formica countertops, a two-burner stove, stainless-steel sink, portable refrigerator and oak cabinets took up one wall. An alcove held a bistro table and chairs. The living area claimed a leather sofa and a table spanning its width. Books and magazines were stacked on a leather-covered bench positioned under a trio of casement windows. An oak armoire shared another wall with a racing bike attached to a rack.

Her smile was dazzling. "It's charming, Micah. It's the perfect bachelor hideaway, except that it's much neater than I'd thought it would be." Every item was in its own place and there wasn't a speck of dust anywhere.

Moving behind her, Micah removed Tessa's shawl and tossed it onto the sofa. Looping both arms around her middle, he pulled her back against his body and nuzzled the side of her neck. "That sounds like a sexist remark, Miss Whitfield."

Tessa tilted her chin, resting the back of her head against Micah's shoulder. "It is," she crooned. "Most of the men I've known use the floor as their hamper and forget about dirty dishes in the sink."

"A laundry service and paper plates are on my must-have list."

"I don't eat off paper plates, Micah Sanborn."

"Snob," he drawled.

"Hell, yeah," she countered. "My aversion to paper products began many years ago, when the paper plate I was carrying gave way and the front of my white shorts was splattered with barbecue sauce. And, of course, the boy whom I had the biggest crush on thought that I had my you know what and..." Her words trailed off when Micah's low, sensual laugh resonated close to her ear.

"How old were you?"

"Thirteen."

"Was he your first crush?"

"Yes. I was okay until he started pointing and laughing. Then I lost it. I ran into the house and refused to come out for the rest of the day. And that's when I realized there was a very thin line between love and hate. I managed to get my revenge when he asked me to the senior prom and I turned him down, then asked his best friend."

"Ouch! Remind me not to get on your bad side."

Turning in his loose embrace, Tessa smiled up at Micah, her gaze moving slowly over his distinctive features. Meticulously groomed, he was the epitome of tall, dark and handsome.

"You don't have to worry about getting on my bad side because I don't like conflict. In fact, I avoid it at all costs."

He smiled, displaying his perfectly aligned teeth. "That's good because I don't make a practice to get into it with women."

"What about men?"

"That's different because at least we have a level playing field."

She went completely still for several seconds. "Don't tell me you like brawling?"

"Look, baby, why are we standing here talking about arguing and fighting when we're supposed to be partying?"

"Why are you changing the subject?"

He traced the outline of her jaw with a finger. "Because I'd rather do *this* than talk," he whispered seconds before his mouth covered hers in an explosive kiss that sucked the oxygen from her lungs.

Rising on tiptoe, Tessa wound her arms around Micah's neck and leaned into the kiss as if she were holding on to a lifeline. She wanted him! She wanted him so much that she ached, but she knew it would be at least another two, maybe three days before she felt comfortable making love.

Micah had sparked a need, a thirst that only he could assuage. Her physical need was akin to an addiction she never wanted to get enough of or slake. Why him and not some other man? she'd asked herself. How and why had she felt no shame when she lay with him, a man who was still a stranger? It was as if she'd stepped outside of herself whenever they came together, and she hadn't recognized the woman she'd become at that time.

Pulling back to catch her breath, Tessa stared at his throat. "I need to change into something more comfortable."

His fingers tightened around her upper arms. "Not yet, baby." Micah picked up a remote device from the bistro table, pushing a button. Within seconds the soft sounds of music filled the space from concealed speakers. "You owe me at least three dances."

"Fast or slow?" she teased.

"Slow, of course," he whispered in her ear.

Tessa lost herself in the sensual mood created by the sexy man holding her so close she felt the contours of his body molding to the curves of hers. Their dancing together was akin to foreplay, where they communicated silently emotions neither would've openly verbalized.

I'm falling in love with him. The realization shook her to the core. Closing her eyes tightly, Tessa tried eradicating the thought as one would erase a chalkboard, but it lingered because everything she thought she wanted in a man she found in Micah Sanborn. He was mature, intelligent, well-groomed and mannered. To say he was the total package was an understatement.

She'd thought herself in love with Bryce, but once she ended their liaison she realized she'd agreed to see him because his busy schedule had permitted her time to grow her business. Now her bridal and event-planning business was synonymous with elegance and professionalism, so she felt herself ready for a long-term serious relationship. And who better to share it with than Micah? He wasn't looking for marriage and neither was she.

A secret smile parted her lips as she exhaled.

* * *

"Go home, Micah," Tessa ordered softly, pushing him toward the door. "Tomorrow is a workday and you're going to have to get up early."

Closing the distance between them, Micah pressed Tessa's back against a wall, his gaze lingering on her hair. The curls were back. They'd shared several showers, and when he'd held her head under the flowing water to kiss her, the heat and moisture had tightened the waves the stylist had so painstakingly blown out. "What if I play hooky tomorrow and spend the day with you?"

"You can't!"

It was her turn to host the bimonthly Monday-night get-together for her sister and her cousin. She'd admitted to Faith that she had slept with Micah, and Simone had to know there was something more between them than just a business connection, but what Tessa didn't want was for the focus of their meeting to revolve around her relationship with Micah.

Lowering his head, Micah kissed her forehead. "Don't panic, darling. I can't take off even if I wanted to. I'm scheduled to drive up to Albany for a meeting that will probably last all day." He angled his head and brushed a light kiss over her mouth. "I'll call you in a few days. Don't forget—I'm taking you out for dinner and a movie Friday night."

"I'll put it in my planner. And don't you forget that I'm taking you to the opera at Lincoln Center the day after Thanksgiving."

He rolled his eyes upward. "And if I forget, then I'm certain you'll remind me."

She smiled. "You've got that right." Reaching up, Tessa rested her hand along the side of his stubbly jaw. "Drive safely."

Turning his face, he kissed her palm. "I will. Good night, darling."

"Good night, Micah."

The door opened and then closed. Tessa sighed again as she set the alarm and prepared to go to bed. She had to get up early, clean her house, then decide what she wanted to prepare for Faith and Simone.

The past three days had become a blur. She'd spent Friday night with Micah, who'd greeted her Saturday morning with breakfast in bed. He'd driven her back to Brooklyn, where she'd picked up her vehicle for a drive to Manhattan to meet with an Argentinian diplomat to plan his daughter's quinceañera. The girl's parents had set aside a budget of twenty thousand dollars for a tradition that dated back to the 1500s. It would be another ten months before the girl celebrated her fifteenth birthday, but the event normally took a full year of planning.

She'd called Micah to let him know she was on her way back to Brooklyn, and he'd been waiting for her when she drove up. Switching vehicles, leaving his in her space at a nearby indoor garage, they'd returned to Staten Island in her Highlander. Sunday morning, instead of breakfast in bed, he'd taken her to a local diner that offered grits with shrimps served up in a savory cream.

A steadily falling rain had preempted the Sanborns from playing football. Tessa had been introduced to Seth Cohen and been completely charmed by the young man who'd won Bridget Sanborn's love. A mop of dark curly hair and flashing chocolate-brown eyes and an outgoing manner were the perfect foil for the mathematical genius who was purported to calculate complicated equations in his head.

Bridget had changed her mind again when she'd finally selected an oyster-white satin strapless ball gown with a trapunto-stitched crisscross belt with an opulent cascading train. She'd also decided on a rectangular-shaped sheer tulle cathedral-length veil. Tessa had set up an appointment with the bride to bring her maid of honor for a fitting for a gown in a similar style but in black satin. Rosalind had purchased her mother-of-the-bride ensemble: a black silk organza A-line skirt with a white obi sash, a white Mandarin blouse and a jacket with black silk frogs.

The three women had gone over the seating arrangements, involving Seth only when necessary. He had to be literally forced from the media room for input as to where he wanted his relatives seated. His "whatever Bridget wants" had become his mantra whenever he was asked a question.

When Tessa had finally sat down to dinner with the Sanborns she'd felt as if she were on a roller coaster with the various conversations going on at the same time. More than half the responses to the invitations had come in, everyone indicating they would attend. Gifts had also begun arriving, and Rosalind had set aside space in her sun parlor for the gaily wrapped packages.

She'd fallen asleep during the ride from New Jersey to Brooklyn, waking up when Micah shook her gently to let her know she was home. She'd spent three incredible days with a man, two in which they'd slept and showered together, and not once had he attempted to make love to her.

Walking into her bedroom, Tessa flopped down on the bed and stared up at the ceiling. She'd fallen hopelessly and inexorably in love with a man who was her client's brother.

And what she felt for him had nothing to with sex.

It was about trust.

Chapter 16

Tessa heard the soft chiming that indicated someone had opened the front door. She smiled when she heard her sister's and her cousin's voices. Both of them had keys to her home and she to theirs.

"Hello!" Faith shouted.

"Are you decent?" Simone asked with a hint of laughter in her voice.

"Come on back!" she shouted. "I'm in the kitchen."

The two women walked into the kitchen. Simone, cradling an enormous bouquet of exotic orchids in colors ranging from white, coral-pink and jade to a sensual purple-blue in clear cellophane, placed the flowers on the countertop. Faith followed suit with a white box stamped with the name of her bakeshop. Both were bundled up against the cold weather.

"Where did you park?" Tessa asked her sister as she

hugged her, then kissed her chilled cheek. She repeated the gesture with Faith.

Simone pulled off her gloves and knitted cap, then fluffed up her wealth of curly hair with her fingers. "I used your garage. It's going to cost me a grip for a few hours, but it's worth not having to walk at least ten blocks in the cold."

Tessa nodded. "One of the drawbacks of living in the city is a scarcity of parking spaces."

Faith sucked her teeth loudly. "That's why I don't have a car. Whenever I need one I rent it." She removed a stylish mink cloche before slipping out of a matching tuxedo-style jacket.

"That's not the only drawback," Simone said as she took her cousin's hat and coat. "What folks pay here for rent is double or maybe even triple what I pay in mortgage."

Faith headed for the half bath. "It's the same difference when you factor in property taxes."

"It's not the same, Faith," Simone retorted, following her cousin. "You pay as much for your tiny Greenwich Village studio apartment as I do for a four-bedroom, two-and-a-half-bath house in the suburbs. Not only do I have lots of living space but also enough land to build—"

"Give it a rest," Faith drawled as she gave Simone a warning look that communicated silently that she didn't want to argue about something she had no intention of changing. She loved living in the city and couldn't believe her good fortune when she found the studio apartment in a charming building in the West Village. The location was perfect because it was within walking distance of Let Them Eat Cake. The two women washed their hands before making their way back into the kitchen.

Faith, resting her hands on slim hips, peered over Tessa's

shoulder as she checked a wide pan with shallow sloping sides. She was making paella. "That smells incredible."

Tessa smiled up at her. "I got the recipe from the mother of a friend who uses chicken broth instead of bottled clam juice and achiote oil rather than saffron to color and flavor the rice."

"You've turned out to be a very good cook. Now you can get married," Faith teased, repeating what their paternal grandmother told them after they mastered her unique recipes.

"Yeah, right," Tessa countered.

"Who's getting married?" Simone asked, joining the two at the stove.

"Not I," Faith said.

"Nor I," Tessa intoned.

Simone moved closer, dropping an arm over her sister's shoulder. "You may want to rethink that statement."

"What are you talking about?" Faith asked.

"Tony and I ran into Tessa and her boyfriend last week, and there was no mistaking the heat coming off both of them."

Faith gave Simone an incredulous look. "You met Micah? And what were you doing with Tony?"

Simone's eyes widened. "You know Micah?"

"Answer my questions first, Simone Whitfield. What were doing with that sorry-ass excuse of an ex-husband?"

A rush of color darkened Simone's cheeks. "We're just talking."

Tessa shot her baleful look. "Talking about what?"

Lowering her gaze, Simone stared at the floor. "We're thinking of reconciling."

"Is he still unemployed?" Faith spat out.

Now you know the answer to that, Tessa mused as she turned her attention back to the pan filled with rice, chicken, andouille sausage, clams, mussels, shrimp and green peas. Faith had just verbalized what she'd wanted to ask her sister, but she had learned to bite her tongue whenever the subject of Anthony Kendrick came up.

"He says he has something lined up."

Faith's dark eyes flashed fire. "You know good and well that that bum—"

"Drop it, Faith," Tessa ordered firmly as she adjusted the heat under the pan and covered it with a lid. "You and Simone will never agree about Tony even if he becomes CEO of a Fortune 500 company."

Faith opened her mouth, then closed it just as quickly. Tessa was right. She'd never liked Anthony Kendrick— not because she thought of him as worthless and shiftless but because he'd had the audacity to cheat on her cousin not once but twice during their short-lived marriage. Her expression brightened. "So you and your Micah are going at it hot and heavy."

Simone, grateful that the focus had shifted from her to Tessa, smiled. "He didn't take his eyes off her the entire time."

"What does he look like, Simone?" Faith asked as she crossed her arms under her breasts.

"He's tall, dark and very much a manly man."

"You've got to tell us everything," Faith insisted. "Well not *everything*," she said when Tessa rolled her eyes at her.

Simone looped an arm around her sister's waist. "I can't believe you've been holding out on me."

"I could say the same thing about you and Tony." Tessa touched fingertips with Faith when she sucked her teeth loudly.

"You know you're going to hear it once Aunt Lucy gets wind of you and Tony getting back together."

"And I'm going to have to remind her that I'm a thirty-three-year-old woman who can take care of herself, thank you."

Faith shook her head. "Let me know when you're going to tell her so I can stay away from Mount Vernon until the smoke clears."

"What did you bring, Faith?" Tessa asked, deftly changing the topic.

"It's a spicy Scandinavian apple cake with chopped walnuts. You don't have to refrigerate it because it's best served at room temperature."

Simone picked up the bouquet of flowers. "Do you want me to set the table?"

Tessa shook her head. "I did it already. I decided we would eat in the dining room tonight. What you can do is arrange the flowers. You know where I keep the vases. Faith, could you please take the salad out of the refrigerator and put it on the table?"

The three women moved around the kitchen in synchronized precision, carrying bowls and bottles of white and a fruity rosé into the dining room, where Tessa had set the table with a set of fine bone china she'd inherited from her grandmother.

All thoughts of Anthony Kendrick and Micah Sanborn were forgotten when they sat down to eat and discuss their upcoming projects. Simone had made an appointment to visit Franklin Lakes on Thursday, while Tessa would meet with Bridget's maid of honor on Wednesday. Faith revealed that Bridget and Seth were scheduled to come to Let Them Eat Cake on Saturday to select their cake design and filling.

Simone had offered to stay and help clean up, but Tessa shooed her and Faith out the door, saying there wasn't much to clean up because she'd used only one pan when making the paella.

The hands on the clock inched closer to nine when she finally turned off the lights, set the alarm and went upstairs to her sewing room to cut out a pattern for a size-twelve gown in black satin. Losing herself in the task, she basted the garment together before draping it over a dress form. The bridesmaid gown would be similar to Bridget's with the exception of the train. It was after two when she made her way down to her second-floor bedroom. Showering quickly, she pulled a nightgown over her head and got into bed.

Tessa was asleep within minutes of her head touching the pillow. She slept soundly without the erotic dreams that usually kept her from a restful sleep.

Tessa huddled closer to Micah as they left a small movie theater in Greenwich Village that featured two-week runs of foreign films. She'd sat, her gaze fixed on the screen as she'd read English subtitles to Jean Cocteau's 1946 black-and-white masterpiece, *La Belle et la Bête.*

The below-freezing temperatures had abated, the mercury reaching a balmy fifty-four midday, and the streets were teeming with New Yorkers taking advantage of the warmer weather.

Micah had come directly from work to pick her up to take her to Il Mulino, advertised as the best Italian restaurant in the Village. Even with reservations they'd had to wait to be seated in the dimly lit restaurant with exposed brick walls and bentwood chairs. The wait was more than worth it because of the lagniappe of delicious fried zucchini served within minutes of their being seated.

She hadn't expected to see a classic French film with English subtitles but quickly became engrossed in the beautifully filmed version of *Beauty and the Beast*. Tessa found herself moved to tears whenever the beast tortured himself when he thought Belle wasn't coming back to him.

Micah's arm tightened around Tessa's waist over her coat. "Were you crying, darling?"

Tilting her chin, she met his gaze. "I admit to shedding a tear or two because I felt sorry for the beast."

His expressive eyebrows lifted. "He knew he was taking a risk when he permitted Belle to return home."

"But he loved her so much."

"And it was apparent that she'd fallen in love with him, because she did come back."

"Yes, but only when he was close to death."

Micah smiled. "But he didn't die, and like in all fairy tales, they get to live happily ever after."

"Do I detect a hint of cynicism, Micah?"

"No," he countered. "It was just a grown-up version of a classic fairy tale."

"Fairy tale or not, I really enjoyed it."

"So did I," he admitted.

What he wanted to admit to Tessa was that he'd enjoy anything as long as she shared it with him. He'd spent the week traveling between New York City and Albany for meetings that had been extended from one to four days. After the first night, when he'd returned home too late to call Tessa, he called her within minutes of leaving the historic landmark courthouse. Their conversations had been light and playful, and when he'd rung off he'd made certain not to blurt out how much he missed her, missed her and couldn't wait to see her again.

Activating the remote device, he opened the passenger-side door to his car. Tessa got in and he closed the door and came around to the seat beside her. Shifting, he stared at her profile. "Come upstate with me."

She turned and stared directly at him. "When do you want to go?"

"Tonight."

"Now?"

He nodded. "We'll stop at your place so that you can get a change of clothes."

"When do you plan on coming back?"

Reaching out, he pushed tendrils away from her satiny cheek. "Tomorrow."

"You want to drive more than three hundred miles, then turn around to come back the next day?"

"When do you want to come back?"

"Sunday."

"I thought you had business to take care on Sunday."

"It's something that I can do over the phone. May I make a suggestion?"

"Yes, you may, as long as you don't change your mind."

"Can we take my truck?"

Micah's smile was dazzling. He'd consider himself lucky if he was able to spend one night with Tessa. Two days with her was akin to winning the lottery. Wrapping a hand around her neck, he pressed a kiss to her hair. "That sounds like a plan to me."

In order to save time, Tessa didn't bother to change out of her dress and heels. She filled her overnight bag with sweatpants and shirts, jeans, socks, running shoes, a pair of boots, nightgowns, underwear and personal items while Micah left his sports car in her parking space at the garage, then drove several blocks to fill up the Highlander. She'd suggested taking her vehicle because she could relieve Micah if he was too tired to drive. She wouldn't mind driving his racy two-seater, but it'd been a while since she'd driven a car with a stick shift.

The doorbell rang as she closed the bag and slung the strap over her shoulder. Walking out of her bedroom, she pushed a button on the intercom next to a hallway wall switch. "Yes."

"Micah."

Depressing another button, she disengaged the lock to the front door. Less than a minute later she handed the bag to him, set the alarm and made her way off the stoop to where he'd double-parked. The official placards he usually stored under a visor in his car rested on the windshield.

Waiting until she was seated and belted in, Tessa pointed to the placards. "Are those for me?"

Micah buckled his own belt and shifted into gear. "Sorry, sweetheart, but I can't give them to you."

She stared at his distinctive profile, pushing out her lower lip in a pout. "But I thought I was your girlfriend."

"You are my girlfriend. But if you're ever stopped by the police, then call me."

"What if I can't reach you?"

"Accept the citation and I'll handle it."

"Well, well, well," she crooned softly. "What happened to the straight-laced former police officer who said he wouldn't fix a parking ticket for me?"

A hint of a smile softened Micah's firm mouth. "That was before you became my girlfriend."

"So now it's different?"

He nodded, grinning. "Oh, yeah. Very different."

What Micah wanted to disclose to Tessa was that he was a different man from the one who'd first walked into

Signature Bridals. Before meeting her, it'd been all about Micah Sanborn and what he wanted for himself. He understood himself well enough to acknowledge that he was selfish—selfish with his time, his emotions, while always withholding a part of himself from others. This is not to say that he didn't love his family and wouldn't give up his life to protect them, but it had never been that way with a woman.

Tessa had changed him—inside and out. She was independent, spunky and brutally candid. She'd established the rules for their relationship, and if he'd been less secure, he would've walked away from her. The reason he hadn't was because she wanted what he wanted: a relationship that was open, trusting and comfortable; a relationship where they would enjoy what made them male and female without the fairy tale ending of happily ever after. His father had warned him about dating a woman for more than a year and not committing to a future with her, but what Edgar didn't know was that Tessa was content to date him without a promise of marriage. For them it'd become a win-win arrangement.

He planned to enjoy the woman sitting beside him, enjoy what she willingly offered, and in return he would give her most of himself. The only thing he would withhold was something he'd given away as a child—his unconditional love. That he'd given to his mother.

Once Micah maneuvered onto the interstate, he increased his speed. It was close to midnight, vehicular traffic was light and there were stretches of unlit roadway that permitted him to exceed the limit by twenty miles. He and Tessa sang along with a station that played old favorites and golden oldies as the darkened landscape whizzed by. The trip which he normally accomplished in under four hours was accomplished within three. They'd stopped at a twenty-four-hour supermarket to pick up enough groceries to last several days.

Outdoor solar lights highlighted the converted barn as he parked in front of his vacation retreat. He rested a hand on Tessa's arm as she attempted to open her door. "Stay here while I check inside."

Tessa waited, watching as Micah disappeared inside. Seconds later the entire first floor was ablaze with light and then so was the second story. She couldn't wait to kick off her heels and stretch her legs.

Micah reappeared, opening the passenger-side door. "Everything's okay. Why don't you go upstairs and bed down while I unload the truck?"

"I'll help you."

He shook his head. "I've got it, darling. Keep my side warm for me," he teased, handing her her overnight bag.

She didn't have to be told twice. Reaching for her purse, she made her way toward the house, across the yawning living/dining area and up the winding staircase to the loft.

Micah walked into the bathroom and found Tessa, eyes closed, her head resting on a folded towel, in the tub as pulsating jets swirled the water covering her breasts. When he'd walked into the bedroom he'd expected to see her in bed, not lounging in the bathtub.

Going to his knees, he leaned over and brushed his mouth over hers. "Do you want company?"

Moisture spiking her lashes, Tessa's lids fluttered as she struggled to open her eyes. The warm, pulsating water had relaxed her so much that she'd drifted off. Micah had stripped down to his boxer-briefs.

"I was getting out."

"When?" he whispered against her parted lips. "Tomorrow morning?"

She met his gaze. "It's already tomorrow morning."

"True." Rising, Micah reached for a towel, then hunkered down again and lifted Tessa from the tub as if she were a child. He headed for the bedroom. "After I dry you off, I'm putting you to bed."

Her arms went around his neck. "I can't go to bed until I do things."

A frown creased his smooth forehead. "What things, Tessa?"

Tessa pointed to a number of bottles lining the marble countertop. "I need my deodorant and my moisturizer for my face and to put crème cologne on my body."

A smile replaced his frown. "Relax, baby. I'll take care of everything."

Minutes later she lay on the bed as Micah straddled her, blotting the moisture from her face, arms, back and legs. Light from a bedside table lamp shimmered off her rosewood-brown skin. She pointed, indicating which bottle contained the creams she used on her face and body. His ministrations were slow, deliberate, gently massaging her muscles as if it were something he'd done many times before. Tessa closed her eyes and gave in to the comforting touch of his long fingers, the strength in those digits when he kneaded several knots in her calves. There was no area he left untouched.

Pressing light kisses along the length of her spine, his mouth lingered on the area at the small of her back. "Don't go anywhere, darling. I'll be back as soon as I take a shower."

She nodded. Never had her body felt so supple,

relaxed, stress-free and at rest. "Where would I go, Micah? We're in the middle of nowhere and I'm not ready to have a face-to-face with a bear."

He kissed one buttock, then the other. "You won't see any bears because they're hibernating."

"Whatever," she drawled.

Moving up, Micah kissed her shoulder. "You smell good enough to eat."

Pinpoints of heat found their way up her body to her face before reversing and settling in the region between her legs. Vivid memories of the first time they'd made love were burned into her head. She'd begged him to make love to her and he had. His lovemaking was strong and passionate enough to make her forget the men with whom she'd lain. Tessa lay facedown, eyes closed and shrouded in a cocoon of warmth as she waited for Micah to return to the bed. And he did return, smelling of soap and toothpaste. He got into bed, his body covering hers, most of his weight supported on his arms.

"What took you so long?" Her voice was low, sultry.

Nuzzling her ear, Micah pressed his mouth against the side of her neck. "I wasn't gone more than fifteen minutes."

Tessa smiled without opening her eyes. "That was five minutes too long."

"What's the rush, baby? We have all night."

"Do you know how long I've been waiting for you to make love to me?"

Pressing her down to the mattress, Micah fastened his mouth to her nape. "Do you think it has been easy for me, too? Every time I talk to you on the phone I get aroused. There's something about your voice that sends my libido into overdrive. I wanted you last weekend, but you were on your period. I wanted to tell you that I've never been

turned off by blood, but I didn't want to gross you out."
He smiled when she gasped. "You're not good for me,
Tessa Whitfield, because since meeting you I've become
an insomniac. I've lost count of the number of times I
stopped myself from getting in my car in the middle of
the night to drive over to your place just to be with you.
Even if we didn't make love, I just wanted to feel you,
smell you."

"You're feeling and smelling me, Counselor. Now can
you please finish your summation and make love to me?"

Micah's response was to move down the bed and press
light kisses over the heels of her feet. His teeth and tongue
nipped and tasted every inch of flesh in his journey to
brand Tessa his most precious possession. He lost himself
in everything that made Tessa Whitfield who she was and
would become. He wanted her—all of her.

Tessa clamped her knees together when she felt
Micah's erection pressed to her hips. A gush of wetness
bathed the folds at the apex of her thighs, indicating her
body was preparing itself for his penetration.

"Oh, Micah." The two words were barely audible.

He heard her entreaty, echoing his own need to be
inside her. Reaching over, he removed a condom from the
bedside table. The seconds ticked off as he slipped on the
latex covering. Wrapping an arm around Tessa's waist,
he eased her to her knees and, using his free hand, guided
his throbbing sex into her, her gasping in surprise. Once
fully sheathed inside her, he cradled her waist as he
pushed slowly into her flesh closing around him. Then
he set a deliberate rhythm that had both close to climax-
ing. The press of buttocks against his belly as she rocked
back and forth, the position allowing for the deepest
penetration and sight of her firm swaying breasts, made

him close his eyes to shut out the erotic vision. It was either make love to her with his eyes closed or withdraw from Tessa to turn off the lamp. And the pleasure he derived from her body was too intense for any interruption.

Tessa's breathing deepened before quickening until she found herself gasping for her next breath. Each time Micah pushed into her quivering flesh it was as if he touched her womb before withdrawing to thrust again. His motions quickened as he cupped her breasts. The weeks, days, hours, minutes and seconds that had passed since he'd last made love to her vanished in a nanosecond when she climaxed. Waves of ecstasy washed over her like the ocean rocked by a violent storm, and she was helpless to swallow back the surrendering moans of pleasure that left her with an incredible feeling of completeness.

Micah's hoarse groan overlapped hers as he threw back his head and gave in to the dizzying intensity of his release. Looping his arms around Tessa's waist, he held her in an almost death grip until the pulsing eased, then stopped. His knees shook, his heart pounded like a jackhammer in his chest and he felt light-headed as if he were going to faint. Easing forward, he collapsed on her body.

"Micah! Micah, get up! You're crushing me."

Somehow through the lingering sensual haze he heard Tessa's voice. Rolling off her, he lay on his back, his chest rising and falling heavily. He reached for her right hand and gently squeezed her fingers. "I'm sorry, baby."

Tessa lay down, peering over at the man beside her. She knew it was time she stopped lying to herself. She'd fallen in love with Micah Sanborn.

Chapter 17

Tessa sat on the rug between Micah's outstretched legs in front of a blazing fire. She'd just finished talking to a client who'd referred her to the wife of a bank president who wanted her to coordinate her husband's retirement party. The celebration, more than five months away, would be held in their penthouse on the Upper West Side with panoramic views of the Hudson River and New Jersey. Reaching for her PDA, she entered the information she'd jotted down in a small spiral notebook. A shiver raced up her spine when Micah's fingers snaked around her neck.

"Don't."

"Don't what?" he whispered close to her ear.

"Let me finish entering my notes." Her thumbs moved with lightning speed as she tapped keys as her speedwriting raced across the small screen. "M-i-c-ah!" His name came out in several syllables when he looped an arm around her waist, lifting her effortlessly off the rug.

"Finish it later. If we're going for that walk, then we better get going before it gets dark."

She held up two fingers. "Give me two minutes and I'll be done."

Cradling her face in his hands, Micah lowered his head and kissed the end of her nose. "If you're not ready in two minutes, then I'm leaving without you."

"Remember to leave a trail of bread crumbs for me to follow." She'd asked him to take her out to survey the area. The last time she'd come, the weather had kept them indoors.

He dropped his hands and she sank back down to the floor. "Two minutes, Tessa."

Turning on his heels, he walked out of the space toward the rear of the house. He and Tessa had slept late, and when they'd finally left the bed after another passionate session of lovemaking the sun had passed its zenith. He'd prepared a hearty brunch before driving into town to pick up a supply of firewood. By the time he'd returned Tessa had cleaned up the kitchen, put up a load of wash, made the bed and cleaned the bathroom. She gave him a bit of attitude when he told her that he didn't bring her with him so that she could do housework. She'd come back at him, saying she wasn't raised to sit on her hands and have someone wait on her. The warning look in her eyes had spoken volumes: the subject was moot.

He wanted to spend time with Tessa, make love to her and not waste time arguing. They got along so well that for a few brief moments he'd tried imagining what it would be like to be married to her. However, as soon as the notion came it fled. Marriage meant a lifetime commitment, possibly children and a happily ever after. Fairy tales were dreams not reality. He'd laced up his boots and had just reached for his fleece-lined jacket when Tessa stood in the doorway to the mudroom. Her eyes appeared abnormally large in her bare face.

"You really were going to leave me, weren't you?"

He met her obviously shocked stare. "Yes, I was."

"Are you always so dictatorial?"

He took a step. "You think I'm being dictatorial because I want to leave on time?"

She waved a hand. "Perhaps I used the wrong word. Is *anal* more appropriate?"

Micah's expression stilled as he struggled to understand the woman standing inches away. Why was she so damned determined to fight with him? Well, if she was spoiling for an argument, then she was out of luck.

"Are you coming, Tessa?"

Tessa didn't know what to make of the enigmatic man to whom she'd given her heart. She hadn't wanted to argue with him, but she'd needed something—anything—to keep her from blurting out how much she'd come to love him.

"Yes, Micah. I'm coming."

Walking over to a bench, she sat down and reached for her boots. Her effort to put them on was thwarted when Micah bent down and slipped them on her sock-covered feet and tied them up. He took her coat off a wall peg and held it while she pushed her arms into the sleeves.

"Do you have a hat?" he asked as he buttoned her coat.

She shook her head. "I didn't bring one."

"You're going to need one because the temperature is dropping." He opened a plastic storage bin and pulled out a ski cap. "One for you and one for me."

Bundled up in her wool coat, hiking boots, ski cap and gloves, she reached for Micah's hand. "I'm ready."

He pulled her against his chest, rocking her gently in his embrace. "You're going to have to stop fighting with me."

Tessa pressed her nose to his shoulder. "I don't want to fight with you." *It's just that I don't want to love you,* she added silently.

Micah kissed the top of her cap. "Are we still friends?"

She smiled. "Yes." Why, she asked herself, was Micah deluding himself? Friends don't make love to friends the way he'd made love to her. He'd offered all of himself, holding nothing back, and vice versa.

They left the house through the door in the mudroom, making their way down a sloping hill until reaching a narrow, curving one-lane road. They walked along the side of the road in silence. Ancient trees with massive trunks so wide it would take the arms of two men to span them, stood like motionless sentinels, their branches reaching upward and outward like skeletal limbs. The stillness and silence were frightening and comforting at the same time. It was as if time had stood still and she and Micah were the only two human beings left on the planet.

"Don't move."

Tessa went completely still, inhaling and holding her breath. It wasn't until Micah pointed to his right that she slowly let out her breath. They'd come upon a family of deer nibbling on the branches of a bush covered with dark red berries. It was a doe with two fawns. Their spots were barely visible.

"They're beautiful."

Micah nodded, then turned to look at Tessa, whose eyes were glistening with unshed tears. His heart stopped before starting up again. He didn't understand her. She was the consummate businesswoman who had just enough edge to be taken seriously, yet she cried over fairy-tale movies and feeding deer. He felt her vulnerability as surely as it was his own. Wrapping both arms around her body, he held her as they watched the deer strip the berries from the bush. A hoot of an owl disturbed the silence, sending the deer scurrying into the woods for safety.

They started walking again. Tessa found breathing difficult with the rising elevation. The thinner air was a reminder that she was in the Adirondack mountain range. "Do you ever go skiing up here?"

Micah eased her farther off the road when he heard the sound of an approaching vehicle. An updated Volkswagen Beetle with a ski rack sped past them. "No. I usually ski in New Jersey. Would you like to learn to ski?"

"No."

He laughed. "You said that a bit too quickly."

"I don't like cold-weather sports."

"If you dress appropriately, then you won't feel the cold."

"Thanks but no, thanks, Micah. I much prefer a tropical beach."

"If I had a preference between a ski slope and the beach, then I'd certainly take the beach. That's not to say that downhill skiing isn't enjoyable."

The sun dipped lower in the horizon, casting lengthening shadows over the countryside, and there was just a hint of light in the sky when Micah and Tessa returned to the house.

Tessa, her back supported by a mound of pillows, stared at the leaping flames behind a decorative screen in the bedroom fireplace as she waited for Micah. The soft sound of an acoustic guitar playing flamenco filled the space. She'd shared cooking duties with Micah when they'd prepared a creamy shrimp fettuccine, but he'd shooed her out of the kitchen while he'd cleaned up the remains of dinner. He walked into the bedroom carrying a bottle in one hand and two wineglasses in the other. A pair of pajama pants rode low on his slim hips.

Micah sat on the side of the bed and filled the glasses with wine. Smiling, he handed Tessa a glass. "I hope you like it."

Touching her glass to his, she took a sip. "It's a nice, dry Riesling."

His eyebrows lifted. It was apparent the woman who'd enthralled him was full of surprises. "You can identify wine by taste?"

She gave him a sensual smile. "I've attended more than my share of wine-tasting competitions. Where did you get this?"

"Bridget gave me a case as a housewarming gift."

She took another sip. "I like it," she said, scooting over when Micah got into the bed next to her. Tessa snuggled against him, their legs intertwined. Everything was perfect: the wine, the music, the warmth and smell of burning wood and the man who'd unwittingly awakened a need she hadn't thought possible.

Tessa gave her name to the doorman, who picked up a phone and dialed the apartment of a prospective client. The woman had called her frantically earlier that morning, sobbing hysterically because the wedding planner she'd hired to coordinate her daughter's upcoming wedding had terminated their contract. The young woman's wedding was scheduled for a Valentine's Day candlelight celebration.

The man in bottle-green livery smiled at Tessa. "Mrs. Pendergast is expecting you. The elevator that will take you to the twenty-fourth floor is on your left." She crossed the opulent vestibule in the luxury high-rise apartment building on Park Avenue and made her way toward the elevator.

The frantic telephone call from Mrs. Adele Pendergast had interrupted the conversation she'd been having with Micah. He'd called to tell her how much he'd enjoyed sharing the weekend with her, and Tessa had been forthcoming when she'd told him that she looked forward to doing it again. It was as close as she would come to admitting that she wanted to spend more time with him. Weekends were no longer enough. She wanted more— much more than a few nights together every two weeks.

She pushed a button and the elevator door opened. Walking in, Tessa pushed the button for her floor, the doors closing and the car rising smoothly upward. The doors opened and she saw a framed Monet print on the wall. Every six feet another framed print graced the papered walls of the carpeted hallway.

She rang the bell to the Pendergast apartment, and within seconds the door was opened by a petite dusky-skinned woman wearing a pale gray uniform. Smiling, she introduced herself. "I'm Tessa Whitfield. Mrs. Pendergast is expecting me."

The door opened wider. "Please come with me."

Tessa followed the woman through an enormous entryway and down four steps to an expansive sunken living room. Floor-to-ceiling windows let the outdoors in with startling vistas of Central Park and downtown Manhattan. The furnishings looked as if they'd been chosen for a layout in *Architectural Digest*.

A tall, incredibly slender woman with shimmering

blond hair rose from a silk-covered chair. A younger woman who was an exact replica of the older woman stood up, flashing a weak smile.

A slight frown marred Adele Pendergast's perfect face. "Hilda, please take Ms. Whitfield's coat." There was a slight edge in her voice that did not bode well for the woman in her employ. "And please bring us some coffee and tea."

Slipping out of her coat, Tessa handed it to the house-keeper. "Thank you."

Adele waved a hand with an enormous South Sea pearl-and-diamond ring. "Please sit down, Ms. Whit-field." Waiting until Tessa sat down on a maroon-and-au-bergine-striped love seat, Adele sat down again. Her daughter repeated the motion, her movements resem-bling a marionette manipulated by several strings.

Adele, beautifully attired in a Chanel suit, Ferragamo pumps, a magnificent strand of pearls gracing her neck and matching studs in her ears, leaned forward in her chair. "Ms. Whitfield, this is my daughter Samantha. Darling, this is Ms. Whitfield of Signature Bridals. She's agreed to coordinate your wedding."

"I do believe you're being a bit premature, Mrs. Pen-dergast," Tessa said calmly. "I told you that I would have to talk to you first before committing to anything."

Adele Pendergast stared at the young woman in the ubiquitous New York City black: turtleneck sweater, tailored wool slacks and suede pumps. Tessa's hair brushed off her face and secured in a chignon and her lightly made-up face played down the natural beauty that didn't require the services of a plastic surgeon or esthe-tician—unlike Adele, who'd practically drained her husband's bank account when she underwent a complete makeover to hold back the hands of time.

"But isn't that why you're here, Ms. Whitfield? To commit to coordinating my daughter's wedding?"

Tessa felt a shiver of annoyance snake its way up her back. Counting slowly to three, she forced a smile she didn't feel. "I'm here for a consultation, Mrs. Pendergast."

Adele met Tessa's unflinching stare. "There's not much to talk about, Ms. Whitfield. My daughter is scheduled to marry James Cullen Siddell at a Long Island country club, and her father and I are prepared to pay top dollar for your services."

Crossing her feet at the ankles, Tessa shifted her gaze from mother to daughter. A brilliant platinum engagement ring with an Asscher-cut diamond circled the third finger of her tiny hand. Tessa had seen enough diamonds to recognize the cut and carat weight with a single glance, and Samantha's ring exceeded three carats. Although exquisite, the ring was overpowering given her fragility.

"Samantha, what is it you want for your wedding?"

"We want a formal affair," Adele said quickly before Samantha could answer Tessa's question.

"What about invitations?"

"They've been mailed." Adele answered again.

Tessa's impassive expression concealed her exasperation with Samantha's mother. "How many guests are you and your fiancé inviting, Samantha?"

"The last count was two hundred and twenty-five." Adele had answered for her daughter a third time.

Tessa had had enough. Adele was obviously a controlling, overbearing mother and there was no doubt she'd become a certified monster-in-law. "Mrs. Pendergast, I'd like to talk to Samantha—alone?"

Adele sat up straighter at the same time her eyebrows

lifted slightly. A blush suffused her pale face. "Why, Ms. Whitfield?"

"It's going to be *her* wedding and that means she should be the one answering my questions."

"But my husband and I are paying for everything, *Ms. Whitfield.*"

"Who's paying for what is of no concern to me, Mrs. Pendergast—that is *if* I decide to coordinate your daughter's wedding. Must I remind you that this is not about you or your husband but Samantha and her fiancé?"

The rush of color to Adele's face was so intense that Tessa thought she was going to stroke out on her. Not only didn't she want to take on Samantha as a client but she didn't need the extra revenue. No amount of money was worth having someone micromanage what she did quite well.

"What's it going to be, Mrs. Pendergast?"

Fingering the pearls hanging from her neck, Adele affected a thin-lipped smile. "Okay, Ms. Whitfield. I'll permit you to be alone with my daughter."

Tessa refused to relent. "I'm not asking your permission." She turned to look at Samantha, who'd fixed her gaze on the pattern of the priceless Persian rug under her feet. "Samantha, do you want to speak to me alone?"

The flaxen head came up, and when Samantha met the wedding planner's resolute stare she felt a measure of courage to finally stand up to her controlling mother. Ms. Whitfield was the third wedding planner she'd hired since her yearlong engagement to the son of one of her father's business associates. She wasn't in love with James, but with time she knew she could learn to love him.

"Yes, I do, Ms. Whitfield."

"Sammie!" Adele gasped.

All the resentment she'd harbored over the years to conform to her parents' standards welled up inside her and spilled over like bile. "Don't call me that dreadful name, Mother!" Her bright blue eyes gave off angry sparks. "And, yes, Ms. Whitfield, I'm willing to talk to you without my mother's interference."

"How dare you speak to me like that," Adele countered.

"I'm not a little girl, Mother. In case you've forgotten, I'm all of twenty-three years old and I'm quite capable of making my own decisions. Either I become involved in planning *my* wedding or James and I will elope."

Adele's eyes widened until they resembled silver dollars. "You can't."

"I can and I will."

"James will never become a party to an elopement."

"That's where you're wrong, Mother," Samantha countered angrily. "James was the one who suggested it."

Falling back against her chair, Adele closed her eyes, her chest rising and falling heavily. It was a full minute before she was back in control. She opened her eyes. "Okay, Ms. Whitfield." Her voice was pregnant with resignation.

Tessa and Samantha watched as Adele stood up and walked out of the room as Hilda walked in carrying a silver tray with matching pitchers filled with coffee and hot water. They shared a knowing smile as the housekeeper set out delicately painted porcelain cups and matching dessert plates. Within minutes she'd set the coffee table with several varieties of imported tea, butter cookies filled with jam, lemon slices, sugar cubes and chilled heavy cream.

"Would you like coffee or tea, Ms. Whitfield?" Samantha asked when Hilda left the room.

"I'll take tea with cream. And please call me Tessa."

Samantha flashed a bright smile. "And when it's just the two of us you can call me Sammie," she said like a coconspirator.

Tessa nodded. "Now tell me what you want for your wedding."

As Tessa rode the subway to Brooklyn she mentally went over what she'd discussed with Samantha Pendergast. She'd agreed to take her on as a client after Sammie reassured her that her mother would remain in the background until it was time for her to make her appearance as mother of the bride. She'd dealt with her share of Bridezillas, but Adele Pendergast was her first monster-in-law.

A smile softened her mouth as she climbed the subway stairs at her stop, and she was still smiling when she unlocked the door to her home. She kicked off her shoes, hung up her coat and went to check her voice mail. She had three messages, but it was the last one that quickened her pulse.

Depressing a button for speed dial, she listened intently for a break in the connection. The call was answered after the second ring. "Good afternoon. Wildflowers and Other Treasures."

"Simone, it's Tessa. What's up?"

"Are you going to be home tonight?"

"Yes. Why?"

"I need to talk to you."

Tessa heard a tremor in her sister's voice. "What's going on, Simone?"

"I'll tell you when I see you."

It'd been a while since they'd had a heart-to-heart sister talk. "Do you have anything on your calendar for tomorrow?"

"No, I don't. Why?"

"Bring clothes so you can stay over."

There was a pause before Simone's husky voice came through the earpiece. "Okay. I'll see you in a bit."

"Drive carefully," Tessa countered, knowing her sister's penchant for speed.

She hung up, wondering what was so critical that Simone wanted to see her. As much as she didn't want to acknowledge it, she knew it had something to do with Anthony Kendrick.

"Not again," she whispered to herself. Each time Simone had a crisis or dilemma her ex-husband was always the usual suspect.

Faith was the one who was the brutally honest Whitfield, while Tessa assumed a role as either peacemaker or neutralist. If Simone was coming to bitch and moan about Anthony, then Tessa was prepared to take Faith's approach and go right for the jugular. Either she would endear herself to her sister or alienate her.

Chapter 18

After Judge Andrew Carr heard the second case on the calendar, a tall figure entered the courtroom through the door that led to the hallway and the judges' chambers. Micah clamped his teeth together when he recognized the probation officer. His appearance did not bode well for a defendant who hadn't attended any of his treatment sessions or completed his hours of community service. There was no doubt he would violate and be forced to serve out his sentence.

The court clerk called the defendant's name. The sullen-looking young man stood up and glared at the judge as two court officers took positions behind him, handcuffs ready. Micah had talked to the defendant's court-appointed lawyer to try and keep the nineteen-year-old out of jail, but she hadn't fared any better than the D.A.'s office.

It took less than thirty seconds for Judge Carr to render his decision to send the defendant to jail to serve out the rest of his sentence. Then all hell broke loose in the courtroom. The defendant sprang at Micah, landing a punch on his jaw. Reacting quickly, Micah's right fist came up under the enraged youth's chin. He fell backward from the force of the blow, two court officers pouncing on him and holding him down while a third cuffed him. A swarm of white shirts crowded into the courtroom, most with hands on their firearms, and they quickly cleared the courtroom. Frothing at the mouth, his eyes rolling back in his head, the trussed-up prisoner was dragged out to a corridor behind the courtroom, into an elevator and downstairs to a holding cell.

A female court officer touched Micah's arm. "Are you all right?"

He opened and closed his mouth, wincing. "I'll live."

"You better put some ice on your jaw before it blows up."

Judge Carr came down off the bench and approached Micah, his gaze filled with concern. "The idiot didn't realize you were trying to keep him out of jail." He peered closer. "You better to see about your jaw. It's swelling."

"I'm good, Judge."

"You're not good, Sanborn. Now get the hell out of here and get yourself X-rayed. And I don't want to see you in my courtroom again until you get medical clearance."

Micah gathered his files and made his way out of the courtroom, stopping short when he saw the small crowd standing in the waiting area, talking quietly amongst themselves. All eyes were on him as he headed for the exit.

A court officer slapped him on the back. "Nice right, Sanborn."

He nodded but kept walking.

"You clocked his ass good," said the clerk who'd gone outside for a cigarette break.

The news of the courthouse altercation reached Micah's office before he did. He lingered long enough to put away his files and call his primary physician to let him know he was coming in for an X-ray of the left side of his face.

Tessa opened the door and went completely still. She was expecting to see Simone, not Micah. She hadn't realized how fast her heart was beating until she realized her hands were shaking. The left side of Micah's face was so grotesquely swollen that she marveled that he could see out of his eye.

She caught his arm, pulling him into the foyer. "What happened to you?"

Wrapping an arm around her shoulders, Micah leaned heavily on Tessa to support his sagging body. An X-ray technician had taken pictures of his face, and thankfully he hadn't lost any teeth and no bones were fractured. The doctor gave him a prescription for a painkiller, instructed him stay home until the swelling went down and return for a follow-up visit within a week.

"I got into a little scuffle at the courthouse."

"Who hit you?"

"A pissed-off defendant who'd violated the terms of his probation."

"What happened to him?"

"He's in jail." His knees buckled again. "Do you mind if I lie down for a while?"

"Don't faint on me, Micah."

"I'm not going to faint. I took a painkiller."

She gave him an incredulous stare. "When did you take it?"

"It's been about twenty minutes."

"You drove here under the influence?"

Micah's uninjured eye fluttered. "Not now, Tessa."

Tessa managed to get him up the staircase, undressed and into bed without mishap. He was asleep before she left the bedroom. The doorbell rang again, and this time she was certain it was her sister.

"Thanks, Tessa, for taking time out for me," Simone crooned as she stepped into the foyer.

"That's what sisters are for," Tessa said as she reached for Simone's overnight bag.

Slipping out of her coat, Simone stared at the trench coat hanging from the mahogany coat tree. It definitely was too large for Tessa. Her hands halted as she turned and fixed her hazel eyes on her sister. "Do you have company?"

"Yes. Micah's upstairs sleeping. He took a pain-killer, so he came here rather than attempt to drive to Staten Island."

"Is he okay?"

"He says he is."

"Look, Tessa, I don't have to stay over."

Tessa waved a hand. "Micah being here shouldn't change anything. Besides, we hadn't planned to see each other today." Simone opened her mouth again, but Tessa stopped her. "Please don't say anything else. Have you had lunch?" Simone shook her head. "If that's the case, then hang up your coat and put your bag in one of the bedrooms. I'm going to throw something together before we sit down and talk."

* * *

Three-quarters of an hour later, Tessa sat in the dining area in the kitchen with Simone enjoying skirt-steak BLT with basil mayonnaise on thick slices of toasted French bread, washed down with mugs of warm rose-hip tea. The radio on the countertop provided a soft backdrop to the conversation conducted in hushed tones.

"I'm confused," Simone admitted.

"What are you confused about?"

"It's Tony."

Tessa set down her mug and dabbed her mouth with a paper napkin. "You claim you still have feelings for him and you've talked about reconciling, but what's stopping you now, Simone?"

A fringe of long lashes touched Simone's honey-gold cheeks when she stared down at the crumbs on her plate. "Tony says he's changed."

"Has he?" Tessa asked.

"I don't think so."

"Are you sleeping with him?"

Simone looked up, seemingly startled by her sister's query. "No. That would complicate everything."

Tessa was hard-pressed not to smile. At least Simone knew enough not crawl back into Tony's bed, although she'd once admitted that he could be very persuasive. "Last week you said you were reconciling. What happened to make you change your mind?"

"He turned down a position with one of the largest auditing firms in the northeast."

The seconds ticked off as the sisters regarded each other. "I know you don't want to hear this, Simone," Tessa said in a quiet voice, "but Anthony Kendrick will never get a job as long as his mother continues to take care of him. Your first clue when you met should've been why is a grown-ass man still living with his mother? He has an MBA and is a CPA, so he can't say he isn't qualified to hold down a nine-to-five. And all that bull about 'he's so fine' doesn't pay rent or mortgage or put food on the table. He's a baby boy, Simone, and he'll always be a baby boy. Remember why you kicked him out the first time. Please don't go back to wallow in the same slop you managed to extricate yourself from.

"As human beings we're not made to be solitary creatures, but sometimes it's what we have to do in order to take a good look at who we are and where we want to go. I've had less relationships than you and Faith combined, yet I don't mind being alone. In fact, I enjoy my own company. I get up when I want, go wherever I want and I'm not beholden to anyone."

"Mama always said you were selfish."

"And you're generous to a fault, Simone. And where has it gotten you? You've put up with a spoiled, lazy good-for-nothing that's looking for a substitute for his mama. It's a good thing you didn't have any children from that bum or you never would've gotten rid of him. His excuse would've always been the kids. I'm glad that you're having second thoughts because that means you haven't completely lost your mind."

There was a swollen silence before Simone spoke again. "Are you telling me not to go back to Tony?"

Tessa shook her head. "No. You know I'm not one to tell you what and what not to do when it comes to your love life. All I'm saying is that he's not good for you."

Reaching across the table, Simone grasped Tessa's fingers. "I know that, but I had to hear someone else say it." She released her hand, pushed to her feet and walked over to the kitchen's wall phone. Removing the receiver from its cradle, she tapped in a number.

Turning her back to her sister, she listened for the break in the connection. She froze when she heard the deep, velvet voice that never failed to send shivers up and down her body. "Tony, this is Simone."

"Hey, now, baby. What's up?"

She pulled her shoulders back. "Nothing's up, Tony. I called to tell you no." A profound silence ensued.

"What do you mean no?"

"It's no to us getting back together. Not now and not ever. Goodbye."

"Don't hang up, Simone!"

She heard the panic in his voice, but what Anthony Kendrick didn't realize was that Simone Ina Whitfield wasn't the same woman she'd been when they first met what now seemed aeons ago.

"What do you want, Tony?"

"Can't we talk, baby?"

Simone shook her head, curls floating around her face like a reddish cloud. "I'm done talking. Goodbye and good luck with your life." She hung up, then turned to see her sister giving her a thumbs-up gesture. "Right about now I could use something stronger to drink than tea."

"What about a wine spritzer?"

Simone's eyes sparkled like precious stones. "I said a drink, not Kool-Aid, Tessa."

Tessa stood and headed for the cabinet that doubled as her bar. Simone had surprised her with the request because her older sister usually didn't drink anything stronger than wine. "I can make you a cosmopolitan, a martini or a margarita."

"I'll take a margarita. In fact, make it a double. Don't look at me like that, Tessa Whitfield. I'm not driving, and as soon as I finish my drink I'm going upstairs to sleep it off."

Tessa couldn't help laughing. It appeared as if her residence had become safe haven for the injured and the brokenhearted. First it'd been Micah and now her sister. She took out the ingredients for the margarita, then filled a pitcher with crushed ice from the refrigerator door. Her uncle had taught her to mix drinks, and she'd lost track of the number of times she'd assisted the regular bartenders during the many affairs held at Whitfield Caterers.

It took Simone nearly an hour to finish her drink. Then, as promised, she climbed the staircase to the second-floor bedroom she usually occupied whenever she stayed over in Brooklyn Heights. Her thoughts were too muddled to realize that Micah Sanborn slept in her sister's bedroom down the hall as she undressed, then slipped under several handmade quilts that had been passed down through several generations of Whitfield women.

"Where do you think you're going?" Tessa asked Micah as he sat up and swung his legs over the side of the bed.

"Home," came his hoarse reply.

She pushed off the chair in her sitting room where she'd sat reading for the past hour. Micah had slept through the morning and the entire afternoon. She moved closer, watching as he reached for his shirt.

"Are you sure you're going to be able to drive?"

"Yes." Micah swayed before righting himself as Tessa's hand caught his forearm. "Please don't touch me."

Her hand dropped. "What are you trying to prove, Micah Sanborn?"

He ignored her strident tone. "I'm going home." Instead of driving to Staten Island, he'd stayed in Brooklyn and come to Tessa. He'd come to her because he'd needed her. And it was the first time since his mother had walked away from him that he realized he needed a woman. Somehow he'd permitted Tessa to slip under the barrier he'd erected to keep all women at a distance; because what he felt and was beginning to feel for her went beyond friendship with fringe benefits.

Micah sat down on the side of the bed as he pushed his legs into his trousers. He managed to dress himself, albeit very slowly. Turning, he met her confused stare. "I'll call you when I get home."

Tessa nodded and managed a small smile. Even with his battered face he still had the power to make her heart beat a little too quickly. "Okay."

They walked out of the bedroom together and down the staircase, where Micah retrieved his trench coat. He opened and closed the door, leaving her staring at the spot where he'd been.

Micah pressed a button on one of the remote devices on his car's visor and the iron gates swung open. He drove through the gates, and they closed automatically when the tires depressed a metal plate. Switching to the high beams, he maneuvered along the road leading to the house where he'd grown up. When he'd told Tessa that he was going home it wasn't to the studio rental in Staten Island but Franklin Lakes. He found his parents in the kitchen. Edgar stood behind Rosalind, his arms around her waist as she stirred a pot on the cooking island.

Rosalind saw him first. Her face became a ghostly

white as a gasp escaped her parted lips. "Micah!" His name came out in a whisper.

Edgar seated Rosalind on a stool and rushed over to his son. "What the hell happened to you?"

Micah gave his father a reassuring grin. "It's not as bad as it looks. A defendant facing a misdemeanor charge decided to up the ante with felony assault because he'd violated the conditions of his probation."

"Why you?" Rosalind asked.

"He couldn't hit his lawyer, so I was the closest target."

Rosalind, having regained her composure, slipped off the stool and closed the distance between them. She touched his swollen face. "Did you see a doctor?"

He repeated what he'd told Tessa. "I can't go back to work until I get medical clearance, so I'm going to hang out here for a week." He pressed a kiss to Rosalind's forehead. "I'm going upstairs to take a shower, then I'm going to pop another pill and go to bed." The numbing effects of the painkiller had begun to wear off and the pain had returned with a vengeance.

Rosalind hugged him, then kissed his uninjured jaw. "Have you eaten?"

Micah shook his head, then thought better of it. "No, Mom."

"I know it's going to be a few days before you'll be able to chew anything. What if I make you a smoothie?"

"I'd like that, Mom." He kissed her again. "I'll see you later."

Rosalind knocked on the bedroom door, waited, then walked in. Micah hadn't turned off the lamp on a side table. He lay in bed on his back, eyes closed, his chest rising and falling in a deep, even rhythm. She neared the bed, setting the glass filled with a fruity liquid and a straw on the nightstand. Without warning, he opened his eyes and stared at up her leaning over him. Sitting on the side of the mattress as she'd done countless times whenever her children were sick, she placed a hand on his forehead. Thankfully it was cool.

"How are you feeling?"

Micah affected a lopsided grin. "Good."

She removed her hand. "Are you in pain?"

He let out a lingering sigh and closed his eyes again. "No."

Rosalind noticed a sheet of paper on the nightstand next to a pile of loose change. The doctor who'd treated her son had completed an incident report. With wide eyes she noted the time of the attack and the time that Micah had received medical treatment. Where, she wondered, had he been for the past eight hours?

"Mom."

"Yes, dear?"

"Please give me the phone. I have to make a call." Rosalind retrieved a cordless phone from the hallway table and handed it to him. Pushing up on his elbows, Micah pressed his back to the headboard. His dark eyes watched his mother as she waited for him to make and complete his call. Under another set of circumstances he would've asked that she leave because he didn't want her to overhear his conversation. However, the controlled substance he'd taken clouded his thoughts to where he felt as if his head were detached from his body. Squinting, he punched in the number to Tessa's cell phone.

"Hi," he whispered when hearing her greeting.

"Where are you, Micah?"

Why, he thought, did her voice sound as if she were in tunnel? "I'm home."

"You left my place more than two and a half hours ago, and I've been worried sick about you. And I don't have to remind you that it doesn't take *that* long to go from Brooklyn to Staten Island, even with traffic delays. I—I thought something had…" Her voice trailed off, then complete silence.

"Tessa, are you there?"

"Yes—yes I'm still here."

Her soft sobs came through the earpiece and his heart did a flip-flop; he felt her vulnerability. "Baby, are you crying?"

"No."

"Liar."

"You're not worth my tears."

He managed a smile that felt more like a grimace. "You're not a very good liar, Tessa Whitfield."

"Now that I know you're still alive I'm going to hang up."

"I'll call you tomorrow. I promise."

"Now who's a liar, Micah Sanborn? Weren't you the one who said you don't make promises?"

"This is one promise I'll keep. Are we still on for Lincoln Center Friday?"

"We don't have to go if you're not up to it."

"I'll be up to it."

"We'll see. Now hang up, because you sound as if you're under the influence."

"As a matter of fact, I am. We'll talk again tomorrow." Depressing a button, he ended the call, handing the receiver to his mother. "Thank you."

Leaning over, Rosalind kissed his forehead. "Drink your smoothie, Micah."

She left the bedroom, closing the door behind her.

What she'd suspected the first time Tessa Whitfield had come to her home had just been verified. It was quite obvious her son was taken with the very beautiful and very talented wedding planner.

Chapter 19

Tessa reread the e-mail before sending it. It was only five weeks before the Sanborn-Cohen nuptials, and she wanted to remind Bridget and Seth to schedule a time for their rehearsal and rehearsal dinner, write their wedding vows and, more importantly, obtain a marriage license. Pressing a key, she sent the e-mail.

Glancing at her planner, she noted December seventeenth for Bridget and her maid of honor's final fitting with shoes, accessories and lingerie. She couldn't ignore the slight flutters in her belly. She'd lost count of the number of weddings she'd coordinated, yet as the day grew closer to the time when a Signature bride was to exchange vows her anticipation shifted into high gear.

She consciously hadn't thought of herself as a bride because she would be faced with several dilemmas. Would she plan her own wedding or let someone else assume that responsibility? Would she make her gown or select one of Lucinda Whitfield's LCW designs? Did she want a small, intimate affair with close friends and family or a formal extravaganza with a five-course sit-down dinner?

A wry smile twisted her mouth as she slumped in her chair. Her fantasies would remain just that because Micah had been forthcoming when he'd admitted that he wasn't the marrying kind.

Incredibly she'd struck out not once but twice with the last two men with whom she'd become involved. Bryce was a married man and Micah a confirmed bachelor. She was batting a big fat zero. When, she mused, had Theresa Anais Whitfield become a masochist, a glutton for punishment?

She'd agreed to a relationship with Micah based on friendship with the added bonus of sharing a bed. Sleeping with him wasn't an issue because, as consenting adults, it was what they both wanted. However, she wanted more, and the man she loved was unable to offer more.

Straightening, Tessa reached for the telephone. She still had a number of calls to make before picking up Faith. They'd decided to go to Mount Vernon before the Thanksgiving holiday to help with the cooking and return to the city Friday afternoon.

Micah had kept his promise, calling her twice each day; she laughed when he complained about Rosalind serving him copious amounts of food with the edict he finish everything on his plate. However, he admitted that convalescing at his childhood home wasn't all that bad because it permitted him to spend more time with his parents.

She called Juan Cruz to see if he'd completed the order for Bridget and Seth's personalized thank-you cards and touched base with several suppliers to get a final price for their services.

Simone walked into the kitchen filled with mouth-watering smells and bustling with activity, cradling a large crystal bowl filled with colorful flowers in autumnal colors to her chest. Her mother stood at the cooking island watching Malcolm Whitfield lift a large turkey from a pan, while her uncle Henry expertly removed corks from bottles of wine. Tessa tossed the contents of a bowl filled with salad greens at the same time Faith and her mother placed pies on trivets to cool.

"Happy Thanksgiving!"

Lucinda's expression brightened when she saw her eldest daughter. "You're just in time. We were just sitting down to eat." It was a rare occasion when Simone made it to traditional family holiday get-togethers in time to eat with the Whitfields. Easter, Mother's Day, Thanksgiving and Christmas were the busiest times of the year for the flower business. She turned to her husband. "Mal, please take the flowers into the dining room."

Simone gave her father the floral centerpiece, then rose on tiptoe to kiss his cheek. "Hi, Daddy."

He kissed her forehead, winking. "Hi, yourself."

"Hey, Tessa, I got a confirmation just before I left that the Sanborns received their floral centerpiece and your boyfriend his get-well bouquet." Everyone stopped and stared at Tessa with Simone's announcement.

"What boyfriend?" Lucinda asked.

"Theresa, dear, you didn't tell us that you were seeing anyone." It was Edith Whitfield's turn to question her niece.

Tessa smiled at her aunt. Edith and Lucinda were the only ones, aside from her teachers in school, who called her Theresa. "He's not a boyfriend in the traditional sense of the word."

Edith's dark eyes impaled her. "Are the two of you dating?"

"Mother, stop with the interrogation," Faith whispered in protest.

"I just asked her a simple question, Faith. It's not as if I'm asking for intimate details."

Henry Whitfield moved over to his wife, brushing a kiss over her mouth. "Edie, leave the young folks to their business," he said softly.

Tessa wanted to throw her arms around her uncle's neck and kiss him for smoothly defusing what would've become a very uncomfortable situation for her. Edith had earned the reputation as a certified busybody. Whenever she lowered her voice to a crooning tone it signaled that she was going in for the kill. Her "darling" and "sweetheart" was a prelude for breaking down one's defenses to figuratively spill their guts to the charismatic woman. And with her still-incredible beauty it was hard to resist the former model's charm.

Edith smiled at her husband. "I just wanted to know whether I had to prepare for a family wedding, that's all."

"I'm certain when it's time for Theresa to get married she'll let us know. Won't you?" Lucinda asked.

Tessa flashed a brittle smile. "Of course I will."

"I don't know about the rest of you," Simone said, waving her hand, "but I'm ready to eat." She'd worked nonstop for the past three days filling orders for select clients, stopping only long enough to eat takeout from her favorite Chinese restaurant and drink gallons to keep her alert.

"Amen to that," Faith intoned, for once agreeing with her first cousin. She knew her mother was in rare form when Edith began her inquisition as soon as she arrived the night before with Tessa. Edith wanted to know if she was dating anyone and, if she was, then when was the last time they'd gone out. She knew she'd annoyed her mother because she'd refused to answer her questions. And instead of spending the night with her parents, she'd called Tessa and asked her to come and pick her up so she could spend the night with her aunt and uncle.

"Lucy, baby, can you please cut me another piece of pumpkin cake?" Malcolm Whitfield's wife had baked his favorite pumpkin roll cake filled with toffee cream, served with a caramel sauce.

Lucinda Whitfield shook her head. "No, Mal. You've already had two slices."

Malcolm glanced at his daughters, seeking their assistance. "You see how she treats me?"

"Mama's right," Tessa and Simone chorused.

Malcolm's hazel eyes darkened as he glared at Tessa then Simone. "The only time you two agree on something is when your *mother* decides what's good for Malcolm's stomach."

Lucinda rolled her eyes at her husband of nearly four decades. "That's because your daughters know much you complain whenever your belly starts acting up."

Simone narrowed her gaze at her father. "Mama's right. The last time you had an upset stomach you sounded like a wounded buffalo. It was something awful."

Henry, the consummate peacemaker and four minutes older than his twin, gestured to his dessert plate with a generous slice of pumpkin cake. "If y'all keep snapping on my brother, I'm going to give him my piece." There was a chorus of gasps followed by complete silence from those sitting around the formally set dining room table.

Malcolm's smile was as bright as the rising sun. "Thanks, brother."

Henry winked at him. "No problem, brother."

"I know they're not trying to gang up on me," Lucinda whispered under her breath.

Tessa patted her mother's arm. "Let it go, Mama. You can take care of Daddy when you get him alone."

Lucinda's scowl vanished as she leaned closer to Tessa. "When did you get so smart?"

"I learned it from my mama," she crooned as if they were coconspirators.

Hours later Simone and Faith crawled into Tessa's bed with her as they'd done when they were much younger. Faith lay on a pillow next to Tessa, while Simone supported her back on a pillow at the footboard of the queen-size sleigh bed.

"What happened, Tessa, that you sent your manly Micah flowers?" Faith asked with a wide grin.

Tessa repeated what Micah had eventually revealed to her about the courtroom brawl. He'd decided to tell her everything before she heard from another source, because the news had spread throughout the judicial grapevine like wildfire. A judge who'd attended law school with Edgar Sanborn had called to tell him that his son was a hero because he'd coldcocked a defendant who'd attacked him because he'd been remanded to serve out his sentence.

"He said he got in a good punch before the court officers subdued and cuffed the man."

Simone sat, slapping her thigh covered by a pair of flannel pajama pants. "I told you he was a manly man!"

"Hot damn, Tessa!" Faith whispered. "You found a lawyer who moonlights as a pugilist."

"He wasn't always a lawyer."

"What was he?" Simone asked.

Tessa stared at her sister, then her cousin. She'd neglected to tell them about Micah's prior law-enforcement career. "He was a cop."

Faith's eyes widened. "Does he carry a gun?"

"No," Tessa laughed.

"Is he licensed to carry one?" her cousin asked.

"Yes." When Tessa had questioned Micah about carrying a firearm he'd admitted to having two, but they were locked in a safe in his apartment.

"That's what I'm talking about, Simi," Faith said, calling Simone by her childhood nickname. "Tessa's found a prince with brains and brawn."

"You deserve someone good, sis. I'm glad you have Micah."

Tessa forced a smile through her expression of uncertainty. Her cousin and her sister were happy for her when she wasn't that happy for herself. She'd been the one to set the rules for her relationship with Micah, and along the way it had come back to bite her.

Tessa walked down her block after she'd parked her SUV in the garage, her steps slowing when she noticed the tall figure of a man leaning against the door to a gray sports car. She came closer, a smile parting her lips. Micah was waiting for her. For once, he'd found a legal parking space in front of her home. He straightened as she approached him. He hadn't shaved, but she could discern some puffiness along his jaw, and a darkening bruise was visible below his left eye.

He extended his arms, and seconds later her face was pressed against the softness of a bulky sweater. "How long were you waiting?"

Micah buried his face in the fragrant flyaway curls tickling his nose. "I got here about an hour ago."

Pulling back, she stared up at him. Simone had called him a manly man, and that he was, and the hair on his face served to validate her sister's claim. "Come inside. We don't need to give my busybody neighbor anymore to gossip about."

Lowering his head, Micah brushed a kiss over her soft mouth. "I could really give her something to talk about, but you have to live among these people."

"Come inside," she said, repeating her command.

"Let me get my bag."

She nodded. He was prepared to spend the night. Waiting until Micah retrieved a dark brown satchel with his initials branded into the supple leather and a garment bag, she made her way up the steps. Tessa unlocked the door and deactivated the alarm. She didn't have time to catch her breath when she found herself lifted off her feet and her mouth smothered in a burning kiss that stole the remaining breath from her lungs.

Cradling Micah's bearded face between her hands, she kissed his forehead, eyebrows, lashes and the bridge of his nose, then found his mouth again. He carried her up the staircase and into her bedroom.

It was as if the whole world held its breath when he undressed her, then himself. Holding out her arms, she welcomed the man she loved into her arms, between her legs and inside her.

Their reuniting and joining was frantic, as if both feared it was a dream and would be over whenever they woke from the erotic coupling. They climaxed simultaneously, hearts pumping against their ribs as they returned from their shared flight of free fall.

There was only the sound of breathing as Tessa snuggled against Micah's damp body. She closed her eyes and fell asleep in his embrace. However, sleep didn't come as easily as Micah wanted. He'd come back to New York earlier than he'd planned because talking to Tessa only served to enhance his dependence on her.

He'd retreated to New Jersey because he feared emotionally he was in over his head with Tessa. But time and distance did little to quell his craving for a woman who claimed she only wanted friendship with fringe benefits.

The truth was he liked Tessa Whitfield, and the liking had nothing to do with friendship or fringe benefits.

Chapter 20

Micah shielded Tessa's body from the crush of well-dressed couples filing out of the Metropolitan Opera House. He hadn't known what to expect yet had thoroughly enjoyed the spectacular production of Mozart's *Magic Flute*.

It was his first time inside the magnificent building with five great arched windows offering views of the opulent foyer and two murals by Marc Chagall. Tessa revealed that the exquisite starburst crystal chandeliers were raised to the ceiling just before each performance.

She also told him that one of her clients, a patron of the arts who sat on the board of the Met and several museums, held seasons tickets to the Metropolitan Opera and the American Ballet Theater and each year she mailed her two tickets as a Christmas gift. Once she revealed this Micah wondered who Tessa had taken the year before.

Tessa tugged at Micah's arm. "Look, it's snowing."

Softly falling snow was accumulating on the sidewalks. It was New York City's first snowfall of the winter.

He smiled at her animated expression. When they'd dressed for the evening's affair he hadn't thought Tessa could improve on perfection, yet she had. He'd thought she was stunning the night of the National Latino Officers Association dinner-dance, but tonight she was the epitome of elegant sophistication. She'd chosen to wear a black wool gabardine suit with a pencil skirt and a peplum jacket, sheer black stockings and matching silk-covered pumps. On her ears a pair of diamond studs, and a delicate white strand necklace sprinkled with diamond spacers graced her slender neck.

It had taken all of his willpower not to remove her fur-lined silk three-quarter coat, then strip her naked and make love to her until he passed out or his heart stopped beating—whichever came first. But he'd known Tessa was looking forward to attending the opera, so he'd quickly dispelled his erotic thoughts.

"Do you feel like walking to Rockefeller Center to see the tree?" Tessa asked as snowflakes settled on her curly hairdo.

Micah lifted his eyebrows. "You want to walk in the snow?"

She smiled, bringing his gaze to linger on her mouth. "Yes."

"Aren't you afraid of ruining your shoes?"

She shook her head. It wasn't often that she got into Manhattan to see the tree in person. "No. Now, if you're afraid of a little snow, then we can—"

"Hello, Tessa. I'm a skier," Micah said, interrupting her.

"Then let's go, Micah. I'll treat you to a latte if you get too chilled," she teased.

Tucking her gloved hand into the bend of his elbow, Micah escorted Tessa down Columbus Avenue. They'd come into Manhattan several hours before the start of the performance to share dinner at Les Célébrités, a luxurious dining room off the lobby of the Essex House Hotel. When Tessa had invited him to accompany her to the Lincoln Center he'd wanted to make the night special and take her out to eat. When he'd called the restaurant he was told they were booked solid. Not one to accept a first refusal, he left his name and a call-back number, adding that he was a Kings County assistant district attorney. Three hours later he got a call with the news that they were able to seat him and a guest at one of their much-sought-after fourteen tables. He'd grown up watching his parents navigate and circumvent near-impossible situations by surreptitiously dropping names and titles, and usually with remarkable results.

"Do you bowl?" Micah asked Tessa after they'd walked several blocks.

"I haven't bowled in a while. Why?"

"Some guys from the four-four are forming a bowling league after the new year. They'll meet on Wednesday nights in the Bronx. I'd like you to partner up with me."

"Will I be the only female?"

He chuckled softly. "No, Tessa. There will be female officers. Speaking of women, why don't you invite your sister and her husband to join us? We could use another couple."

"Simone and Tony are not a couple. They were divorced several years ago."

"But, didn't you introduce him as your brother-in-law?"

She inclined her head. "I did because I didn't want to embarrass my sister by referring to him as her ex."

"They looked rather friendly toward each other."

"They have their ups and downs." Tessa wanted to tell Micah that Simone had more bad times than good with Tony but decided Simone's personal business was just that—personal.

"Invite her anyway. There'll always be someone to pair her up with."

She gave Micah a sidelong glance. "Are you match-making, Micah?"

"Oh, hell, no," he countered quickly. "I tried that once and the result was I lost two friends."

"I can't promise anything, but I'll call Simone to see whether she'd like to join us."

The snow was falling harder the closer they came to Rockefeller Center. Surprisingly the streets were crowded with native New Yorkers and out-of-town tourists. No one seemed to mind the frozen precipitation as they stared up at the towering, gaily decorated Norway spruce.

Retracing their steps, they stopped at the garage to pick up Micah's car. The city had become a winter wonder-land with the falling snow and the holiday lights shining from the many apartment windows as they headed in a westerly direction toward Brooklyn. Donnie Hathaway singing Ray Charles's classic "A Song for You" came through the speakers of the BMW Roadster.

She met Micah's amused gaze when he stopped for a light. A dreamily sensuous light passed between them moments before he shifted into gear and sped off again. He reached for her hand the next time he stopped, placed it over the gearshift, holding it in place as he shifted gears. He still held her hand when he maneuvered into the twenty-four-hour garage where she kept her sport utility vehicle.

Three-quarters of an hour later Tessa carried the

steaming mugs of chocolate topped off with a frothy cream into the bedroom, smiling at Micah as he took the mugs from her. Droplets of water from his recent shower clung to his coarse, closely cropped hair.

They got into bed, pulled up the quilts and sipped hot chocolate as the snow continued to fall, blanketing Brooklyn and most of the tristate area. The day that had begun with them wrapped in a passionate embrace ended with them talking about everything but themselves.

Early December found Tessa beset with a number of corporate holiday parties that made her reconsider an initiative she'd proposed to her sister and her cousin earlier in the year: she needed an assistant to set up appointments and follow up with orders from vendors. She made a notation in her planner to contact her alma mater to advertise for a part-time fashion student.

The first two weeks in the month she was in Manhattan three out of five nights at hotels or upscale restaurants, conferring with head chefs and banquet managers. As with her wedding business, coordinating private parties all came from referrals.

The doctor had cleared Micah to return to work, and he'd revealed that his first day back at his office he was greeted with a pair of boxing gloves while the theme song from *Rocky* blasted from a boom box. He took the gloves home and hung them on the handlebars of his bike suspended on the wall rack.

Tessa exchanged telephone calls with him every night; she'd outlined to him the details of her hectic monthly schedule, and although she wanted to see Micah, she knew it would prove disruptive to her busy schedule. Whenever she was with Micah or shared her body with

him he took precedence, not Signature Bridals. But it was
Signature Event Planners and Signature Bridals that she'd
worked long hours to grow, and it was her dedication and
work ethic that gave her the resources to live a very comfortable lifestyle.

Two weeks before her wedding Bridget and Melissa
Knight, her maid of honor, came for their final fittings.
As instructed, both brought their shoes, accessories
and lingerie.

Removing a pin from the cushion strapped to her left
wrist, Tessa adjusted the bodice to Melissa's gown. "I'm
going to insert a binder to minimize your breasts."
Melissa reminded her of a porcelain doll with her milky-
white skin. She was petite with a full bosom, raven-black
short hair and large brilliant eyes that changed color from
blue to violet depending upon her mood. "You don't want
to show too much flesh to the religious officiates. I'd
planned a wedding where the bride's gown was cut so low
that the rabbi was definitely shocked *and* embarrassed by
the wanton show of flesh."

A becoming blush found its way up Melissa's chest to
her hairline. "I've always had to wear separates because
of my chest."

Tessa met her gaze in the full-length mirror. "That's
not a problem with this dress because it was designed to
fit your body's proportions." The black satin strapless ball
gown had the same trapunto-stitched crisscross belt as
Bridget's; it emphasized Melissa's slender waist without
the cascading train. She'd excluded the train because it
would've overwhelmed the bridesmaid's diminutive
height.

After Tessa made the final adjustments she told
Bridget and Melissa the dresses would be delivered to

Franklin Lakes within the week by special messenger. They gave her a perplexed look until she explained that she was willing to pay the extra cost to have a bonded courier deliver the garments.

She spent the remainder of the evening making altera- tions, praying neither Bridget nor Melissa would gain or lose any appreciable weight over the next two weeks.

Tessa's eyes were tired and burning slightly when she finally crawled into bed. She shut off her phone's ringer. She didn't want to talk to Micah because hearing his voice before going to sleep elicited erotic dreams that made her ache for him like an addictive drug. Closing her eyes, she exhaled. Within minutes she'd fallen asleep.

Tessa had just finished going over the checklist for the Sanborn-Cohen wedding when the sound of the doorbell chimed throughout the house. She glanced at the small monitor perched on a side table in her office. The security company had installed a hidden camera over the doorway so everyone coming to or leaving Sig- nature Bridals was filmed.

The corners of her mouth inched up in a beguiling smile as she went to answer the door. The scent of pine wafted in the air from the large wreath attached to the solid oak door. Christmas was two days away, and lights, wreaths and menorahs hung from doors of the brown- stones lining both sides of the street.

"Hello, stranger," she crooned when he stared down at her as if she were truly a stranger. He was causally dressed in a black pullover sweater and jeans, a sheep- skin jacket and leather slip-ons.

Micah drew in a breath, holding it, then exhaled. It'd been a month, four long, lonely weeks since he'd seen

Tessa, and seeing her under the glow of the lanterns on either side of the door made him weak in the knees. She appeared thinner, almost fragile. Her eyes looked haunted as though she hadn't had enough sleep. There was no doubt she was working too hard. When he'd asked to see her she'd said her schedule was so full that she barely had time to sleep. It was only when he told her that he wanted to give her his Christmas gift that she'd relented.

"Merry Christmas, Tessa." He handed her a small shopping bag containing a gaily wrapped box.

Tessa peered into the bag. "Thank you. Please come in."

He lifted his expressive eyebrows. "Are you sure you want me to come in?"

"Of course I am. I want to give you your gift."

Micah didn't move. "You didn't have to get me anything."

"I could say the same thing for you," Tessa countered. "Come in, Micah. You're letting out the heat."

Grasping his hand, Tessa led him into her parlor. Wrapped gifts with matching tags covered the length of a mahogany credenza. Picking up a box covered with black-and-silver paper, she handed it to Micah.

"Merry Christmas, Micah."

He angled his head. "Should I open it now or wait for Christmas?"

"Read the tag."

"'Do not open until Christmas.'"

"Does that answer your question?"

Micah stared at Tessa staring up at him. "Yes, it does."

There was an uncomfortable silence until she asked, "Would you like something to eat or drink?"

The muscles in Micah's face relaxed. How could Tessa not know that he could go without food or water for extended periods of time but not her? "No, thank you. But I would like something from you."

Her expression mirrored confusion. "What?"

He took a step, bringing them within inches. "I'd like to kiss you."

Her sexy mouth opened, closed, then opened again. "If you hadn't asked me, then I would've asked you the same thing."

Reaching for Tessa, Micah cradled her to his chest. "What happened to us?"

"What do you mean?"

"You were right when you called me a stranger. There was a time when we wouldn't go more than a week without seeing each other."

Tessa buried her face between his neck and shoulder. "I've been busy."

"We're both busy with our lives and our careers. But that's no excuse for not finding time—quality time to see each other. Isn't that what *friends* do?"

Easing back, she tried seeing what was going on behind Micah's intense dark eyes. "We're not friends, Micah."

He blinked once. "If we're not friends, then what are we?"

"We're lovers. We sleep together. We don't have sex, we make love."

Micah's eyebrow nearly met in a frown. "What are you trying to say, Tessa? I'll acknowledge that you're busy, but is there another reason why you don't want to see me or answer your phone at night?"

She knew it was time she stopped lying to herself and to the man with whom she'd fallen in love. Straightening her shoulders, Tessa took a deep breath. "I don't answer my phone at night because I can't to talk to you."

"Why?

"I can't because I have a hard time falling asleep."

"What do I have to do with you falling asleep?"

"I have dreams—erotic dreams."

His frown deepened. "And you think I don't, Tessa?" The tendons in his neck bulged. "Since I began sleeping with you I go to bed with a hard-on and wake up with one. I'm forty-one years old, Tessa, not an adolescent boy. I should be able to control my sexual urges, but I can't. All that says is that we're both horny. You're going to have to come up with another reason—one that makes sense to me."

"I…I love you." There. She'd said it. She'd finally told him what lay in her heart. A bright smile softened her eyes and mouth. "I love you, Micah Sanborn." His expression changed to one of shock. "I know I'm not sticking to our original agreement but—"

"No, Tessa," he gasped. Micah felt as if someone had driven a stake through his heart. "Please don't love me."

"Don't tell me what I should feel."

He shook his head. "I'm not—I can't tell you what you should feel. But it's not going to work."

The seconds ticked off as they regarded each other. Tessa's eyes narrowed. "Do you think I'm going to ask you for a commitment? Do you actually believe I'd ask you for more than we have now?"

She hesitated, swallowing the screams of frustration welling up at the back of her throat as realization dawned. Micah thought she wanted a happily ever after with him. Yes, she loved him. Yes, she thought about when she would marry—but he hadn't figured into the equation. What they shared was too new, too fragile to ask for more.

"I'm not asking you to fall in love with me, Micah,"

she continued, this time her tone softer, more concilia-tory. "You wanted to know and I told you. Perhaps it was a mistake for us to sleep with each other. Perhaps we should've stuck to friendship without the fringe benefits."

Micah closed his eyes for several seconds. Tessa didn't understand. She couldn't understand how much she'd frightened him when she told him that she loved him.

"I don't regret sleeping with you."

"Nor I you," Tessa countered. "In fact..." She swal-lowed the words poised on the tip of her tongue. "I made a mistake, Micah. I never should've gotten involved with you."

"How can you say that, Tessa?"

"I just did. Now will you please leave?"

Micah managed to conceal the dread he hadn't felt since he'd sat in the hospital's clinic waiting for his mother's return. He'd loved his mother unconditionally, and it'd taken four weeks away from Tessa for him to realize he loved her—unconditionally.

He admired her spunkiness, candor and beauty, re-spected the drive it took for her to own and operate her own business single-handedly and loved the unbridled passion she willingly offered him.

Her eyes filled with the shimmer of unshed tears, tears he knew he'd put there. "I'll call you."

The words washed over Tessa like a cold wave. "Please don't. Let's make a clean break while we still can be civil to each other."

The soft chiming of a clock on the fireplace mantel signaled the half hour. It was six-thirty, the same time as when he'd first walked into Signature Bridals and the same time he'd leave Tessa Whitfield and Signature Bridals for the last time.

Turning on his heels, he walked out, leaving Tessa staring at his broad-shouldered back. She hadn't realized her legs were shaking until her knees buckled. She managed to make her way to a club chair and sit down, willing the tears blurring her vision not to fall.

Tessa stared at the wood on the grate in the cold fireplace, replaying all that she'd shared with Micah. A wry smile twisted her mouth. She had established the rules and she had broken her own rule. There was no way she would blame Micah. The blame was hers to shoulder—alone.

Chapter 21

"Are you all right, Micah?"

His head came up and he saw the look of distress on his mother's delicate face. When he'd left Tessa's house he hadn't bothered to stop in Staten Island but continued on to New Jersey. He hadn't wanted to go home because he didn't want to be reminded of the time Tessa had come for a sleepover. It was a weekend when they had slept together but hadn't made love, and that was the first time he knew he'd fallen in love with her. It hadn't been about sex but friendship *and* companionship. She'd become his partner in every sense of the word, the half that made him whole.

"I'm fine." Pushing back his chair, he stood up. "I'm sorry, but I don't have much of an appetite."

"I can..." Rosalind's words trailed off when Edgar gave her a warning glance. She was more than familiar with the look. It meant *Back off.* There were occasions when she tended to smother her children because she feared losing them. It took her husband's sage advice to put her mind at ease that no one was going to come and take them from her—and if that did occur, then he would call in every legal favor owed him to keep their family intact.

"What do you think is bothering him, Edgar?" she asked when they were alone.

Edgar's brow knitted in a frown. "I don't know. Perhaps we should back off for a while. If he wants to talk, then he'll come to one of us."

"I hope you're right," Rosalind mumbled under her breath. She had an idea of what had Micah distracted but decided to reserve comment.

Micah knocked on the door to his father's study, waiting for him to acknowledge his presence. As expected, he was jotting down notes from his law books. "Dad, can you spare a few minutes?"

Edgar rose to his feet, waving him in. "Of course I can. Come on in."

The two men sat down on matching leather chairs, facing each other. The study had become Edgar's sanctuary and museum. A number of tables held scaled-down models of sailing ships, from Chinese junks to frigates. Built-in floor-to-ceiling bookcases were packed with law journals, books, copies of briefs. The shelves on one wall were crowded with notebooks, report cards, book reports, papers, theses, a dissertation, drawings, finger-painted posters and doodlings, chronicling his sons' and daughter's education from pre-K through college.

It was in this room that he graded papers, researched arcane laws, conferred with some of the state's most brilliant legal minds. And it was also where he'd sternly lectured his children whenever they'd broken curfew or failed to achieve the grades equal to their aptitude.

Pressing his hands together between his knees, Micah stared at the fading pattern of the Turkish rug under his sock-covered feet. "I need your advice on something," he said quietly.

Edgar's impassive expression did not change. "Is it advice or my opinion?"

Micah's head came up and he met his father's steady gaze. "It's not about the law."

The older man's mouth curved into an unconscious smile. "If it's not the law, then it must be a woman."

A muscle quivered at Micah's jaw. "It is."

Leaning forward, Edgar reached out, resting a hand on his son's knee. "It's been a long time since I've had to concern myself with matters of the heart. I'm honored you trust me enough to confide in me."

"This isn't about me, Dad."

"If not you, then who is it about?"

"Tessa Whitfield."

Edgar's fingers tightened before he withdrew his hand. "What does she have to do with you?"

"We've been seeing each other."

A flash of humor crossed Edgar's face. "You're dating Bridget's wedding planner." His question came out like a statement. Micah inclined his head. "How long have you dated her?"

"We met for the first time in October."

"You're talking less than three months. You're practically strangers. So what's the problem?"

Much to his chagrin, Micah laughed. "It's ironic you say that because tonight she called me a stranger."

Edgar sobered quickly, crossing one leg over the opposite knee. "Talk to me, son." He listened, as he'd done when he sat on the bench hearing cases ranging from petty misdemeanors to felony murder. He'd spent less than a decade in the criminal court before opting for a professorship at a law school.

"Do you love her, Micah?" Though he didn't answer, his son's expression said he did. "Why is it so hard to tell the woman you love her?"

"It's because I don't want it to happen again."

"What are you talking about?" Again Micah didn't answer. *Because I don't want it to happen again.* Edgar replayed Micah's statement over and over in his head, suddenly realizing why his son couldn't have a healthy relationship with a woman. Despite all he and Rosalind had given him, Micah still did not trust a woman enough not to abandon him.

Rising to his feet, he walked over to his desk and opened a drawer. He took out an envelope that had yellowed with age and handed it to Micah. "I probably should've given this to you years ago, but I felt it wasn't necessary because I didn't want to open up old wounds."

Micah took the envelope. "What's in it?"

"Open it, son."

He lifted the flap and removed a single sheet of lined paper. There were four short sentences and a signature written with the broad point of a pencil. The words were barely legible: *Please take care of my son. His name is Micah. I cannot take care of him because I am not well and I don't want to hurt him. He is a good boy who needs a good home. Evelyn Howard.*

Micah closed his eyes, pressing a fist to his mouth. He remembered his mother slipping a piece of paper in his jacket pocket, but at four he wouldn't have been able to read any of the words.

He lowered his hand. "What did she mean that she didn't want to hurt me?"

"I don't know—and I guess we'll never know."

"Was I physically abused?"

Edgar shook his head. "There was never any evidence of physical abuse. When Rosalind and I first brought you home you were much smaller than most children your age, but within a year you were in limits of all the milestones." Shifting his chair, he moved it closer to Micah's. "Your biological mother loved you, and because she did she left you in a safe environment. She could've taken a bus, gotten off in the middle of nowhere and walked away, leaving you in harm's way. Before your adoption was finalized I had an investigator check out every Evelyn Howard who'd given birth to a baby boy in the entire state of New Jersey with the birthdate and address you'd given the social worker, but he came up blank. I wanted to reassure Rosalind that once she got her son there wasn't going to be someone who'd come to claim you."

Micah didn't know why, but he felt like shouting at the top of his lungs. Evelyn Howard or whoever she was hadn't abandoned him after all. She'd left him at the hospital because she couldn't care for him.

He returned the note to the envelope and handed it back to Edgar. "Thanks, Dad."

Edgar stared at the envelope. "What do you want me to do with it?"

"Shred it, burn it. I don't care."

"Where are you going?" he asked when Micah stood up and headed for the door.

"I have to make a telephone call."

Taking the stairs two at a time, Micah marched into his bedroom to retrieve his cell phone. Scrolling through the directory, he punched in Tessa's number, counting off the rings until he heard her voice-mail greeting. Not bothering to leave a message, he called her cell phone. Again he got her voice mail.

A knowing smile deepened the lines around his eyes. There was no doubt she was avoiding him, but she couldn't elude him forever. There was just a little matter of Bridget's wedding.

Tessa felt a lump in her chest where her heart lay as she identified herself, speaking into the microphone attached to a post outside the gates leading to the Sanborn property. It'd taken a little more than a week of telling herself to get over Micah Sanborn. What they'd had was a fling, a very passionate fling based on friendship with a few fringe benefits. She couldn't deny she had fallen in love with him, yet unlike her association with Bryce, she'd gone into the relationship knowing what to expect. However, in less than four hours she would come face-to-face with Micah Sanborn again for the very last time.

The gates opened and she drove through. Several vans were parked alongside the house. The vendors she'd hired to decorate the house and set up the tables had arrived. There hadn't been a need for her to arrive early to oversee their work because they knew exactly what she wanted and expected for her clients.

Rosalind, her hair coiffed for the evening's festivities,

was waiting for her when she alighted from her truck. "Welcome, Tessa. You look beautiful."

Tessa gave her the first genuine smile she'd been able to summon in days. She'd shared Christmas dinner with her family in Mount Vernon, smiling and responding when necessary. She'd become the consummate actress, because no one suspected that she'd banished from her life a man she had fallen in love with.

"Thank you, Rosalind. Your hair is exquisite." Rosalind's silver hair was styled to feather around her small, round face.

Tessa wore one of her "wedding" uniforms: black silk tunic with silk frogs running diagonally from neckline to hem, quilted cuffed sleeves and side slits, over a pair of matching slacks and low-heeled suede quilted pumps. Her stylist had cut her hair, applied a gel and lifted the remaining curls with her fingers to give it a modified spiked appearance. At first Tessa thought it too extreme, but the next day she'd discovered she liked her new look. In a matter of hours she would celebrate a new year, and what better way than with a new look?

Her smile in place, she stepped into the entryway. All of the furniture in the living room had been removed, leaving only a table that would double as an altar for the ceremony.

The railing to the elaborate winding staircase was entwined with white calla lilies, cosmos, orchids, gardenias and deep magenta roses, the same flowers that made up Bridget's bridal bouquet. A four-tier wedding cake, with layers of red velvet, carrot, mocha and hazelnut fillings, sat on a lace-covered table in a corner. Delicate piping adorned the sides of the stunning white fondant-covered creation that gave it a look of heirloom quality.

Bouquets of white and black roses, softly curling white ribbon and green leaves, all made with piped royal icing, surrounded the first layer and remaining three layers. Nestled cozily amidst the *pastillage* flowers between the top two tiers was a charming miniature of a bride and groom. On closer inspection Tessa saw that the bride wore an exact replica of Bridget's wedding gown. Cake designer Faith Whitfield had gotten every detail right. All of the guests would receive souvenirs of the cake with their favorite filling presented in pale gray boxes tied with black satin bows.

Tessa followed Rosalind into the formal dining room. She'd ordered white, black and silver paper lanterns be suspended from specially constructed scaffolding that created a beautiful canopy over the dining room and connecting ballroom. It was the first time she'd suggested using the lanterns, and the effect was stunning.

"I like it."

"Bridget and Seth like them, too," Rosalind confirmed. "Come check out the seating arrangements."

The bridal table was set on a raised platform in the ballroom with a rectangular table with seating for eight. Bridget and Seth had requested that their parents sit at the bridal table.

Family members and guests would sit at five rectangular tables that were surrounded by the same number of round tables, each seating ten. Straight-backed chairs swathed in alternating black and silver organza repeated Bridget's Art Deco color scheme. After dinner, some of the tables and chairs would be removed to allow room for dancing.

Workers were covering the tables with tablecloths and centerpieces of stalks of bamboo held together with red

satin ribbon in delicate cylindrical vases set in the middle
of a quartet of small rectangular glasses filled with black
shiny marbles and white votive candles. Everyone
worked in silent, practiced precision, putting out place
settings with crystal stemware, silver and china.

Tessa followed Rosalind down a hallway that led into
the smaller of the two kitchens, where the caterer and her
staff were preparing dishes for the cocktail hour.

"How is Bridget holding up?"

Rosalind clucked her tongue behind her teeth. "I hope
she's better tonight."

Tessa's eyes grew wider. "What happened?"

"She was so nervous at the rehearsal last night that she
kept forgetting her lines. I found a masseuse willing to
work on the eve of a holiday. Of course, I had to pay him
three times his hourly fee, but it was worth every penny.
Right now she's sleeping sitting up in a chair so she
won't ruin her hairdo."

Tessa wanted to ask Rosalind about Micah.

How was he? Where was he?

Was he angry because she hadn't taken his calls?

"Where's Edgar?"

"The menfolk are camped over at Abram's. Seth and
his best man are staying at the hotel with his parents and
out-of-town relatives."

"Is Melissa here?"

Rosalind nodded, smiling. "She's upstairs with Bridget."

Pushing back her sleeve, Tessa noted the time. It was
four-fifteen. The guests would begin arriving at six for
an extended cocktail hour. Seth and Bridget were scheduled to exchange vows at eight, followed by a sit-down
dinner and reception.

The musical program included prerecorded music for the

cocktail hour and dinner, while a live band would alternate with a DJ for nonstop music during the reception. Bridget wanted her special day captured on tape and film, so Tessa had to contract with two photographers, one to capture images with his digital camera and the other on videotape.

An hour later the bartender arrived with his staff, the band with their instruments and sound equipment, followed by the DJ and his electronic equipment.

Tessa went completely still for several seconds when she thought she heard Micah's voice behind the closed pocket doors to the dining room. Forcing herself back to the task at hand, she checked and double-checked the names on her clipboard with the place cards at each table. The wedding menu was eclectic. Aside from the ubiquitous prime rib, roast chicken and sole, the caterer offered a white asparagus soup with Tsar Nicoulai sturgeon caviar, Thai-style lobster with grilled black mussels, Kaffir lime-coconut milk infusion, fried Thai basil, bok choy and baby carrots. There were other seafood dishes: chilled marinated lobster with fresh lychee; a mock ravioli of wild salmon carpaccio and avocado topped with caviar and roasted beets; wild-caught prawns with watermelon, Hami melon, serrano ham and watercress; and a smoked salmon roll wrapped in English cucumber with lemon cream and salmon caviar. A raw bar, set up in the living room, offered grapefruit-infused gin, lemon-verbena-and-red-currant-infused vodkas, mignonette-and-lemon gelée, littleneck clams and oysters on the half shell, rock shrimp ceviche and crab-and-celery-root salad.

The wait staff in white tunics and black slacks filed out of the kitchen carrying cloth-covered trays of risotto-stuffed calamari with black trumpet mushrooms, quail eggs with crème fraîche and caviar on rye-bread crackers. They were followed by others with trays of crab cakes, chilled shrimp with accompanying sauces, puffed pastries and dim sum.

Rosalind and Edgar had spared no expense to give their daughter a wedding to remember.

Tessa, standing off to the side of the crowd that had gathered in the living room to witness Bridget Sanborn exchange vows with Seth Cohen, caught a glimpse of Micah as he cradled Marisol to his shoulder. Her gaze caressed his broad shoulders under his tuxedo jacket, the stark white collar against the darkness of his throat and the ruggedly handsome profile that she knew with her eyes closed.

Her gaze shifted to Bridget and Seth as they exchanged vows. Her Signature bride was ravishing with her dark hair pinned up in an elaborate hairdo under her veil. Chandelier diamond earrings dangling from her ears matched the diamond fringe necklace around her neck. Seth's uncle, a jeweler, had given Bridget the exquisite jewelry ensemble as a wedding gift, while the platinum-and-diamond bangle on her right wrist was an estate piece she'd inherited from Rosalind's mother.

There was a strange hush as Seth turned to face Bridget. He'd cut his mop of dark, unruly curls and covered his head with a white yarmulke. "I was not looking for love, but I knew the moment I saw you it became obvious that love had found me. And it took only a matter of weeks for me to tell you that I loved you, I needed you and that I wanted you in my life to make it complete."

Tears were streaming down Melissa's face as she struggled not to break down completely. However, she wasn't the only one in tears.

Bridget's voice was amazingly clear when she looked into the eyes of her groom. "A quote from Helen Keller is most appropriate at this time. 'The most beautiful things in the world cannot be seen or even touched. They must be felt in the heart.' Seth, you've touched my heart as no other man has or ever will. I knew you were the man I wanted to spend the rest of my life with because you knew every word to 'Fields of Gold.'" A smattering of laughter followed her admission. "Love was not on my schedule either, nor was it a necessity. You have come so quickly into my life and have completely taken my heart. I vow on this day before God, our families and loved ones to love you forever as my husband and friend."

Tessa, who'd lost count of the number of weddings she'd witnessed, didn't know what was wrong with her. She, who never cried at weddings, was practically sobbing. Reaching into the pocket of her slacks, she withdrew a tissue to blot her face. She caught movement out of the corner of her eye and found Micah staring directly at her. His gaze widened before narrowing. An expressive eyebrow lifted slightly before he averted his eyes to see his sister slip a ring onto Seth's finger. The minister, the rabbi and the priest placed their hands over the couple's joined hands and blessed their union.

Seth and Bridget Sanborn-Cohen turned to face the assembly as husband and wife, their bright smiles mirroring the vows that had come from their hearts as the videographer paused to change a cassette. He and the photographer had begun taking pictures as Rosalind and Melissa had helped Bridget into her gown and accessories while her guests were downstairs eating and drinking.

The younger children were permitted to witness the

wedding and eat at the reception but knew they would have to retreat to the upstairs bedrooms once the dancing began.

Tessa slipped out of the living room to find the DJ and instruct him to turn on the prerecorded music. The soft selections would play throughout the time when Seth and Bridget would circulate to greet their guests and would continue throughout dinner.

She hadn't gone more than ten steps when she felt someone grasp her upper arm. She didn't have to turn around to know the man holding her was Micah. His warmth and the familiar fragrance of his cologne swept over her.

"I have to talk to you," he whispered close to her ear.

"Not now, Micah. I'm working."

"How about later?"

She glanced down at the large, well-groomed hand on her arm. Peering over her shoulder, her gaze inched up to a silver-and-black-striped silk tie, to his firm male mouth that conjured up a flood of memories that brought a wave of heat to her face.

"I'll still be working later."

His hold tightened as he turned her to face him. "Look at me, Tessa." Her wet lashes fluttered before she met his eyes.

"We've said all we needed to say the last time we were together. Now please leave me alone."

He took a step, forcing her back against a wall. "I can't do that because I love you. And to echo the words of my brother-in-law, I wasn't looking for love, but on October thirteenth when I walked into Signature Bridals for the first time I had no idea that love would be there waiting for me. I've run from love and women who professed to loving me because that was what my biological mother did. She told me that she loved me minutes before she walked out of my life. I've been screwed up in the head for years, and there's no doubt I'm still a little crazy. After I left you I had a long talk with my father. He gave me a note Evelyn Howard had slipped into my jacket. That note helped me understand that she wasn't able to take care of me, that she loved me enough to give me up so I would have a better life than she could give me."

Leaning closer, Micah shook his head. "I'm tired, Tessa. Tired of running from love. I want to stop and settle down with a woman who completes me. I want a family of my own that I can protect and provide for. I'm not perfect, but with you by my side I'll work at trying to make you happy."

For the second time that night tears filled Tessa eyes and overflowed. Curving her arms under his shoulders, she held him. "We'll talk about this later, Micah."

"You promise?"

She sniffled. "Yes, I promise."

Reaching into a pocket of his dress trousers, he pulled out a handkerchief. Cradling her chin in his free hand, he gently blotted the moisture on her cheeks. When Tessa took the square of cotton from him he saw a flash of light from her wrist. He caught her hand, pushing back her sleeve.

"You wore it."

Shaking her hand, Tessa let the bracelet slide down her wrist. Micah had given her a delicate diamond bracelet for Christmas. It was a close match to the necklace she'd worn the night they'd gone to the opera.

"Yes, Micah, I wore it. Thank you. It's beautiful."

"You're beautiful, Tessa Whitfield. By the way, I like your hair."

Her lids lowered in a demure gesture as she inclined her head. "Thank you."

Someone cleared their throat and Micah and Tessa sprang apart like guilty children caught in a compromising situation. Edgar Sanborn, resplendent in formal dress, stood in the hallway staring at them. "Flirt on your own time, son," he drawled, repeating what he'd said to him when Tessa first came to Franklin Lakes to play football with the Sanborns. "Tessa, is my son bothering you?"

"No, sir." Stepping around Micah, she went to find the DJ.

Edgar dropped a hand on his son's shoulder. "I hope you got it right this time."

"I believe I still have a chance."

"Perhaps she needs a little persuading."

"What are you talking about, Dad?"

Edgar shook his head. "Damn, Micah, do I have you tell you everything?"

"Yeah, Dad, sometimes you do."

Looping his arm around Micah's neck, Edgar pulled him closer. "Let me tell you how I changed your mother's mind and got her to agree to marry me."

With wide eyes, Micah listened as his father whispered in his ear how he'd convinced Rosalind that she would be making a grave mistake if she didn't marry him. "No, Dad. That would never work with Tessa."

"How can you be sure it wouldn't work?"

"Because not only is it illegal it's also immoral."

One pair of dark eyes regarded another equally dark pair with amusement. "You're really as tight-assed as they say you are."

"They who?" There was a hint of defensiveness in Micah's voice.

"The folks at the Kings County D.A.'s office."

"Who of your old legal cronies do you have spying on me?"

"No one in particular. But that's not to say I don't hear good things about you. You know that I'm proud of you."

The seconds ticked off. "I know that, Dad. As proud as I am to be your son."

Edgar tightened his grip. "Your mother and I have waited a long time to see all of our children married. Don't make us wait too much longer for you."

A genuine smile softened Micah's rugged face. "I won't. And that's a promise."

"Liar."

"Why would you say that?"

"You never make promises."

"Well, this is one I intend to keep."

Edgar watched Micah as he turned and walked back into the living room. He hadn't realized he'd been holding his breath until he was forced to exhale.

"Why do you look like the cat that swallowed a canary?"

He shifted to find Rosalind several feet away. Had she overheard his conversation with their eldest son? He held out his arms and wasn't disappointed when she came into his embrace. Lowering his head, he whispered what he'd overheard and seen.

Rosalind's blue eyes shimmered like brilliant topaz. "I knew it, I knew it," she crooned over and over. "Darling, I just hope Micah gives us more time than Bridget did."

"Not to worry, sweetheart. Remember—the Whitfields are in the wedding business."

Rosalind looked at her husband. "How many grand-children do you think Micah and Tessa will give us?"

"Rosie! I don't believe you're counting grandchildren even before they're married."

"I can dream, can't I?" she quipped, winking at Edgar. "Let's join the others before they come looking for us."

Arm in arm they returned to the living room in time for the photographer to snap what would become a memorable family picture.

Chapter 22

After toasts by the best man, the maid of honor and the parents of the bride and groom, Seth and Bridget cut the cake as waiters served slices of the confectionary masterpiece with the nontraditional fillings. The members of the eight-piece band moved into position on a raised dais when the tables in the ballroom were moved to the living room to provide adequate space for dancing.

The extremely talented and versatile male singer picked up a portable microphone as the band opened with Sting's classic "Fields of Gold." Having removed her veil, Seth walked Bridget out onto the dance floor so they could share their first dance as husband and wife.

Seth changed partners, dancing with his mother—an attractive brunette that didn't look old enough to have children who were in their thirties—while Bridget danced with Edgar.

Tessa watched Edgar's tender expression as he gazed down at his daughter staring up at him. He'd given his princess a wedding to remember. The band alternated with the DJ, playing nonstop music from every decade beginning with the forties.

Following Jewish tradition, Seth and Bridget were hoisted in chairs for the *hora* as friends and family members danced around them, and because Ephraim and Chavva Cohen, wearing crowns of orchids, were marrying off their last single child, they were honored with the *mezinka,* a congratulatory dance.

Everyone was up and dancing when the DJ put on the "Cotton-Eyed Joe," then the "Cha Cha Slide." Tessa didn't have time to react when she was pulled onto the dance floor by Abram and Micah. Caught up in the infectious rhythms, for a brief time she forgot that she was working. She dipped, swayed, threw her hands up, smiling whenever she met Micah's gaze. Even Seth's octogenarian grandparents tried keeping up as the minutes ticked down the old year. The crowded dance floor and the continuing flow of champagne equaled a successful reception.

The volume lowered at the same time the chandelier dimmed. A table with a large flat-screen television was rolled into the ballroom. Waiters circulated, handing out flutes of champagne. There was complete silence as gazes were trained on the images of the boisterous throng in New York City's Times Square filling out the screen. It was less than three minutes away from a new year.

Tessa went completely still when she felt a hard body pressed to her back. "Where's your champagne?"

She smiled. "I'm working, Micah."

Angling his head, Micah pressed a kiss to the column of Tessa's scented neck. "Can't you forget work for a minute?"

"Why?"

"I'd like to ask you something."

"Will it take more than a minute?"

"No." Wrapping an arm around her waist, he eased her back. "Come with me."

"Where are you taking me?"

"You'll see. Let's go so we can get back in time to see the ball drop."

Tessa followed Micah like a trusting child as he led her down a wide hallway, passing rooms with closed doors. At the end of the hallway he turned left and opened a door. He touched a wall switch and the space was filled with soft gold light from a table lamp.

"This is my father's study," Micah explained before she could ask.

The masculine room was filled with leather chairs, sturdy mahogany tables, a collection of model ships, shelves packed tightly with leather-bound books and a credenza with crystal decanters filled with an assortment of liquors.

Pulling her closer, Micah put the flute to Tessa's mouth, waiting until she took a sip. His gaze fused with hers when he took a deep swallow. Glancing over her head, he watched the hands on the fireplace mantel clock inch closer to midnight.

"What do you want to talk about?"

Tessa's query pulled him back to why he'd wanted to get her alone. "I need to ask you something."

"What is it, Micah?"

He took another swallow of the premium wine, buying time and watching the sweep hand ticking off the seconds. His gaze came to rest on her questioning eyes. "What are you doing with the rest of your life?"

His question did not register on Tessa's confused thoughts. Why, she asked herself, was Micah talking in riddles? "I don't understand."

He moved closer. "What's there not to understand?"

"Why are you concerned about *my* life, Micah?"

"Is it possible for me to become a part of your life?"

She was totally bewildered at his behavior. Smooth-talking, silver-tongued, articulate Micah Sanborn was talking in circles. "Either you tell me exactly what you want or I'm leaving."

"Theresa Anais Whitfield, will you do me the honor of becoming my wife?"

Tessa wavered, trying to comprehend what she was hearing. Micah had talked about settling down and starting a family. But for her that hadn't translated into a formal proposal.

She'd slept with a man she'd known a week, but that no longer was an issue.

She'd fallen in love with a man she didn't know as well as she should have, but that no longer mattered.

She'd told herself that she wasn't ready for marriage but knew that to be a lie.

Resting her head on Micah's shoulder, she closed her eyes. "Yes, Micah Edgar Sanborn, I will become your wife. But I'd like us to wait before announcing our engagement."

The joy Micah should've felt dissipated. He was over forty and he'd wasted half his life running from love. Now that he realized he loved Tessa enough to want to spend the rest of his life with her, he didn't want to wait.

"How long do you want to wait?"

Easing back she smiled up at him. "Would you be opposed to a couple of months?"

He shook his head. "No." At first he'd thought she was going to say a year. "When would you want to get married?"

Her smile widened. "June. I've always wanted to be a June bride."

"This coming June?"

She nodded.

Setting down his flute, he wrapped both arms around her waist, lifting her off her feet until her head was level with his. He swung her around and around. "Thank you," he whispered over and over against her parted lips.

Looping her arms around Micah's neck, Tessa opened her mouth to his passionate kiss, shocked at her own eager response when her tongue curled around his, tasting the lingering slightly sweet taste of champagne.

They were still locked in a passionate embrace when a roar went up in another part of the house. It was now a new year. Micah and Tessa registered cries of "Happy New Year" at the same time. They shared a smile.

"Happy New Year, Micah."

"Happy New Year to you, too, baby." He kissed her again. "Can I interest you in a post-celebratory New Year's Eve party after you get off from work?"

"Whatever do you have in mind, Counselor?"

His expressive eyebrows lifted. "How about checking in to a hotel with impeccable room service and a suite with a bathtub big enough for two?"

Pressing her breasts to his chest, Tessa gave him a saucy grin. "And what do you plan for us to do in that hotel suite?"

He lifted a shoulder under his wool jacket. "I don't know. You tell me."

Tessa ran her hand down the length of Micah's tie. "I still have at least an hour before I'm off, so that should give you time to come up with a plan as to how we'll spend the first day of the new year together." Pushing against his chest, she stepped around Micah and walked out of Edgar's study with an exaggerated wiggle of her hips.

Micah stood in the doorway, watching the sensual sway of her bottom. "I'm going to make love to you all night, all day, all afternoon, then all night again," he called out to her. Tessa stopped, turned and lifted her tunic. He stared numbly at her breasts spilling over the lace of her demi-bra; the flesh between his legs hardened instantaneously.

Groaning, he stumbled backward and sat down heavily in a chair, waiting for his erection to go down. He closed his eyes and said a silent prayer of thanks. He also offered up a prayer for Evelyn Howard, wherever she was, for Edgar and Rosalind for their love and support, then pushed off the chair, rising in one fluid motion, and left the study.

As Micah neared the ballroom the sound of music grew louder, blending with voices raised in song. A knowing smile tilted the corners of his mouth as he saw Tessa talking to his mother. In another six months Tessa would gain a mother-in-law and Rosalind another daughter.

Tessa saw him staring at her. She gave him a demure smile before lowering her gaze.

It had been a long time coming, but Micah Sanborn felt an astonishing sense of total fulfillment for the first time in his life.

Tessa pressed her face to Micah's moist chest amid waves of ebbing ecstasy, unable to believe what'd just passed between them. She'd known of the strong passions within her, but it had taken the man holding her to his heart for her to completely let go of her inhibitions.

"I just changed my mind, Micah."

"What about, baby?" His voice sounded if he were a long way off.

"I don't want to wait to get engaged."

Micah sat up as if hit by a stun gun. "What!" The single word exploded from his mouth.

Tessa sat up and touched the side of his face. "I changed my mind about waiting to get engaged. I want everyone to know that I love you—"

"And that I want to spend the rest my life with you," Micah said, finishing her statement. "We'll go look for a ring whenever you're free, then I'm going to Mount Vernon to meet your family. And, knowing my mother, she'll want to invite the Whitfields over for Sunday dinner."

"Will they be expected to play football?"

He chuckled, the sound rumbling in his chest. "They can, but only if they want to."

"Why are you giving them a choice when you didn't give me one?"

"How else was I going to cop a free feel, Tessa Whitfield?" His hand moved from her hip up to a breast.

"You are a nasty old man, Micah Sanborn."

"You think so?"

"I know so."

"But you like this nasty old man, don't you, baby?"

Tessa crawled up on his lap, her arms going around his neck. "I wouldn't have you any other way."

They held each other, hearts beating as one, until Micah eased Tessa down to the mattress and pulled the sheet up over their naked bodies. She curled into the curve of his body, a gentle peace silently communicating that she'd chosen the right man to become her friend, her lover, her husband and the father of the children she hoped to share with him.

The second title in the Stallion Brothers miniseries...

TAME A WILD
STALLION

Favorite author
DEBORAH FLETCHER MELLO

Motorcycle-driving mogul Mark Stallion falls fast and hard
for gorgeous mechanic Michelle "Mitch" Coleman. But
Mitch isn't interested in a pretty, rich boy who plays with
women's hearts...despite the heat generated between them.

"Mello's intriguing story starts strong
and flows to a satisfying end."
—*Romantic Times BOOKreviews* on *Love in the Lineup*

Coming the first week of June wherever books are sold.

KIMANI™
ROMANCE

www.kimanipress.com   KPDFM0690608

Wrong DRESS, Right GUY

Award-winning author
SHIRLEY HAILSTOCK

Cinnamon Scott can't resist trying on the gorgeous wedding dress mistakenly sent to her. When MacKenzie Grier arrives to retrieve his sister's missing gown, he's floored by this angelic vision...and his own longings. With sparks like these flying, can the altar be far off?

"Shirley Hailstock again displays her tremendous storytelling ability with My Lover, My Friend."
—*Romantic Times BOOKreviews*

Coming the first week of June wherever books are sold.

KIMANI™
ROMANCE

Destined *to* MEET

Acclaimed author
devon vaughn archer

When homebody Courtney Hudson busts loose for one
night, she winds up in bed with sexy Lloyd Vance, an
Alaskan cop escaping a troubled past. Then tragedy strikes
and they're caught in a twist of fate that threatens
to destroy their burgeoning love.

*"[Christmas Heat] has wonderful,
well-written characters and a story that flows."*
—Romantic Times BOOKreviews

Coming the first week of June wherever books are sold.

KIMANI™
ROMANCE

National bestselling author

ROCHELLE ALERS

No Compromise

In charge of a program for victimized women,
Jolene Walker has no time or energy for a personal
life...until she meets army captain Michael Kirkland.
This sexy, compelling man is tempting her to trade
her long eighteen-hour workdays for sultry nights
of sizzling passion. But their bliss is shattered when
Jolene takes on a mysterious new client, plunging
her into a world of terrifying danger.

"Alers paints such vivid descriptions that when Jolene
becomes the target of a murderer, you almost feel as
though someone you know is in great danger."
—*Library Journal*

Available the first week of October
wherever books are sold.

ARABESQUE®

www.kimanipress.com

KPRA0181007

These women are about to discover that every passion
has a price...and some secrets are impossible to keep.

NATIONAL BESTSELLING AUTHOR

ROCHELLE ALERS

After Hours

A deliciously scandalous novel that brings together
three very different women, united by the secret lives
they lead. Adina, Sybil and Karla all lead seemingly
charmed, luxurious lives, yet each also harbors a
surprising secret that is about to spin out of control.

"Alers paints such vivid descriptions that when Jolene
becomes the target of a murderer, you almost feel
as though someone you know is in great danger."
—*Library Journal* on *No Compromise*

**Coming the first week of March
wherever books are sold.**

sepia™

www.kimanipress.com

KPRA1220308

NATIONAL BESTSELLING AUTHOR

ROCHELLE ALERS

invites you to meet the Whitfields of New York....

Tessa, Faith and Simone Whitfield know all about coordinating
other people's weddings, and not so much about arranging
their own love lives. But in the space of one unforgettable year,
all three will meet intriguing men who just might bring them their
very own happily ever after....

Long Time Coming
June 2008

The Sweetest Temptation
July 2008

Taken by Storm
August 2008

ARABESQUE®

www.kimanipress.com

KPALERSTRIL08